THE BOOK OF IFS AND BUTS

Vintage Tales

THE BOOK

STORIES

RABINDRANATH MAHARAJ

OF IFS AND BUTS

VINTAGE CANADA

To Muldoon and the other hobos

VINTAGE CANADA EDITION, 2002

Published in Canada by Vintage Canada, a division of Random House of Canada Limited, Toronto, in 2002. Distributed by Random House of Canada Limited, Toronto.

National Library of Canada Cataloguing in Publication

Maharaj, Rabindranath
The book of ifs and buts / Rabindranath Maharaj.

Short stories.
ISBN 0-676-97447-3

1. Immigrants—Fiction. I. Title.

PS8576.A42B66 2002 C813'.54 C2002-901319-4
PR9199.3.M344B66 2002

www.randomhouse.ca

Text design by CS Richardson

Printed and bound in Canada

Ancient forest–friendly: Printed on 100% post-consumer recycled paper

10 9 8 7 6 5 4 3 2 1

CONTENTS

Vintage Tales

The Journey of Angels

"... and the beginning is as distant in the past as the ending is in the future, and walking to town, miraculously out of pain, I looked upon the world and remembered."
—William Saroyan

Part One

This is how it used to be. I was the honoured head of the biotechnology department at the University of Armenia. Before I moved to America three years ago, I was examining the possibility of introducing an antifreeze gene from a cold water fish into *Triticum urartu*, the wild grains located in the Ararat valley—progenitors of the first cultivated wheat in the world. It is very regrettable that I had to leave, because I feel that my countless years of experimentation will either have been wasted or more likely will be appropriated by Zoravar, who is well known for his drinking and his plagiarism.

None of this is true, of course. Not the language, not the facts. I was never the head of any biotechnology department, and Zoravar was a brilliant scholar whom I have seen tipsy just once. On that occasion I was picking the dried mazzards from his gardens when he strolled out of his house with a beautiful woman on his arm. The woman was about thirty years younger than his fifty-five, and from the way she was waving around a bottle of cognac and ceaselessly laughing at everything he said, I reasoned she was one of his students.

Zoravar's back door and the window overlooking his garden were always open, even when he was away at the university, and a variety of young women strolled in and out. The exact purpose of their visits was never clear to me, though I suspected that Zoravar with his massive forehead, aquiline nose, white hair swept back and gangly frame, always outfitted in slightly worn coats, must have cut a charming figure to these women. They were all healthy-looking, and I admired his taste.

Or I used to.

Once, I saw a woman walking past the curtains which, billowing in the breeze, gave her the appearance of a gliding apparition. She might have been naked or clad only in her underwear. I climbed down from the tree, skipped over the hedge beneath the window and pulled the curtains aside.

Five shelves ran along the left wall. All were stacked with books but for the middle, where there were tins of tobacco, a potted palm, a pipe, a brass urn, and a framed photograph of Zoravar with black hair and a neatly trimmed beard. Standing next to him was a tall woman with narrow-set but striking eyes. Directly opposite the window was a doorway, and when I leaned over, I saw, just beyond my reach, a small circular table with a book on the latticed top. Zoravar had brought this book to the garden a few times, not reading or anything but just staring at the plants in an absent-minded way. I bent forward to get a better look at the cover—two white-gowned men pouring liquids into narrow glass tubes—when I heard a small gasp and saw the young woman framed against the door. One hand was against her mouth and the other was clutching the towel wrapped around her waist. She was younger than I had imagined, maybe nineteen or twenty, and with her wet hair and the towel barely reaching her thighs she looked very pleasing. She glanced at the shears in my hand and, without saying a word, walked across to the top shelf, tiptoed, and removed a file. Then she returned through the door.

The next day, Zoravar came up to me and pretended he was examining the cracks in the cobblestone. I blurted my explanation, or rather my lie, before he had a chance to ask his question. His hands were clasped behind his back and he was shifting from one foot to the other. I noticed his pipe's stem protruding from the pocket of his jacket.

I continued mixing the manure for the seedlings he had brought from the university. When I was about to leave, I saw him standing by the window, one hand holding away the curtains. He invited me in.

So, that evening, I walked home burdened with Zoravar's books and with a steadily growing guilt. My wife, Leila, was delighted by my employer's interest. She hugged me tightly, and when I stiffened, she removed her hands from around my shoulders. She said she knew how much I suffered as a gardener, how each day the pain in my body grew worse. She could not bear to see the look in my face, which eighteen months ago she had spotted across the pastry shop where she worked. She had known immediately we would always be together. And Zoravar, wasn't he a kind employer to take an interest in a silly young gardener? She laughed and wiped away a tear.

We made love that night, as we had done almost every night since we were married, with a complete recklessness which I would regret when I struggled up in the morning.

I could never resist her; never resist her plump cheeks, her unfathomable grey eyes and her laughter after she had said, "Always, always you are so serious, Saren." I could not resist, either, when she asked to meet Zoravar. During that first meeting he was the perfect host, ushering us into his living room decorated with rugs and antique vases and trailing vines, pouring us tea into his delicate cups, inquiring if the tea's temperature was all right, standing at the doorway and stuffing tobacco into his pipe while we sipped nervously. In his soft, studious voice he told us how gratified he was by our visit—Zoravar who had hosted so many educated people. He plucked out a book from a scrolling corner shelf and held it against his nose as if it were one of his prized flowers. He pushed the book into my hand. We were conquered, my wife and I. We had never been in the presence of such an educated man, or the recipients of such generosity.

Leila began visiting me at work, sometimes with snacks of *basturma*, dried meats and *subjuk*, the spicy sausages which made my mouth water. One afternoon, Zoravar told her that she could use the kitchen to prepare her delicacies for me. She hesitated at first, perhaps afraid that she might break one of his handcrafted cups, but when Zoravar persisted, she surrendered. She had never been in a kitchen like his, or been a student of such an authority. He taught her to make meatballs with raisins and pine nuts and stuffed fruits, and my favourite, *paklavas*, a pastry filled with walnuts and pistachios and cinnamon. Her face was always flushed with pride when she came to me about ten minutes or so before I was ready to leave. Occasionally we took the pastries home, together with his books. I had never seen my wife as happy. Each day, she returned with some new recipe, some titbit about Zoravar's life at the university. In a sense he was the tutor of both of us.

I was overwhelmed. I could not yet grasp the purpose of these unselfish acts. Later, I found out, of course. But even on that day when I entered Zoravar's house to ask about a potted fern he had bought from the university and saw my wife sitting on the table, Zoravar bent over her, kissing her forehead, his hands lost beneath her dress, I could not blame him. I blamed my wife, I blamed the dolmas and *paklavas*, I blamed the pain in my back which had recently caused me to feign tiredness so many nights.

When my wife moved in with Zoravar, I could tell he was just as embarrassed as I was. I knew that I could not continue working there, and I was sorry that Zoravar's tutelage—of me, at least—would end. Exactly four days after my wife moved into his house, I put aside the fern, dusted my hands and knocked on his door. I had planned my speech all day, but when Zoravar emerged in his flannel pyjamas, I didn't know what to say. He tapped out some ash from his pipe and walked to the side of the house. I followed him. And Zoravar, with his pipe in his hand, looking at the ground rather than at my face, said everything I had rehearsed. He spoke for about twenty minutes and I could see that the speech was tiring him.

Then he told me of a friend from Brooklyn, a retired professor who had grown too old to tend his garden. His friend wanted a gardener from Armenia.

So we parted as friends, with Zoravar making the necessary arrangements. On the day of my departure, my wife hugged me and gave me a bag of *paklavas*. She was crying and laughing at the same time. Zoravar drove me to the airport, about two hours away. Throughout the trip he remained silent, occasionally slowing to light his pipe. Once or twice he cleared his throat, but said nothing. Then, finally, he asked what was troubling me. I wanted to thank him for taking in a humble gardener; for helping me with my stumbling English; for teaching me the way of the world. But instead, I stammered out my confession about the young woman, who, two days after she had seen me peeping through the back window, had overcome her fear sufficiently to invite me into the house. That time, she was not holding a towel against her body.

Zoravar smiled when I revealed this, and a few minutes later he said that a beautiful woman should not be hidden but savoured and shared as a dolma would be. And with that one statement he completely erased the small, lingering bit of embarrassment that existed between us. I thought, Without Zoravar, I would be nothing.

When I wrote him two months after my arrival in Brooklyn and mentioned that my back was worsening, he replied almost immediately with a long, comforting letter. He explained the stress of relocating to a new country and the effects on the body of a sudden change in temperature. Perhaps the work was too strenuous, he said, in which case I should take little rests and bend my knees while lifting heavy objects. He offered a number of useful tips, but to tell the truth, my job at Panos's was easy. His backyard garden was barely the size of a large room, and I enjoyed misting and pruning the cacti and orchids and anthuriums and roses in his even smaller greenhouse. If anything, I idled too much, but when I confessed as much to Panos, he gazed stupidly at me with his yellow eyes.

Panos looked like a sick crab. He had a huge, craggy face and very short legs with which he would shuffle sideways in his greenhouse. He had no friends, and from Zoravar I gathered that his wife was living in a sanatorium of some sort. He disappeared every evening and I assumed he was off visiting the poor, sick woman. I grabbed this time to walk about the street, venturing further each day. I tried to picture the people inside these locked-up houses. There were no verandahs or galleries or children running along the small yards, and I felt that in our street there were only old, sick people. But the outsides of the houses were tidy, and the hedges and vines with purple, bell-shaped flowers were neatly pruned. Maybe these old people each had a foreign gardener who also took care of them. At the end of the street was a small telephone cubicle, and a few times I thought of surprising Leila and Zoravar with my voice, thousands of miles away.

One evening, as I passed the telephone cubicle and crossed the street to a more busy section with old, ugly shops, I heard a terrible commotion, with sirens and vehicles racing in my direction. Three police cars pulled up at a convenience store and the police rushed out with drawn guns—just like in the American movies I had seen in Armenia.

People were walking by hurriedly, but I stood across the street, admiring the cars and curious about the commotion. After about ten minutes or so, one of the police emerged from the store and crooked his finger at me. I looked up and down the street and waited for a car to pass before I crossed to the other side. The policeman seemed annoyed. He was quite tall, and the skin on his face and hands was smooth and pale. "Whaddya staring at?"

I smiled a bit and tried to compose a thoughtful reply. "Your vehicle." The flashing lights reminded me of the American airport.

He took a step towards me and placed his hands on his waist. Now another policeman came up and asked, "Where're you from, buddy?" His voice was friendly, but his hand was on his holster.

"Armenia."

"Armynah? Wait here." The first policeman returned to the store. The second looked me over and smiled in a friendly fashion.

What happened next still puzzles me. We are an expressive people with rich, purposeful gestures, but when I attempted to explain how I happened to come to America, I was thrown against the police car with my face on the hood while my pockets were emptied. When I was finally allowed to stand upright, I was asked a series of pointless questions about Armenia, drugs, guns, the Russian Mafia, and crime rings. The smiling policeman was still smiling, but all the time I was thinking, What have I done? I pondered that question as I raced to Panos's house, as I huddled in a corner of the greenhouse, as I shaved off my beard, as I took off the gold chain my wife had given to me when we were married.

From then on, whenever I heard the sound of sirens, I continued walking, my head bowed, not looking to see if anyone had been shot or killed.

Panos began spending more time in his greenhouse, hunched over some plant for half an hour sometimes, his slowly blinking eyes the only sign of life. I guessed his wife's condition was worsening. Although I was worried about his behaviour, I never asked him about his problems.

One evening, I saw him slumped face down next to a large, spreading anthurium. I shook him, gently at first.

He slipped off the stool. In a panic, I wrapped my arms around him and dragged him into the house. His short legs bumped up the steps to the front door. I set him on the couch, heaved his foot over the soft cushion and called the operator. Fifteen minutes later I heard the sirens outside. I began to tremble. I expected to be thrown against the couch or the table, but the white-gowned officials (looking a bit like the men on the cover of Zoravar's book) were very polite. They pulled up Panos's eyelids, they felt his pulse, they attached clamps to his chest, then they turned to me.

I answered all their questions. They wrote on their pads and seemed satisfied.

Later that evening, a woman with a square jaw, and round breasts pushing out from beneath her sweater, came into the house. She was followed by a balding, middle-aged man dragging a suitcase. I sprang up from the couch to help him, but he grasped the suitcase's handle tightly and proceeded to haul it up the inside steps. Midway up, he stumbled and rolled down the stairs. He glanced at the woman, then at me. "You!" I could not place his accent. "What you fookin' staring at?" They both looked at me. I grabbed the suitcase, pulled it up the stairs and felt a searing pain in my back. "Whatsa fookin' matter with you now?" I heard the man jabbering as I dragged the suitcase up and laid it in a room's entrance.

When I came down, he pointed to a chair. "Sit here." I sat and he commanded the woman, "Okay, now you talk to him."

They were, as I suspected, Panos's family, the woman, Ani, his daughter, and the quarrelsome man his son-in-law, Bagrat. Ani said that they were here to sell off the property. And for the funeral too, Bagrat added. Not a fookin' day more. He stamped a bony foot on the floor, and I couldn't decide whether he was funny or hateful. He said that I would have to clear out of the house.

That night, for the first time since I arrived in America, I lay in bed and despaired. What madness had overtaken me when I decided to leave my village? How could I possibly survive in this place? Under Zoravar's tutelage my English had greatly improved, but here I knew no one, and I had no skills other than gardening. And it was in that state that I got out the books Zoravar had given to me. I read in a fever, not bothering to understand the words. Before, it was an obligation to Zoravar; now, it was an escape. I read throughout the funeral, I read in the basement while Ani and Bagrat were arguing upstairs, and I read when Panos's sick wife, a wizened old woman with her mouth open as if she had swallowed a roll of copper wire, was brought out from her sanatorium and installed in her dead husband's room upstairs.

Everything changed then.

I tended to the old woman all day, until Ani and Bagrat came home from their work at the library. I fed her liquefied fruit and a variety of pills, I cleaned her mess, I changed her diapers, I sponged off her disgusting body. The garden suffered. And I suffered. But I had no choice.

The room was medium-sized, maybe about fifteen feet by ten feet, with the bed set against the wall to the right of the doorway between two mahogany side tables. There was no furniture in the room other than a high-backed chair, on which I sat and kept watch over her, and a stool against the far wall. A small, frosted window faced the bed, and sometimes I would shift the curtain aside, peep out at the garden, and notice brown leaves smothering the shrubs and weeds springing up between the flowers. The old woman's eyes were always closed and I was tempted to slip out of the room to the garden, but I was afraid that she would croak during my absence.

When I was a boy, I was told that the simplest solutions are always before us, always within reach, if we can just recognize them. Until then I had never realized the truthfulness of this observation. Zoravar, so far away, rescued me once more. Each morning, I carried one of his books upstairs and, sitting on the stool, read from about ten in the morning to four in the afternoon. Now I tried to make sense of what these educated people were saying. The only interruptions were the feeding-and-cleaning routine, and even that began to bother me less and less. By the end of the first week in the room, I had finished his book on fish research; by the end of the second, his book on transgenic applications. I read with a passion that surprised me, but I was fearful that the old woman would suddenly croak and that this opportunity would be snatched away. I redoubled my attention to the old woman. I sapped her face with warm water, and rubbed her soft, wrinkled shoulders and legs with one of my mother's concoctions: lemon and camphor and olive oil. I patiently fed her every last drop of soup. She responded to my ministrations. One afternoon, I felt the frail muscles on her arms and legs loosening and yielding while I kneaded. Her eyelids fluttered when I moved to her neck. The next day, she raised an arm about two inches from the bed, as if to direct me to massage her scrawny fingers.

She was improving, gradually but surely. At night, I knelt before my bed and offered prayers of gratitude. I was grateful, but frightened too. I prayed for the old woman, for Panos, for myself, for Zoravar, for my wife. I also prayed for an end to the pain in my spine.

On a Saturday, while I was massaging the old woman's leg, she began to twitch. The sheet rode down her shoulders. She uttered a low groan which, broken into melodious syllables, sounded like a sheep's bleat. I stood up and made the sign of the cross. She was getting a call from above, I was sure of it. Her time had arrived.

I heard footsteps scurrying up the stairs and then I was pushed roughly aside. Bagrat bent over the bed, his nose just a few inches from the old woman's. One of his eyes was blinking faster than the other.

Then the old woman did something completely unexpected. I think she was straining into a smile, but maybe the muscles had been locked into place for too long, because half of her face remained completely frozen. The result was a dreadful, mocking sneer. Bagrat jumped back and bumped into me. I grabbed his arms to steady us both, but he shrugged me off and ran out of the room. Then I noticed Ani at my side, looking puzzled. She took a step forward and squeezed her mother's wrist. The old woman spread her fingers on the bed, like a dog's paw when it is being stroked.

When Ani was leaving the room, she took up my book from the floor, glanced at the title and held it out to me. I took the book and heard her walking slowly down the stairs. About six in the evening, when it was time for me to leave, the couple was still quarrelling downstairs, so I opened my book once more and read for another hour. The old woman did not bleat again.

When I went down, Bagrat had left and Ani was leaning forward on the sofa, her chin resting on her cupped palms. The old television, almost hidden in its long wooden console, was on. I did not want to disturb her, so I tiptoed in the direction of the basement. She looked up at me. I felt silly walking on my toes. Not knowing what to say, I smiled, but she remained serious.

"Who are you?"

She seemed nervous, but because I had rehearsed the answer to such a question many times, I replied immediately. "I am Saren. I am thirty-one years old and have spent the last three years of my life employed as a gardener for the esteemed Zoravar, a celebrated—"

She cut me short with her eyes. "I have only returned to Armenia once, but I have never seen a gardener reading a book like yours."

I began to feel uncomfortable. How could I tell her about the dishonest acts that had led to my interest in the books? How could I tell her about my encounter with the young woman in Zoravar's house? Or the evening I caught Zoravar over my wife, his long fingers poking about beneath her dress? Or the embarrassment that followed and Zoravar's honest attempts at reparation?

So I said nothing and just stared at the leather sandals I had brought with me from Armenia. She too stared at my sandals. My back began to hurt. I felt that if I stood there for another minute, I would drop. The pain radiated upwards and shot into my shoulders. I started to walk away and stumbled on the sofa. She uttered a soft shriek, like a baby gasping for air, when my head brushed the nape of her neck and her right breast. She was well padded and felt warm and cozy, like a cow.

Later, I lay in bed, more humiliated and embarrassed than I had ever been in my entire life. I was unable to think clearly. She must have been shocked by my assault. I was sure she had seen my erection rising from my flannel pyjamas as I stumbled up. Perhaps she had already contacted the police.

It was time to pack.

I crept out of my bed, withdrew my canvas suitcase from the cupboard, tugged my clothes off the rack, then knelt and emptied the drawers. I heard her walking down the basement stairs. I squeezed and whacked my shorts and trousers to make more space. I must have looked like a madman with my hair waving about and my trembling hands lunging at my clothes.

She stood in the doorway and said coolly, "This arrangement cannot work."

"Yes, yes, yes," I heard myself saying. I set about thumping with renewed vigour.

Small patches of her speech dripped through my haze. "We have to travel an hour from work each day . . . it is very tiring . . . and Mama . . . it is a miracle . . . we may have to stay here longer than we anticipated . . . and Bagrat is miserable . . . we would both be grateful if you could spend more time with Mama . . . I know it's a heavy task . . . we will double your salary . . . it is only fair . . . please . . . "

I stopped thumping. A balled piece of underwear was in my hand. I dropped it hastily and turned to Ani, who was still standing in the doorway, slightly tilted on one foot, a hand on her waist and the other running through her hair.

"Yes, yes, yes."

She smiled, but tiredly. I tried not to look at her breasts. When I felt a hardening in my pyjamas, I snapped my legs together and almost fell backwards. Then, once more, the pain. I waited for her to leave.

"Oh, I almost forgot. You left your book upstairs."

I motioned to the bed. "Leave it there. Please."

She went to the bed and placed the book carefully on the pillow.

The next morning, the sickroom was completely redecorated. The curtain had been replaced, pictures of lakes and rivers placed on the walls and two candle holders set on the side tables. And my chair had been dragged across to the window so that I now had a view both of the old woman and of the garden.

That was how I spent the next three weeks: tending the old woman, reading my books and sneaking small peeks at the garden from the frosted window. Zoravar had suggested that improper lifting and bending was responsible for my pain, but sitting on the chair for such long periods seemed even more afflicting. Most nights I would wait until I heard the clinks of cups and saucers on the kitchen table before I grasped the railing and walked slowly down the stairs.

In the basement, I would lie on my back and feel waves of pain pulsing through my body. One morning, as I bent down to put on my slippers, my left hip was seized in a clenching spasm. I fell to the floor, grasped the sheet and pulled myself slowly to the bed. Half an hour later, when I went upstairs, the old woman's eyes were opened and I felt her gaze following me around. By midday, the pain had subsided enough for me to clean and sponge and feed her. Her skin was warmer and seemed less grey than usual.

Each day, her skin felt more supple and alive, but my own situation was worsening. Ani and Bagrat began arriving later than usual from the library, and sometimes I would doze off in my chair while I was waiting for them. One night, when I awoke, I noticed that the candles had been lit. I was about to check the old woman when I was caught by a movement on the wall. The hair on my hands stood on end. Huge claws were grabbing at the walls, reaching for the paintings, clutching the old woman. I bolted up. Her eyelids snapped open. She looked at me and smiled horribly. A candle flickered and the shadows danced in black waves over her.

I was so relieved that I began to laugh, loudly and nervously. For a moment I had imagined that the room was haunted with the spirits Mother had told me of while she was waiting for my father. Each night he would come home later and later. Then, one morning, he did not show up. Whenever I asked my mother, she told me that he had left to find work in the town. But as time passed, her story changed. Sometimes he had been stung by a poisonous giurza snake that lived in the rock canyons, and at other times he was murdered by robbers. Once, she told me that he had been seduced by the *nhangs*, the mermaid creatures that lived in the valleys.

I heard footsteps running up the stairs. "What was that sound? Was it Mamma?"

"Yes," I lied, and saw the old woman looking at me hatefully.

Ani went to the bed and straightened the sheet around her mother's neck. As she was leaving the room, she stopped by the door and smiled. "I have something for you."

"Yes?"

"You were asleep when I came in to light the candles, so I left it in your room."

"My room?" I tried to remember if any underwear was carelessly strewn on my bed.

Later that night, I read the book she had brought from the library for about half an hour, but when I fell asleep, I dreamed of my father living in a valley between two cloudy slopes. In the dream, he was dancing with the *nhang* creatures.

Two days later, as I dozed, I was awakened by a terrible argument downstairs. Something crashed on the floor, there was silence, then Ani came into the room, holding a small handbag. She sat at the foot of her mother's bed and said she was grateful I had agreed to take care of her mother. She seemed a bit flustered, maybe because Bagrat was pacing about downstairs and grumbling in Armenian, *"Vay yes ko mayrt taghem"* ("I should bury your mother"). Ani told me that he had suggested her mother be carted off once more to the sanatorium. He quarrelled daily about the distance to the library, the traffic jams, the gloomy house and, above all, the expense of taking care of the old woman. I pretended to be surprised, as if I didn't know all of this already. Ani looked at me and sighed. I had never noticed how long her eyelashes were. I tried to focus on her eyes instead of her breasts. She didn't know how she could repay me. She parted her legs slightly and the handbag settled in the fold of her dress. She had something she knew I would enjoy. She had thought of surprising me in the basement, but Bagrat was in such a bad mood, she had decided to wait no longer. She stood up suddenly and thrust out her hand shyly. "Take it."

I took the handbag and retrieved the two hardcover books. They looked new, but I noticed the library's stickers on the spines. I opened the books and smelled the dusty paper. Unexpectedly, I was overcome—just like when one of my uncles had offered me a drink of his wine and winked in the direction of the kitchen where my mother was cooking his favourite meal.

I blinked away the tears. Ani was staring at me with a puzzled look, then I noticed that her eyes too were misting over. I admit she was a bit blocky and had the kind of squarish jaw which makes some women look rough and quarrelsome, but at that moment I felt like throwing her on the bed and leaping on her. The old woman would undoubtedly be crushed, but I didn't care. Ani took a step towards me, placed a hand on my cheek and left.

For half an hour, I paced the room. I was just thirty-one. I had not had a woman for five months. My wife had spoiled me. And besides, it was Ani who was pushing me to these thoughts. Even Zoravar's analogy about women and dolmas kept running through my mind. By the time I went down to the basement, I was convinced of my hopeless corruption.

I awoke twice that night. In the morning, I felt like my back had been twisted out of shape. While I was hobbling up the stairs, I was seized all at once by the idea that I should return to Armenia. I had been poor but comfortable. I did what I knew best. Perhaps Zoravar would re-employ me.

In this mood, I made plans to return. I was not stupid; I knew my life was here in Brooklyn, but it gave me a strange comfort to make these little plans. I imagined how it would be, working once more for Zoravar, and Leila bringing me her tasty snacks each evening.

These fantasies ambushed me at odd moments and, while I was left miserable afterwards, the act of planning momentarily calmed me. I knew I would have to get another wife, but there were many young, healthy women in the village. Some had even sulked and pretended to be jealous when I took up with Leila.

Maybe Ani sensed I was unhappy. Sometimes at night, when she came to relieve me from my shift, she would glance at me seriously while she was rubbing her mother's joints. Then one night she asked what was bothering me.

How could I explain? I pressed my palms together and prepared to leave.

Still massaging her mother, she told me that she too missed Armenia, even though she had left with her parents when she was just six and had returned only briefly three years later. After she got the job at the library, she had sought out books on Armenian history and culture, and was astonished by what she had not known. She discovered that Armenia was the world's first Christian state, and that in 1620 it was divided between Turkey and Persia. She learned about the massacres inflicted on our people from then until the horrible period between 1915 and 1922, when more than a million Armenians were killed—the first genocide of the twentieth century. She began to view her parents and the relatives she barely remembered, the cousins who had shamed her with their loud ways when they visited America, in a different light. One night, she stopped massaging and asked if her father had spoken to me in the weeks before he died. I shook my head. She remained silent for a while, then said that her grandparents had been rounded up with the other villagers by the Turks and sent to a desert in Syria, Der Zor. At first no one realized what had happened. Her grandfather had been asked to turn in his hunting weapons to the Turkish gendarmes to assist with the war effort, and then told that he, together with all the able-bodied men in the village, would be temporarily relocated. No one suspected, but later on, the women and children too would be forced to undergo these death marches across Anatolia. And the weapons collected by the Turks were used as proof that her grandfather and the other men had been planning a revolution. Her father was four years old then. He had been rescued by a person he later called "a good Turk." But that was all he was prepared to reveal. He said nothing of the circumstances following his escape or anything about what had happened to his mother. Perhaps she had been raped, then starved or murdered.

Poor, poor Panos. I tried to imagine the old, silent, craggy-faced man from the greenhouse watching his mother being tortured.

Ani looked at me. Her breasts heaved. I didn't know what to say.

For the next few nights, she continued to talk of Armenia. I thought it strange that someone would understand a place only after she had departed it. Ani spoke about the liturgical music, the stone carvings, the churches, the waterfall flowing into the Araks river—all of this with such feeling that I could see these places before me. I had nothing to offer her in return; nothing to match her broad knowledge. I told her about the night I met my wife in the pastry shop and about my work at Zoravar's. I remarked on his brilliance and his generosity. I mentioned his gift of books to me, and the recipes for *plaki* and *bourek* and *paklava* he had taught to Leila. The old woman's mouth creaked open and a dribble of saliva ran down her chin and settled between two long strands of hair.

The following night, Ani brought up a bowl of *basturma* and a cup of *jajik*—yogurt and cucumber dip. She placed the food on the side table and left. I stared at the food and covered my face with my hands. I heard a sniffing sound. At first I thought it had come from me, but then I heard it once more from the direction of the old woman. She was staring at me out of the corner of her eyes, her mouth slightly open and the tip of her tongue protruding like the *moghesakul*, the lizard-eating snakes I had caught as a boy. I dragged my chair further away. I dipped the *basturma* into the *jajik* and held it before my mouth, savouring the aroma. Then I heard the sound again, a pronounced clack.

I should state right now that there are few things that annoy me more than a wet clacking sound. I felt like walking across the room and shoving a towel in the old woman's mouth. Instead, I took the cup of *jajik* and spooned a few drops down her gullet. She slurped noisily. I fed her another spoonful. And another. I was patient. When she twisted her mouth as if she was choking, I waited. In half an hour the cup was completely empty. I stood up to ease away the stiffness in my back and saw Ani standing at the doorway. I had no idea how long she had been standing there, and before I had a chance to ask, she turned and left. Just like that. A few minutes later, I heard Bagrat quarrelling in his strange accent.

I realized that Bagrat did not approve of the time Ani was spending with her mother, which was stupid of him. The old woman was her mother, after all, and needed constant care. I could not understand his attitude one bit and, even though he rarely spoke directly to me, I began to hate him. That same night I had even more reason. Usually, his quarrelling stopped after a few minutes, but this time it went on and on, with Bagrat's voice growing louder and angrier. I stood by the doorway and listened, even though it was none of my business.

Bagrat was in a fury. He was screaming about how the old woman didn't plan to die in the immediate future and that the decision to take care of her was a big mistake. What use was all the property if it was tied up in an invalid's hands? She was a spiteful old witch who was hanging on just to deprive everyone of their rightful inheritance. Maybe she would outlive both of them.

I had heard enough. I went down the stairs, holding the railing and taking my time as usual. When Bagrat saw me, he stopped pacing and shrieked, *"Etti parazzi megna!"* He was wearing slack, oversized shorts which reached to his knees. He looked small and knobby and dangerous. People like that always scare me because I know they are capable of crazy acts which they will regret later. Now he reverted to English. "What you standing there for?" When it dawned on him that I was in pain and could not walk any faster, he erupted into a high-pitched, clattering laugh. He pointed to me. "Two fookin' invalids now." I glanced at Ani, thinking she would defend me. Bagrat continued his spiteful insults as I limped to the basement. "She suck him out. She suck him out dry. Now she strong and he fookin' invalid."

The next morning, Saturday, I went to the greenhouse instead of the sickroom. It was the first time I had been there in five days. The plants looked dry and powdery. The orchids were drooping and petals from the roses were strewn on the floor, but the anthuriums had suffered the most. The leaves, used to daily misting, were now brown and curled at the tips. I felt like I had contributed to their suffering. I had been too preoccupied with my miserable back and with the old woman to take care of the plants. I was, after all, a gardener. I walked over to the end of the greenhouse and opened the valve. A few drops of water trickled from the overhead vents, and as the pressure adjusted to a fine mist, I imagined the leaves stretching and dancing to receive the water. I closed my eyes and turned my face up towards the vents. The water felt warm and gentle and comforting. When, after about five minutes or so, I opened my eyes, the glass walls were steamed over and the air in the greenhouse was as foggy as the Ararat mountain in the morning.

Once, my mother had pointed irritably in the direction of the Ararat mountain when I asked about my father. I thought he was cavorting with the *nhangs*, but as I grew older, I realized he would never return, and I understood, too, the real reason for the visits from my various "uncles." I began to hate my mother. But I hated my father even more. I was not a slouch at school, yet I would never be able to attend university. I would never again receive presents like my friends and, worst of all, I would be compared to my father for every simple mistake. Like the night of my nineteenth birthday when I stumbled home smelling of wine. I was drunk because it was my birthday and also because I had, on that night, decided that if my father was ever to return, I would kill him.

~

I tried to get these thoughts out of my mind, but the fogginess of the greenhouse made me think of ghosts and spirits. I blame my father, my mother and these invisible ghosts for what happened next.

When Ani stepped from behind a trellis which was wreathed with orchids, I placed my hands around her waist and pulled her to me. I could smell her pleasant, cow fragrance and feel her heavy breasts against my chest. Only when I jammed my lips against hers did she push me away. I felt like a fool with my open mouth dangling over her forehead. Hastily, I tried to think of some excuse: the mist had made me light-headed, my back had collapsed. But Ani smiled. Just a little. And standing there before me, she said that she was not interested in men. I could not understand. Not interested? Then why was she married? She must have noticed my confusion, because she leaned forward and gave me a small smack on my cheek. "Don't bother with it. Everyone is entitled to one secret."

Some secret, was all I could think. Some secret.

"Just like you. I always see you with all that suffering in your eyes."

I said it was my back. I told her that, most mornings, I would awaken curled in a ball and had to uncoil myself slowly and in different stages.

"Take off your shirt." For a moment I had this wild hope that she had, for some reason, made me an exception to her taste, but when I fumbled with my pants' zipper, she said, "No, no, no," but more amused than annoyed. She guided me to a bench, and for the next twenty minutes or so she massaged my back and neck and shoulders, kneading the muscles and tracing her thumb over the knotted areas. At first I was worried she would notice my erection, but as her fingers rubbed and stroked, I felt more relaxed and all those nasty thoughts flew away. I had almost fallen asleep when she said, "A snake."

I got up swiftly. "What?"

"Like a snake. Your back. I would like you to see someone. My doctor."

So, three days later, I visited her doctor and learned that I had a disease called spondylitis. Eventually my spine would curve out of shape and I would become a cripple like Abgar, the old man whom we had taunted and teased on our way from school.

When Ani and I returned from the doctor, the old woman was completely still, and for a moment I thought that Bagrat had strangled her while we were away. He cast me a funny look and stomped out of the room, but I was too worried by the doctor's prediction to pay him much attention. My life had been cut short. I would be a disfigured old man in a few years. The old woman opened her eyes and stared at me. Two fookin' invalids. Now *I* felt like strangling her.

Late in the night, out of desperation, I wrote a letter to Zoravar. I asked him to read it to my wife. For weeks I waited, but there was no response. I felt like they had abandoned me. In the meantime, Ani massaged me in the greenhouse, brought more books from the library and finally installed a thirteen-inch television on one of the side tables. All of this was supposed to cheer me up, but I felt more like an invalid. The only times my mother had paid me any attention was when I was sick. Maybe in a short time I would become weak and feverish and be confined to bed in a room with no windows. Once, an uncle had called me a nuisance and made a simpering baby sound. Although I was fifteen then and with fever, I sprang up from the couch and reached for his throat. He fell backwards, tumbling on the floor. Then he staggered up and left, cursing my mother and me. She didn't speak to me for more than a month, and I noticed that she began to confine the uncles to her bedroom. Around this time I began taking my books outside to the remains of an old house just behind ours.

I could not give in; I could not allow this disease to disfigure me. I would fight it. The doctor had given me a few stapled pages of a spine-strengthening and -stretching routine which, he assured me, would decrease the pain. I began to exercise in the sickroom, stretching and twisting and rotating. The old woman's eyes followed my every movement. One morning, while

I was forcing my fingers to touch my toes, she uttered a soft grunt. Her face was strained as if she too were struggling to touch her toes. The next day, I exercised closer to her bed and kept a careful eye on her. Once more I noticed the tortured expression. She grunted and raised her arm an inch or so from the bed.

Her progress during the following weeks shocked me. I believe it stunned Ani too, and she conveyed her gratitude by massaging me down in the basement for longer durations. She also spent more time in her mother's room, sometimes coming up as soon as she arrived from work. Most of the time, she just sat at the foot of the bed, glancing from her mother to the television. One night, she leaped from the bed with a scream. The old woman's withered hand was trembling towards a saucer of *jajik* on the side table. Bagrat ran into the room. He looked excited and hopeful, but when he noticed the bony hand vibrating towards the table, anger flooded his face. He glanced at me hatefully.

If the old woman's progress was startling, my own deterioration was equally unsettling. The pain was so constant that it soon became a dull, grinding ache deep down in my bones. Each morning, I examined myself in the mirror and imagined the curvature becoming more pronounced. My right shoulder was now noticeably higher than my left. I had also developed a slight limp, which I attributed either to weakening muscles or to my body's adjusting to protect the weaker areas. Worst of all, I felt that my face was beginning to resemble an invalid's. My eyes appeared more hollow, my cheeks more sunken. In a short while I would look like Abgar, the cripple.

One day, while Ani was watching television in the sickroom, I asked her if she had noticed how much I looked like an invalid. She continued to stare at the television as if she did not hear me. Finally, she said, "You are a good man. Inside."

That was the last thing I wanted to hear. People usually say such nonsense to horribly disfigured dimwits who cannot think for themselves. Ani spoke distractedly about some politician on television, but I had stopped listening.

The next night, she brought an armful of books on Armenia. While I was flipping through them, she spoke about the glory of the early Armenians and their determination in the face of centuries of violation. They never gave in, never lost faith. I asked her to stop. I didn't want to hear any more. Of what value was all this fortitude to a cripple? I must have raised my voice, because she did not speak for the rest of the night. In the basement, I flung all her books beneath the bed. Invalids didn't read, they sat hunched in their chairs and stared vacantly into space. They dribbled; they provided amusement for schoolboys. They hung on to their miserable lives. Like the old woman.

Bagrat had been right all along. He had the gift of the always bitter—a keen insight into other people's distress. I became even more certain I had judged him too harshly when he came up a few times to the sickroom and smiled crookedly at me. I noticed that he only came, though, when his wife was not there. Once, I noticed him grinning at me, and a horrible thought crossed my mind. What if he was just like his wife? What if he was not interested in women? The more I thought of it, the more it made sense. A perfect arrangement. Perfect, yes—but I preferred if it didn't include me.

I drew my chair closer to the window whenever he was in the room. He drew his chair closer to mine. I got up and looked out. He stood up and gazed with me. I pretended I was examining the old woman. He stood at my side and joined the inspection. I felt I had brought this nuisance on myself. I was being punished for my impure thoughts about a married woman. God had sent her husband instead.

I believe the old woman knew what was going on. I saw her staring at him spitefully as he followed me around, making idle conversation about her health. One night, when he leaned over and whispered that I had resurrected his mother-in-law, she raised a bony hand towards him and crooked a finger. Her hand dropped back on the bed. He giggled and said, "See, see. She can't do without you." After a while, he added, "Anything you ask, she will do." I thought he was joking, but his face was serious now. He walked over to her bed, snatched her hand and wrenched. She opened her eyes wide. I could see she was terrified. "Now she can move hand. In little while she will be dancing and skipping in road." He giggled again. The old woman's lips stiffened. I thought she was going to spit on him. He tugged her fingers and waved her hand around. The loose skin on her arm rippled.

"Stop."

He looked at me and shook her arm again.

"Please."

He shook it once more and giggled like a madman. Finally, he opened his fingers and her hand dropped to the bed. "Shock therapy." He grinned and left the room.

I tried to understand his cruelty, and when Ani came up, I almost told her. As was his habit, he entered the room immediately after his wife had left. His lopsided grin warned me that he was up to no good. I dragged my chair almost against the television and pretended I was watching a thin, balding man with the face of a bad-tempered butcher talking about some court case.

"Now you interested in politics." I felt his breath, hot and upsetting against my face. "He is mayor. Giuliani. A good man." Now a woman with plump cheeks and shoulder-length hair began chatting about her husband. She was smiling in a worried manner. She looked like an overfed bird, but I felt she might have been attractive in her younger days. "The president wife," Bagrat muttered in my ear as if it was a big secret. "She is involve with fraudulent deal." He hesitated, then said, "I think she should sign paper. Of what use is all this property to her? Maybe you get her to sign."

"Me?" I couldn't understand what he was babbling about.

"She trust you. You are only one."

I laughed at his joke. He placed his hand on my shoulder and laughed too. When the old woman looked at him with dread, I understood. I got up and my chair toppled to the floor. "No!" I screamed at him, and he shrank back.

Ani rushed into the room. When she saw that her mother was still alive, she turned to us. "What happened?" She seemed even more puzzled when Bagrat strode away. I returned to the television, and while she was asking over and over, I continued to stare at the butcher and the overfed bird trading insults.

Bagrat never came into the room again. Not once. His quarrelling grew worse, but now, when I was hobbling down the stairs, he didn't make any nasty jokes; he just fixed me a ferocious look. I think Ani expected me to reveal the cause of my alarm, but whenever I heard her coming up the stairs, I pretended I was exercising, and when that became too painful, I just sat before the television.

My mother had complained that I stood at the window and just stared out whenever something was bothering me, looking out at the mountain and not speaking. Now I just stared at the television. Men and women appeared and disappeared like ghosts. I never paid them much attention even though they looked important, with crowds of reporters trailing after them. I felt they were plump American versions of the people I had always known. Like the president with his red, juicy nose and twinkly smile. He reminded me of Leila's former employer, the cheery pastry maker. And the fat dark woman who chatted with other women, mostly slimmer and fairer, about healing and miracles could have been the village midwife. One night, the television midwife was chatting with a group of women who were recovering from drugs and alcohol. Some of the women had dark crescents beneath their eyes, others had fat, piggy faces, and one had a yellow, watery glow on her neck.

They were beautiful.

Then the show ended and they were gone.

The next day, the old woman stared at me holding my back and limping impatiently from one end of the room to the other, but I didn't bother with her. Finally, the show began. The midwife burst on the stage and began talking about spiritual journeys and healing. Her different hairstyle and the way she bounced on the stage should have suggested that this show would be different.

When she introduced her guests, I sank in my chair. They all had excellent skin and shining hair and wide smiles which showed off their teeth and gums. One by one they recounted their spiritual journeys, and while the midwife sat forward on her couch with her chin flat on her palms, they revealed they were now reborn. They confessed that various books had helped them along the way. Two of the writers were there. They were not as young and healthy-looking as the guests, but they too had huge, gummy smiles and shining hair. The midwife asked the writers about their books and they held them up for the audience—who clapped and murmured—as the writers rattled off five or six paths for fulfillment, some more paths for salvation and a couple others for redemption. The guests nodded at these paths and their hair bounced and rippled.

I could understand none of this. Although I was never very religious, I always thought that these paths involved a search of some sort. But the journeys these people were talking about were not journeys at all. In a way, this was brilliant. Everything was made simple and easy. I admit that I was bothered that these guests' strange religion involved only themselves, but they all seemed excited and talkative and meditative.

Ani too was looking contemplative. Maybe she was recalling one of her own journeys. She sat there for a while before she said that these shows had helped millions of people. I got up. "Where are you going?"

"On a journey," I told her.

And that night, I walked until every bone in my body felt as if it was springing out of place. Just three blocks, but I felt that my journey had begun. The next night, I took the same route but paid more attention to the men and women walking tiredly to some destination. I looked at the buildings too, many of them old two-storey structures like Panos's, but also a few that were taller and dirtier, with many windows. I hurried past the convenience store where the police had thrown me against the car, to a red building with teenagers smoking on the steps. Why were they out so late? Did they have parents? Yet they were all well dressed, with colourful jackets and baggy pants.

By the end of the week, I felt confident enough to tackle another block. This new area was crowded not with teenagers but with women standing at the sides of the road. Sometimes a car would pull over and one of the women would hop inside. Once, a car that had stopped to pick up one of the women screeched and reversed towards me. I remembered my encounter with the police and moved away. The woman sitting on the passenger side said something and the man laughed and drove off. It was only when I was walking back that I figured out what she had said: "He's only a fucking cripple." And I realized something else: the woman with her short skirt and red lips was a prostitute.

I should have seen this before, but the fault was all mine. I had imprisoned myself in Panos's house for the last four months. I had delayed my journey.

One cold night when the breeze was whistling through the trees and scattering the leaves on the sidewalk, I contemplated the various stages of my own journey. First I was a carefree vagabond, then a married man, then a gardener, then a reader of books, then an old-woman–overseer, and now an explorer. The journey had not been delayed; it had been going on for a while without my knowledge. Maybe it had begun much earlier—from the time my uncles would glare at me as if I didn't belong in my mother's house.

Walking down into the basement that cold night, I thought that perhaps all journeys begin without our knowledge.

I thought of this while I was tending the old woman that night. Her journey had ended, but she couldn't see this. I wondered how Ani would react if I mentioned this view to her. She rarely spoke to me again, maybe because she knew I wanted to be alone, but I missed her massages. When she came up, I looked at her and smiled, but just a little. She asked about my back.

I told her I missed her massages. She seemed set to say something, then changed her mind. I asked her. Her eyes widened. Here? Now? While she sat there looking surprised, I unbuttoned my shirt. When Ani stood behind me, I heard the old woman clacking. The clacking grew louder and more irritating, disturbing my relaxation, so I began to hum one of my mother's songs. After a while, Ani joined in, though I could tell she didn't know the tune. She hummed more to the beat of what her hands were doing—softly when her fingers were gliding across my back, and faster and louder when she was kneading. It was the best massage yet. I believe this was partly because I was relieved we were friends again. I suspect she too was relieved.

The next night, she brought up a coat and a cane. She looked funny holding the coat in one hand and the cane in the other. My eyes began to water. I was ashamed she would notice, so I slung the jacket across my shoulder and pranced around the room with my cane, looking like these rich old men from television. Laughing, she said, "For your nighttime walks."

"My journeys."

She continued to laugh, thinking it a joke. Finally, she said, "It's going to get chillier each day now. It's fall. Almost the end of the cycle. Things begin to die now."

"Like your mother?"

"Oh no no. I mean the trees and flowers. The plants from Pappa's garden."

"Yes, I know. Autumn. Thanks for the coat and the walking stick."

She smiled. "The cane."

I discovered that by balancing my weight on the cane and shifting most of my movement to the right side of my body, it was possible to walk further each night. The pain was still there, but now I was able to control it. And in a strange way I felt safer now. People glanced at me without much interest, maybe because I didn't pose any threat. Just a fookin' invalid. Now, though, I didn't mind as much as when Bagrat had taunted me.

Whenever I stopped to rest, I looked around. Everywhere is different in some way, but if you look closely, you can always see something that reminds you of another place, maybe another time in your life.

Like the prostitutes.

I began to understand their routine. They stood at the street corners for a while and if no cars pulled up, they moved on. They each had their favourite corner. The younger ones hung around in groups of three, but the old ones with thick legs and hair piled in layers on their head just stood alone, surrounded by cigarette smoke. After a while I felt I could recognize them all. I gave them Armenian names. The tall one who stood like a statue was Mariyam, the impatient one who smoked cigarette after cigarette was Karineh and the one who wore only black was Eraz.

One night, Karineh smiled across the street at me. It was a peaceful, chilly night, and the smoke over her head looked like a silky shawl. I waited for a car to go by and crossed the street.

"Hello." She had a breathless voice. "Whereya off to?"

When I understood the question, I told her, "I'm taking a walk. For my back."

"Oh, you too, eh." She glanced at the cane, flicked away her cigarette and fished into her purse. There was a small welt just beneath her neck. She looked up and caught me staring. "You live around here?"

An approaching car bathed us in its headlights and she lost interest in my answer. The car pulled over and she opened the door. Maybe she knew the driver, a brown-coloured man with oiled-down hair. The car pulled off with her, and she looked at me and smiled.

The next night she waved at me from across the street and said something to her two friends. They glanced at me and resumed chatting. One of them laughed loudly. I walked on. They looked like schoolgirls on their night out, with their short skirts and cigarettes and rowdy laughter.

I decided to explore another block. Most of the buildings were old and abandoned, with broken windows and writing scrawled on the walls. A drain was clogged with paper and bottles. On the other side of the drain was an empty lot with a pile of rotting crates at one end and an old trailer at the other. In the centre were two huge old cars without tires. The place smelled wet and soggy, like unwashed clothes. Where had all the inhabitants disappeared to? My mind drifted to Ani's conversations about the extermination of our people, and the villages empty but for the few inconsolable relatives wandering around.

I was about to walk back when another cripple stumbled by, his head bent low. He was grumbling and cursing. A woman stepped out of the darkness just behind him. The cripple heard the clap of her heels and stopped. Without turning around, he began to curse loudly. The woman stood there, her legs close together, one hand on her purse. She looked away from us, which I found strange. The cripple began to flap his hands, and his body slouched in a lumbering dance. When he collapsed on his knees, the woman rushed to him and tried to pull him up, but he kept wriggling away from her grip. Finally, she gave up. The cripple remained on his knees, shaking like a dog. The woman turned and walked away, her head bobbing forward. She had a long, bony face and high cheekbones, but it was too dark to see her clearly. She might have been wearing a wig.

When I was walking back, in spite of the cold, I was sweating. I knew it was because of the woman.

The next three nights, I walked around the dirty block, resting on my cane whenever I grew too tired. I despaired that I would never see her again. For three days, instead of exercising, I just sat before the television, watching these skinny young women with tiny upturned noses and fleshy lips and bouncy hair, flirting and sometimes quarrelling with an assortment of young men. The skinny women laughed, tossed their heads, showed their legs, flashed their smiles. The mysterious woman seemed even more beautiful in comparison.

On the fourth night, I spotted her. She was standing just beyond the dull circle cast by a street lamp. I hesitated and took a deep breath. An insect, maybe a tiny moth, got into my nose. I rubbed my nose, surprised by its coldness, and tried to snort out the insect. The woman began walking away. I followed, trying to keep up with her unusual bobbing stride. She walked with her legs close together. They were thin and gawky, like a swamp bird's, and I had this silly idea that they might take off from the ground at any minute. I tried to walk faster, but she was getting away. My cane tapped the pavement noisily. I stumbled. When I looked up, she was gone. I hurried to the area I had last seen her and looked around in the shadows of an abandoned four-storey building with windows nailed shut. Had she run up the four steps and entered the building? Yet the only sound I heard was a faint, prolonged cough, a car backfiring in the distance. I remained outside the building for about ten or fifteen minutes.

The next day, from the clench of Ani's fingers on my back and her slow, deliberate motion, I guessed she had something to say. Maybe it was because of my red eyes and my sneezing. She stopped massaging and placed her palms flat on my shoulders. I waited. "Your skin."

"Is it falling off?"

"No, silly. It's hot. You're getting a fever." Then she added, "You're staying out late at nights." I felt this was more a question than a statement, but I remained silent. "It's not safe."

"No one will interfere with a cripple. I'm lucky."

She misunderstood. "Don't say that. You're not a cripple. I don't know why you—"

"I have met a woman."

"Oh." She removed her hands from my shoulders.

"I think she's a prostitute."

"A what?"

"A prostitute." The shock in her voice made me want to invent something about me and this prostitute. Why should she care? She of all persons.

"Be careful." That was all she said. And I felt my little anger slipping away, and wished she had asked other questions so I could explain that although I had not clearly seen the woman's face, I knew she was beautiful; that I had chased after her last night; that I was going to do the same night after night.

As the season progressed and fall faded into winter, I was obstructed in my search for the woman, both by the coldness and by my pain. Some mornings I could barely move. Occasionally, when Ani talked about her mother's improvement, her voice would drift off, and I felt she was thinking of the prostitute. Maybe she was wondering how my knotted body managed. I thought of that too. How I *would* manage. But more and more I believed that I would never feel a woman's warmth against me again, and a few times while I was shivering in the basement, I imagined myself dying alone, with no one to miss me.

These thoughts neither saddened nor soured me. It just seemed so unnatural that someone thirty-one years old would recall his young days as a distant memory. But my own unusual condition was just one of many. There were four of us in the house, and although we were connected to each other in some small way, this attachment was only for some practical purpose. I suppose we needed each other, and when the need was no more, the connection would be cut. How different this was from my life in Armenia! How young and silly and naive I had been. I understood nothing.

One night, I was returning from one of my walks. Light snow was drifting down, and in the faint light the flakes looked like white moths floating around the trees. The air was warmer than usual and I walked slowly. A woman with a scarf on her head passed by. A door creaked open and a black woman placed her garbage into an open container. She returned to her house and the door creaked shut, as if it was jammed. Everything seemed to be moving sluggishly, even the wind fluting through the trees and lightly swishing the leaves. I stopped to look up at the drifting snow and imagined I saw twisting, intersecting tunnels. A window was banging against a wall. Whenever it opened, I heard some opera song. I tried to piece together the tune from these brief snatches, but each time it sounded different. I closed my eyes and tried to blunt out the intervals, and imagined that the song was one of those mournful *pandukht* tunes sung by lonely people crying for their families. Maybe it was the song of the homeless, "Andounee," which my mother often hummed while she was cooking.

It was bewitching. The snow fell on my face and hair, and while I listened to the song, I felt purer than at any time I could remember. *Purer.* I know it's a strange word for someone in my situation. People came and went; that was my life. I expected nothing more.

As I said, I knew nothing.

Part Two

When the air froze over and the birds disappeared from the trees, I continued my journey by bus. I was now able to travel further and experience new places. I got a schedule from the driver and timed my trips to avoid waiting too long at the curb.

I usually chose a seat at the back if one was vacant. Each time I hopped on the bus, I scanned around for the beautiful, bobbing woman who had vanished in the darkness. Sometimes I saw other women sitting alone. Most looked like the stylish variety I saw on television, but occasionally I spotted a real beauty. Once or twice I thought of making some excuse to sit next to these women, but they all seemed too tired and worried. Or in pain of some sort. Perhaps they were returning from long shifts at some factory to houses with quarrelsome husbands and noisy children.

I wondered at their lives, these women. I wished one of them would sit next to me, but they usually chose the front seats. So I started moving up. A few times they came in pairs and I listened quietly to their conversations, memorizing the strange American expressions. *Gee, that's sumptin, aint it? It's driving me nuts. Get outta here, you're kidding. Lissen, girlfriend, you just look Hubert straight in the eye and tell him you're nobody's bitch.*

One night, a darkish woman, like someone from Syria, stumbled next to me. But her features were flat and she smelled oily, like butter or lard. Her fat, stumpy legs were almost hidden in her heavy leather boots, which might have been too tight for her. She tilted her head onto the back of the seat. A few minutes later, I heard her snoring. Her lips fluttered with each breath. The bus stopped. She jerked forward, opened her eyes and yawned. I felt like wiping away the drop of spit at the side of her mouth. Or licking it away with a soft kiss. She tilted back once more, closed her eyes, and the spit glistened like a speck of pearl. I leaned across and swiftly brushed it away with a finger. She opened her eyes and glared at me. When she stood up, I noted her massive hips. She began shouting in some strange language. The driver glanced back. The woman snatched her bag and marched to the front. She continued in her strange language with the driver. I looked out the window. When I was getting off, the driver inspected my face and my cane.

From then on, I took another bus. I didn't expect to see many people, because it was almost eleven at night, but there were just as many passengers. This driver, a thick woman, maybe about two hundred pounds, was not bad-looking, but I kept my distance at the back of the bus, careful to look away before anyone's eyes caught mine. I did not want to be known as some kind of bus pervert. I started bringing along my books. I felt more comfortable to stare now, because it would seem as if I was just reflecting on something I had read. The books became a shield, like my cane.

That was how I met Moira. At first, she chose the seat opposite mine or the one just ahead, but I never paid her much attention because she had the television look. She was not skinny, though, and she walked with a little bounce which caused her coat to close and open with each step. One night, she seemed to be heading for the seat opposite, hesitated and, with a flurry of her coat, sat next to me. I shifted away and tried to read. She said nothing for the entire trip. The next night, she settled next to me once again, which was very distressing. She was humbugging my privacy. The following night, I sat one row further down. It didn't work. I read for the entire trip, not once looking up.

I thought of switching back to the earlier bus, but remembered the driver who had stared at me up and down. Just when I was wondering if she was going to begin a conversation or something, she started bringing along her own books. That made me feel less pressured. Her books were written by authors named Danielle Steel and Maeve Binchy and Michael Crichton. She traced her finger along the sentences while she read, and sometimes she murmured lightly. I always knew when she was staring at my book because her finger would momentarily linger on one spot.

So we read side by side, not bothering each other. In a way it was a sort of friendship. When, occasionally, she brought along a newspaper, I read with her, learning of the various shootings and robberies, and of the attempts by a sour-looking group of conspirators to impeach the cheery-nose pastry maker. *Impeach*. The word confused me at first. It sounded delicious and forbidden—something you might do to your first girlfriend when her parents were away.

One night, I saw a photograph on the second page of her newspaper. My book fell from my lap. When I bent to get it, my head grazed the woman's leg and a sharp pain ran down my shoulder. I felt the pressure of the woman's leg on my face. I braced my hand on the edge of the seat, almost below her thigh, and forced myself up.

"I'm sorry," I said, and for the first time I looked directly at her. Her eyes were wide open and the corner of her lips curved up as if she was controlling a grin.

She reached down for my book and placed it above the newspaper on her lap. I saw her fingers caressing the spine.

"Can I borrow your papers?"

"Why, sure," she said, as if the words had been on her tongue all along. She folded the newspaper and passed it to me, but kept the book.

I turned to the photograph. It *was* her. The long, bony face. The high cheekbones. The cheap wig slanting slightly to one side. She looked sad and foolish, like when she was helping up the cripple. The bus stopped. I grabbed my cane.

The next night, I returned the newspaper and got my book. I started to apologize, and then I noticed the woman's eyes widening and her lips curving, and I changed my mind. We sat in silence, then after about five minutes she said, "I looked through your book. I hope you don't mind. It's very interesting." She paused for a while. "So do you live around here or are you doing some research?"

"Live."

"Do you like it here? I guess it must be different from your old country."

"It's okay."

"I'm sure your work must be very interesting. You're younger than I expected, though." What was she babbling about? And how interesting could my work be?

"Oh, I'm sorry." She extended her hand. "I'm Moira." I grasped her hand. "Last night . . . "

After a while, I asked her, "Yes?"

Her fingers loosened. I slipped my hand away. "You left so abruptly. I hope I didn't offend you."

"No. It was something I read in the newspaper."

"Oh." She exhaled. "I thought so. But I wasn't sure," she added quickly. "Was it the article about the people in . . . where was it now . . . India, I think . . . who burnt stacks of genetically modified seeds?"

"No, no." Why would she think that?

"Well?"

Why did she widen her eyes so often? "It was about a prostitute who was murdered by her crippled brother."

"Did you know her?"

"I saw her twice."

She flicked open the newspaper and turned to the article. "'Neighbours testified that she took care of him since his accident,'" she read. "'He was found shivering on the stairs, too drugged out to escape. He was still clutching the bloodied bowl.'" She looked up at me. "She was feeding him."

"I believe so."

She folded the newspaper, pushed it beneath the seat and got out one of her books. "So were you in an accident?"

"An accident?"

"Your cane." She opened and closed the book as if she were fanning herself.

"Spondylitis." I opened my own book. I knew she had more questions, but the only thing she said before I got out was, "The prostitute you saw . . . I wouldn't have expected it from a man like you."

The words almost came to my mouth: I'm crippled, not dead. It was only later in the night that I remembered that Zoravar had inscribed on the back cover of the book, *Zoravar Aspiarian, Professor of Biotechnology, University of Armenia.*

I was surprised at how comfortable I felt with the lie. I soon convinced myself that I had not said anything untruthful. The assumption was hers, not mine. But sometimes we are conquered by the roles others have given to us, and over the next three weeks I reread all of Zoravar's books. I made connections and cross-referenced the topics that interested me, like bioethics. I memorized. I soon developed a new vocabulary. *Medifoods. Pharm animals. Frankenfoods. Ecocide.* I gave Ani a list of topics and she returned with a stack of books, which I read while the old woman stared at the television. Not knowing the real reason for my scholarly urge, Ani looked on appreciatively.

One night, while she was feeding her mother, I looked up from a book and told her, "She is dead."

She held the spoon above her mother's mouth.

"Who is?"

"The prostitute."

She asked whether it was from a disease, and when I shook my head, she resumed feeding her mother. When I was leaving, she said, "I'm sorry. You will find someone else."

~

On the eleven o'clock bus, Moira made up for her earlier silence. She told me she was "a weary journalist" pounding out her fingers in a "cubicle surrounded by children just out of the university." She had also been a receptionist for a doctor, a travel agent, a computer programmer and a waitress. They were all ventures she had tired of. After her second wedding, also a venture, she settled down to two years of married life. She was paralyzed by the domestic routine and soon moved out to a one-room apartment and began tutoring Chinese children in tap dancing. That lasted less than a year. She was now thinking of writing a novel—her grandest venture. Or maybe it would be a memoir. She mentioned several unfamiliar names: Victoria Principal, Maria Shriver, Tim Robbins, Susan Sarandon. She had also worked briefly in a health club. Some of these people had invited her to their homes. She didn't say which ones.

She asked where I lived, and when I told her the street number, she said, "I can imagine your house down to every detail. Books and plants in every corner." As she went on, I felt she was describing Zoravar's house. She widened her eyes. "I have this gift." I grew uncomfortable with this gift of hers and regretted revealing my street number. I prayed she wouldn't venture there.

One night, she mentioned the name of a pub, the Thistle and Harp. She spent a few hours there after work, writing her articles. It was easier to compose in a place filled with noise and energy.

"Not in your house, then?"

"My apartment?" She smiled. "I reserve there for better things."

"Like what?"

"You'll have to come over to find out."

I laughed at her joke.

I went instead to the pub. The place was crowded with men and women waving glasses around and chatting and laughing. Finally, I spotted Moira in the corner, bent over some loose sheets. Her hair spilled over her forehead, and from a distance she looked like a television moppet.

"Hello."

She glanced up, frowning. Then her face resumed its wide-eyed look. "Oh. Here, have a seat. I didn't think you would show."

"I needed a break."

"Don't we all." She lit a cigarette and inhaled slowly.

"I didn't know you smoked."

"One of my vices. Would you like something to drink?"

I was unfamiliar with American drinks, so I told her, "Whatever you're drinking."

She called the waiter over and, with the cigarette swaying between her lips, ordered two beers.

She sipped and looked at me through her cigarette smoke. "So, I've been doing all the talking."

"Very true."

She smiled. "I mean that you know everything about me. You've never told me anything of yourself."

The moment I dreaded. I took a drink and finished half the glass. "I have nothing interesting to say."

"Oh, I'm sure that's not true. The modest professor—now, that's a turn. You know, that first day in the bus I saw it."

Saw what? I wanted to ask, but instead I said, "Your gift?"

"I noticed the . . . forgive me for saying this, but I noticed your tortured look and I knew immediately that you were an academic. A researcher of some sort."

"It's the pain in my back."

She threw back her head and laughed. Then she leaned forward, more serious. "So?" I noticed her glancing at my hair. I looked away, saw the waitress and ordered two more beers.

I told her my name was Zoravar Aspiarian and that

I was a professor at the University of Armenia. One evening, I had returned from my class and discovered my gardener poking about between my wife's legs. I felt that my life had broken. I left the university, left Armenia.

"Really?"

"Yes, it's true." Well, *some* of the details were true.

She pressed her fingers lightly against her lips. "Don't take this the wrong way, but it's the sort of thing you read about in cartoons over here. The gardener, the milkman, the plumber."

"It was very painful," I said gravely.

"Oh, I'm sure it was. I'm sorry I brought it up. Let's change the topic. Do you live by yourself here?"

"I'm renting from a couple. The wife's mother lives with them. She's an invalid."

"I meant . . . "

"A woman?" She stubbed her cigarette and twisted the butt on the ashtray. I wondered if she was a bit drunk. I told her, "I spend all my time reading."

She looked up at me and her eyes flashed. Perhaps she was thinking of the prostitute. Then she glanced at her watch and lit another cigarette. "Well, I guess we've missed our bus. Would you like another drink?" She held up two fingers at the waitress before I replied. When the drinks were brought over, she hunched over her glass and spun it slowly. "Can I feel your head?"

"What?"

"One of my hobbies was phrenology."

"Then it's okay." The moment I said that, I knew I was becoming drunk.

She reached across and ran her fingers through my head. "You have lovely hair, Zoravar. Soft and silky."

"What are you looking for, exactly?" I wondered if the other customers were staring at us. Maybe they thought we were being romantic.

"Bumps." Her fingers circled my crown. "You have a saddle—a slope at the centre. I've never come across that before. I wonder what it signifies?" Her finger trailed to my temple, over my ear. At this close range I noticed the freckles scattering outward from her nose. Her eyes appeared huge in her small oval face. She looked like a gremlin. I had never realized how beautiful she was.

She glanced at her watch once more. "I think I should call a taxi." She gathered her purse and went to the counter. When she returned, she put on her coat a bit unsteadily and said, "Don't bother, I've paid the bill. Shall we leave?"

She sat at the centre of the back seat. I placed my cane between my legs and looked out at the buildings. The driver slowed at an intersection and asked for directions. Moira repeated the street number impatiently. The driver spoke into his phone in another language. The unfamiliarity of the driver's strange language, Moira sitting at my side, this section of the city with its tall buildings, my dizziness—all of this made me feel like a vacationer in a strange land. I closed my eyes and thought of waterfalls and lakes and mountains and exotic gardens. When we got out and walked from the lobby of her tall building to the elevator, when she fidgeted with the keys and opened the door, I felt even more like an adventurous wanderer in a strange land. A *taparogh*.

Her living room was bare, apart from the one couch set against the corner, but on the walls there were photographs of men and women who seemed to be models, and over a fireplace, a rug with Persian letters. "They are all gifts." She took my coat and draped it over a rack. "Make yourself at home." She went into the washroom and I heard the slap of water. I sat on the couch and waited until she breezed out of the washroom wearing a loose bathrobe. Her wet hair fell in streaks over her face. "There's coffee in the machine," she said, and disappeared into a door alongside the living room.

The upper shelves of her fridge were filled with fruits and small plastic containers, and the lowest with partly filled bottles of wine. I poured myself a glass of apple juice, closed the fridge and walked over to the couch. I tried to read the Persian letters, but the inscription was too decorative and I was too drunk. Moira came out of the room to adjust the fire. Her small waist flared at the buttocks and narrowed again at the legs.

Bent over, she looked like an egg. I decided I would gaze at the flames dancing like dervishes until I fell asleep. Then I heard Moira from the doorway. "Aren't you coming?"

When I went into the room, she was already in bed. In the faint light I saw her knees and toes sticking out from beneath the white sheet. I removed my trousers and shirt and went to the bed. I lay there for about five minutes or so. I felt her pillow shifting and peeped out of the corner of my eyes. Her hand was snaking down under the sheet. She made a soft sound and opened her legs, touching me. Her skin was a bit damp. The sheet ruffled above her belly and she began to breathe heavily. Then she threw a leg over mine and gripped my hand. I had thought of jumping on her, but this was no longer possible. I waited for some signal. She squeezed my hand tighter and guided it along her soft skin, down to her sheer stubbles. She exhaled from deep in her throat, and I felt her buttocks rising slightly as she directed my fingers. Then her legs slumped back to the bed. Her fingers relaxed a little but kept their hold. After a while her breathing grew shallower.

I concentrated on the room. There was a faint fishy odour. I heard a bubbling and imagined there was an aquarium somewhere by the window. As my eyes adjusted more to the darkness, I noticed the mirror above the bed and, in the left corner of the room, a table and bookshelf. Above the bookshelf was a line of stuffed animals suspended on the wall. I remembered a toy bear my father had brought home on my fifth birthday. He had placed it under my pillow, and in the night I had felt the long fluffy ears and screamed. I fell asleep dreaming of my parents. Somehow, our house had been transported to Brooklyn and the old woman was living with us. I think she was quarrelling with my father.

When I awoke early in the morning, it was still dark. My throat felt dry and swollen. I got up, groped for my cane at the foot of the bed, went to the washroom, stepped into the tub and turned on the water. I sat in the tub with my back against the faucet, and the warm water sprinkled over my head and back. I must have dozed off. The curtain rustled and I saw Moira standing over me with her eyes wide open. She pulled back the curtain and I heard her brushing her teeth. With a muffled voice she said, "I have to leave for work in a while. The spare key is on the kitchen table. Lock the door if you leave."

About ten in the morning, I locked the door and walked out to the street. The building and cars looked newer than at Panos's place. People in suits were rushing along on the street as if they were in a great hurry. Maybe they had urgent appointments in the new buildings with glass windows. How uncomplicated these people's lives must be, I thought. Regular jobs and families and savings. Their journeys were all neatly charted.

All at once I felt afraid of this new stage in my own journey. What would I say to Ani?

Maybe to delay the scene in Panos's house, I went into a small diner crowded with old couples eating bagels and sipping slowly from their cups. Immediately after I had ordered tea, a man with his belly hanging over his trousers, and a big head which made him look like an evil baby, sat next to me and punched some numbers in his cellphone. His fingers were stubby and perhaps he was drunk, because he had to redial several times, swearing as if he was the only one around. Finally, he placed his phone on the counter. "Goddamn Sid." He looked at me as if I knew his Sid and should be annoyed too. He made one last attempt before he slammed down the phone and turned to me. "Never trust a Sid. They're all crooks."

He seemed to be awaiting a response, but I was in no mood for chatting. I told him, *"Ara, es-e ordoots egav"* ("Ara, where did this fellow come from"). My response in Armenian was a mistake because it didn't discourage him one bit.

"You're from Tur-kay? Hadda guy from Tur-kay who worked for me. Same big nose."

"Herrika glooks hartookess," I told him. Please stop ironing my head.

"Glook glook." He laughed. "Canya speak English? Speakee speakee?" Now he span in his stool towards me as if we were about to begin a long conversation.

I am from Armenia, sir. A professor in biotechnology. But I told him nothing.

"This Tur-kaish guy, his name was Moose, and he couldn't speak a word of English when he started working in my garage."

Get outta here. You're kidding.

"Hadda fire him, though. Caught him smoking one of them foreign drugs. Hashish." He leaned closer. "Big nose guy. Just like you. Say, you addicted to that stuff too?"

Listen, Hubert, I'm nobody's bitch.

He shrank back and snatched his phone. I hurried out of the diner.

On the way to Panos's house, I noticed the tall apartments being replaced by three-storey buildings with dirty windows and garbage cans at the sides of the steps. I had to change three buses before I finally arrived at the familiar street with its small old houses and neatly pruned hedges. On the way I was worried that I would see an ambulance or police car parked outside, but the house seemed quiet. I raised the latch and walked inside, to the foot of the stairs. A spoon hit a saucer. Someone was feeding the old woman. I stood there for a minute or two, went down to the basement and dragged out my suitcase from the cupboard.

"You're leaving?" Ani asked from the doorway.

I nodded but didn't look up.

"Where are you going? Did you find another job? I was worried."

I didn't know which of these three utterances I should respond to.

"I thought you were in an accident. I couldn't go to work. I almost called the police. You don't know this place, Saren. It's not Armenia."

It was the first time she had used my name. "I must go," I told her. My nervous voice must have sounded angry, because she said nothing else. "I must go. Please," I repeated several times. I could not understand why I was pleading. Over and over, I told her: My journey. My journey.

She counted out some money from her purse, handed it to me and said, "It's all right. I understand." As if I were being perfectly reasonable.

~

When Moira came home late in the afternoon, she seemed less surprised by my presence than by the dishes I had arranged on the cupboard. We ate sitting on the living-room carpet. Moira talked about her day and complained about the young journalists—"glamour girls," she called them. When she was finished eating, she stretched her legs before her and leaned back on the couch. While I was washing the dishes, she asked me to bring a bottle of wine from the fridge. After the bottle was finished, she reclined once more, closed her eyes, complained a bit more about some little bitch at her work, sighed and heaved herself up.

I planned my move.

I waited for about ten minutes after her shower before I entered the room. She was rubbing a cream on her neck. I waited on the bed. When she joined me, she crossed her ankles and I worried that she was going to fall asleep, but then she started her routine. Immediately, I shifted onto her. She made a sharp sound as if she was surprised and her fingers clenched the sheet, but soon they were stroking my hair and shoulders and back. When I slowed, she pushed me off gently and got on top. She slid her legs up the sheet, and when she leaned towards me, I placed my hands on her small breasts. That seemed to please her, and from her fluttery breathing I sensed what she liked. When we were finished, she uttered a soft groan and rolled over. I waited for the pain, but I felt relaxed and warm, like after one of Ani's massages. Moira turned on her side and snuggled against me. I wanted to enjoy her warmth, but I fell asleep quickly.

Each evening, I set out the food on the cupboard. Moira liked to have a few drinks after her meal, and with her feet stretched before her she spoke about growing up in Brooklyn. I tried to imagine her playing handball or eating these strange dishes like knishes and Mello Rolls, and catching tadpoles in the Japanese garden, and going on dates to the Strand Theatre, the

Ambassador, Majestic Theatre and the Palace. The names sounded so magical, so different from the television America I had grown to know. Occasionally, she would close her eyes and I would think she was asleep, then without looking at me, she would say that childhood memories are the best because you remember mostly yourself; there are no intruders. I couldn't understand her, because my memory of that time was overflowing with uncles. Sometimes she would rest her head on the couch and look at the ceiling, and I would think that she was recalling other memories which she preferred not to share. While all of this was going on, I waited for her to go to the bathroom. I now delayed for about twenty minutes before I entered the room, and even forced myself to be still while she squirmed beneath the sheets. Only when she grabbed my hand would I heft my body over her.

She fell asleep soon after. I suspected she was too tired for any conversation. And I was too embarrassed. One night, after she had dropped off to sleep, I remembered a show I had seen on television in the sickroom. A young woman was chatting about her old, wrinkled husband with her friends. The friends were provoking her about the couple's lovemaking, and the young woman had rolled her eyes and said that each night she felt old age creeping up on her. It was a while before I understood the joke; now I wondered if Moira felt that way. Even though she looked about five or six years older than me.

I was relieved that she rushed off early in the mornings, because I had no idea what we would talk about; or worse, what I would say if she asked me about my research or posed some unanswerable question about the university in Armenia. The fear gripped me with each passing day. I tried to anticipate her questions. Each morning, I wrote some observation or explanation or fact that I recalled from Zoravar's and Ani's books. After a while I hit on a plan. I would satisfy her curiosity by placing the notebook on the couch or on her table or on the cupboard. While I was writing these little notes, I was surprised at how much I had grasped from the books. I read of the growing number of scientists who were worried that new, dangerous plant viruses could destroy beneficial insects, and who feared that this trend towards genetic uniformity would wipe out many, many species of plants. Although I was shocked by this new knowledge, I have to say that I was also disappointed. I felt like someone who had been given a new toy, gradually discovering unexplained rattles and faults. One morning, I remembered the name of the book I had spotted on Zoravar's table on that fateful day: *Genetic Genies*. I had thought then that it was about the stories my mother had told me when she wanted me to fall asleep.

One morning, I asked Moira about nearby bookstores. I explained that I had read these books so often that several passages had stuck in my mind, which was true. Later that day, I walked one block to the second-hand store she had mentioned. I used fifty of the three hundred dollars given to me by Ani and left the store with six books. When I opened the books later, in the apartment, I noticed that they were just a year or two old, and that they bore the names of the previous owners and the universities they had attended.

I tackled the smaller books first, reading the underlined sections and paying attention to the notes scrawled alongside. I felt I was beginning to know the interests of these previous owners. Sometimes I would pretend I was studying in a crowded classroom. In three weeks, I filled four notebooks.

One Friday, Moira came home from work late in the night. I was waiting for her on the couch, but she went straight into the bedroom without eating or showering. She seemed in a bad mood, so I packed the food away in the fridge and waited for her to say something. That night, I slept on the couch. In the morning, she said she would be away for the weekend and asked me to feed the fishes.

The next day, I took the bus to some of the places about which she had spoken. I went to the Japanese garden, hunting for tadpoles. I searched for children playing stoopball, and licking at Mello-Rolls. By the time I ended at Coney Island with dirty streets bearing Russian names, I felt that something had died. I felt sorry for Moira. She reminded me of the people whose homes were destroyed by the earthquake when I was sixteen. That night, I lay on the couch and decided that I would try to make her happy once more, and repay her for everything she had given to me and all I had taken.

On Sunday, I set about preparing my Armenian dishes. I substituted apples for pomegranates, and apricot jam for my wife's jellies. The apartment smelled of cinnamon and honey and yogurt. I arranged the fruits like the television hostesses and brought out two long-stemmed glasses from Moira's cupboard. I fell asleep late that night. I have no idea when she arrived, but in the morning I saw her by the stove, munching one of my pastries. She looked paler than usual, or at least the area around her eyes. Her lower lip was slightly bruised, as if she had been chewing at it. My heart melted. She dusted her hands over the sink and left.

In the evening, she did not talk about her childhood, but just sipped at her wine and stared at her fingernails. I wanted to cheer her up, so I mentioned one of the books I had bought. I recalled some of the observations I had made in the notebooks. This was the first time I had spoken about the field Zoravar had bequeathed to me, and like a child impressing a parent with some new knowledge, I went on and on. I told her about the antifreeze protein gene copied from the flounder to enable tomatoes to freeze and thaw better, and I expressed my worry that soon it would be difficult to characterize some plants, and that vegetarians would never know exactly what went into their mouths. But on the other hand, there were also genes found naturally in both plants and animals, like the gene occurring both in rice and in the human brain. Words rushed out of my head; it could have been Zoravar speaking.

I slept once more on the sofa, but I was happy that I had satisfied her curiosity. During the week, I talked to her more about my readings, not concerned as before that she would see through my pretence. I felt proud to use my new vocabulary when I talked about patenting issues and gene transfer to non-target species, and plant vaccines, and bioethics. I mentioned the growing fear of environmental activists and religious groups, and my own stupid thoughts about the effect on the soul of transplanted genes. It occurred to me that this was the sort of thing the television midwife liked to chat about, but I kept this particular thought to myself. Maybe I was a good lecturer, or she a good listener, because not once did she interrupt. I soon grew used to sleeping on the sofa, then on the carpet, which seemed to agree a little more with my back.

One night, I went into the bathroom. I thought she was in her room, because I did not hear the sound of water, but she was standing in the tub with her hands together, blowing a bubble. I remembered the stories she had told me of growing up, and I must have smiled because she looked funny, standing naked and staring at her bubble. She drew the shower curtain across roughly. A few minutes later, I heard her bedroom door slam shut.

I repeated to myself: Routine, Saren, routine. Remember that.

When she emerged, maybe about half an hour later, I expected some quarrelling, but she sat on the armrest with her hands on her knees and looked down at me. "I'm leaving."

"For the weekend?"

She shook her head.

I felt I should ask her. "Where?"

She seemed to be thinking of my question. After a while she said, "With a friend."

She looked unhappy, bent forward and rubbing her knees. I didn't know what to say. At that instant, I decided to tell her that I was a simple gardener who had spent his first months in America tending an old woman, but instead I found myself talking about my books once again. Maybe I wanted to get her thoughts away from this new unhappiness, or maybe I knew this was my last opportunity to talk about what had been growing and growing in my mind. What if a virus infected an already vaccinated plant and incorporated some of the original viral DNA to create some new hybrid virus? What if an allergen from a plant like the peanut was transferred to another crop? How easy sabotaging an edible vaccine would be for some terrorist organization. She glanced at me, and for the first time in a week her wide-eyed look returned. I knew she was no longer worried. I had cheered her up.

I slept on the floor happily that night, thanking Zoravar and thanking my books. In the morning, she told me, "He's coming over for dinner." She smiled and left. After I cooked, I decided to go out for the evening. Remaining in the apartment would be inappropriate while her friend was visiting. I walked to the second-hand store and browsed through the books, and in the section at the back I admired the brass lamps and decorative mugs and delicate crystal figurines. I wondered if the ghosts of the previous owners hung around these places. But maybe the owners were still alive and had replaced the old lamps and plates and mugs because they all had little hidden defects. In Armenia we rarely threw anything away, but I knew that Americans had seasons for discarding their junk. Spring or fall, I couldn't remember.

My eyes caught a cane standing in the corner. The handle was inlaid with a bronze band. I hefted it—light but solid. The owner, an old man with grey, frizzy hair parted in the centre, came over. He seemed annoyed that I wanted to haggle over the cost of the cane. Finally, he spread his arms. "Okay, take it, take it." While he was slowly counting out my change from the cash register, I noticed a mahogany, long-stemmed pipe on the shelf behind him. Immediately after I left the shop, I began to worry about the expense of the cane and the pipe. I tried to calm myself: This is America, Saren. You are becoming one of them. Nothing more.

While I was walking back to the apartment, I decided to pretend that I had only returned to leave my old cane, but to tell the truth I was curious about her friend. I couldn't help it. She didn't say, but I guessed he was a journalist from her office. Tall and slim and wearing a hat like a television journalist. Long hair. Maybe glasses with a round wire frame. I knocked and Moira opened the door. He was standing against the wall. At first I thought his knees were bent, but when Moira stepped aside, I saw that his legs were very short, especially when compared with his strapping chest and huge head. His hair was cropped low and he had a slim moustache. He didn't look one bit like a journalist.

"This is the"—she hesitated—"the professor I told you about. And this is Edward."

"Ed-ou-ard?" In my shock I used the Armenian pronunciation.

Edward, still leaning against the wall, extended a hand. I walked over. He crushed my hand and smiled.

"Are you joining us, Zoravar?" Moira asked me. "Oh, you got another cane." Her voice sounded different somehow, maybe higher pitched.

"I just came to drop off the old one."

"Can I?"

I gave her the cane and she passed it to Edward. He tapped it roughly between his feet.

"Are you sure you won't be staying?"

I shook my head and fled the apartment. How could I tell her that this Edward gave me a rough, dry feeling? That he would crush her as he had crushed my hand? I walked for two blocks. My mind was in a bad state. I stopped to rest at an intersection. A group of women entered a building with a flashing sign above the door. I waited a few minutes, then followed them in.

A naked woman was dancing on a stage. A few couples sat at the bar and some waitresses with exposed breasts strolled around, taking orders. The circle around the stage was occupied by young men clapping and shouting at the dancer, but scattered inside were a few well-dressed older men who just clasped their glasses tightly and stared. I sat at the back. The naked woman came to the edge of the stage, spun around and bent over. There was more shouting and clapping. The woman straightened and danced over to a group of young men. She held her breasts towards them as if she was pointing, went down on her knees, leaned back, swayed her waist up and down a few times, and sprang up. When she climbed down from the stage, the young men hooted and whistled. The old ones held on to their glasses. The waitresses with the exposed breasts walked around, chatting and taking orders.

Then I noticed another woman making her way through the men who were now returning to the bar, but she was fully clothed, and they did not seem interested. As she came closer, I was confused, because to me she was prettier than the dancing woman and the waitresses. A young man with a blue jacket waved his hand in her face and she swore at him. His friend laughed and, while she was heading to a stool, shouted something about a praying mantis. I was about to go over to her when I noticed a short, balding man sitting alone with his hands clasped before him on the table. A waitress bent over and said something to him. He turned and saw me. I was a bit ashamed that he had spotted me in such a place, but when he gathered his coat hurriedly and left, I realized that his shame must have been greater. He was, after all, married, even if to a woman whose taste didn't include men.

I went to the stool next to the praying mantis woman. She looked up anxiously at me and raised her empty glass. Her broad forehead tapered to a narrow jaw and pointed chin. Her fingers were long and spindly. She really looked like a praying mantis. The bartender came up, and I pointed to her glass and ordered myself a soda. He frowned and walked over to the tap. I felt a finger on my shoulder and momentarily thought it was her, but when I turned around, I saw Bagrat. "Please." His eyes were red and he looked close to tears.

"It's okay. I won't say a word to anyone."

"No, no. You don't understand. It's her." He clamped his fingers on my cane resting against the stool. "It's Houri." I thought he was referring to the woman seated next to me, when he added, "All day long, she just stare, stare, stare. Why for you run away?" He dropped the cane and with the fingers of both hands pulled down his lower eyelids. "Whole day, stare, stare, stare." He picked up my cane, laid it against the stool and walked out of the bar.

"Asshole."

"Do you know him?" I asked the woman.

"Maybe." She shrugged and I noticed her protruding clavicles. "Who's counting again?" She coughed in her hand and wiped her mouth. "I've never seen you here before."

"My first time."

By the time we had walked the two blocks and climbed the rickety stairs to her room, she had already informed me of her popularity and had stated bluntly that I should consider myself lucky, because she chose her customers carefully. "That is why it's going to cost you thirty dollars for twenty minutes," she said as she opened the door. But her price seemed ridiculously low.

The room, darkened by a thick brown curtain, smelled of urine and stale clothes. An ash-coloured cat jumped from a bed and came straight at me. I placed my cane between us. The woman bent down, scooped up the animal and kissed the tip of an ear. I walked across the room, stepping over scattered newspapers and magazines, pushed aside the curtain and tried to open the window, but it was stuck. Outside, two men with hoods were walking slowly. They seemed to be arguing.

Now I noticed that the room was cluttered with junk. Broken vases, bits of ceramic flowers, filthy dolls, pieces of burnt logs, and papier mâché were clumped together on a huge wooden shelf.

"Are you finished admiring?" Her breasts looked like two bubbles.

She looked very anxious, so I asked her softly, "What's your name?"

"Christiana." She sat on the bed and the cat slithered up to her. I noticed the litter box at the side of the bed. She stood up suddenly, looking like a beautiful, tormented scarecrow.

I took out my wallet from my coat. She walked over to an old dresser and pretended she was straightening her hair, but I saw her staring at me in the mirror. "Here." As she made no attempt to take the money, I placed the thirty dollars on the dresser. She tilted the mirror upwards, maybe because she noticed me staring, and her annoyed look flashed by. "What's that?"

She followed my gaze in the mirror, turned around

and looked up at the painting on the ceiling. "The journey of angels."

"Angels?"

"Do you have a problem with that?"

The drawing was done on a sheet of paper, grey as the ceiling. I imagined that in the dark the broad strokes would look like watermarks. After a while I noticed other details. The mouths were all open as if they were crying or screaming in pain, and the necks coiling downwards like snakes appeared to be latching on to a mountain, maybe to prevent the angels from being swept away. "They don't look like angels to me. Where are the wings?"

"You a fucking preacher too? I've had a few like you before." She had a tired, angry voice, like someone suffering with the flu.

"I'm a professor."

"Yeah? That's nice, prof. Are you going to stare at the ceiling all night?"

"Who drew the faces?"

She slumped on the bed just beneath the painting. "That's Josie and Latisha and Rita and Ti."

"Do you know them?"

I watched her long, sinewy muscles as she stretched her neck upwards. "They were my friends."

"Where are they now? Have they ever seen this drawing?"

"I told you they were angels. Look, your time is almost up."

"How did they die?"

"The way women die." She glared at me. "Is it your leg? It's okay, you know. I've had people like you before."

Her cat jumped on a shelf and rubbed against a piece of splintered wood fastened to the base of a rusty reading lamp. The lamp fell to the floor, and the woman bolted from the bed and rearranged it between the other junk. She stood back, appraising, and then I noticed that these bits and pieces, pasted and nailed together, looked like deformed bodies. They were her angels too. A roomful of mangled angels. Like the grieving faces on the ceiling.

I glanced up once more. "Tork!"

"About what?" She sounded frightened.

"No. T-o-r-k. A story my father told me. About the god that looked from above the mountain." But the memory was so vague and so unlike anything I ever recalled of my father that I might have imagined it. "He looked down and protected everything that lived in the mountain."

"That's nice. Now it's time for you to go."

"To go where?"

"How the fuck should I know? You can go wherever you want. Just leave." The cat looked up at me.

"I'm sorry I wasted your time."

"It's your loss, prof, not mine. You paid me, didn't you?"

I stood there for a while, then I asked her, "Why are you so annoyed with me?"

She strode to the door and held it open. "Move out, you bastard." As I was walking down the corridor, she shouted, "An angel is just a fucking wandering spirit, asshole." Did I hear correctly?

On the way to Moira's apartment I tried to understand why the woman had been so angry, but my mind kept drifting back to my father. I tried to remember other stories he might have told me, but my mind fastened on the days following his departure. Some nights, when I was at my window, I would hear my mother quarrelling and crying. That was before the uncles appeared. And all at once I knew why Moira's new friend had so frightened me. One of my uncles was a short, brawny man who was quiet and well dressed and always smiling, but I soon began to think of him as the Slapping Uncle.

The simplest solutions are always before us, my father may have said. It is up to us to see them. So I moved back to the basement apartment with my few items of clothing and my books. Moira, thankfully, did not seem too upset when I told her I was returning to my home. She just stared with her wide eyes when I told her that her new boyfriend was not to be trusted. She hugged me for a long while and felt my head. "Goodbye, Saddlehead."

Part Three

It's now twenty-eight months since I arrived in America. I still live in Panos's basement, even though the old woman died nine months ago. Her death had a strange effect on Bagrat and Ani. Bagrat seems forever frightened and he climbs the stairs quickly, as if he expects the old woman to pop out of her room any minute. He disappears a lot, and although I never mentioned his whereabouts to Ani, my guess is that she knows. She too comes home late most nights and is out on weekends. She is still friendly with me, but she has developed some strange views. She thinks that her mother's death on December seventh, which coincided with the huge earthquake in her parents' village, meant *something*. My own arrival was no coincidence either. She speaks often like that now. I think she is grateful to have someone from Armenia around to chat with.

I take care of the house and garden. I am given a small salary, which is enough for my modest clothing, my books and the course that Ani encouraged me to take at the adult school. As I said, she believes that there are no coincidences in life, and that all the small events we sometimes forget are always pushing us in some direction—like my interest in books. If I didn't know her, I would think she was just encouraging me, a gardener, to upgrade myself, but whatever the reason, I have to say that she has been very generous. She persuaded her doctor to prescribe some pills called non-steroidal anti-inflammatory drugs, which now allow me to walk about more normally than before. I am able to walk eight or nine blocks, but I don't go out every night as before.

A few days ago, during one of my walks, I noticed an old man waiting for the bus. At first I thought he was a boy wearing an oversized coat, but as I drew nearer, I saw his trembling, wrinkled hands. His slanted eyes and sallow colour reminded me of the Ukrainians I had seen walking along in groups. But this trembling man was alone. He was the same age my father would be. As I passed by, I heard him mumbling to himself. He could have been muttering the song with which my father often provoked my mother when he came home drunk at nights. *Oh, not for me will be a grave / With cross-marked stone to view.* I tried unsuccessfully to remember the rest of my father's song.

Sometimes, I see traces of my father in these old men walking alone. Maybe it's just my imagination.

Last night, Ani was talking, as usual, about Armenia. Midway through she stopped and asked if I had ever considered returning. Maybe she didn't expect a reply, because she went on about her own dreams to return, but all the while I was thinking of my father, and the prostitute with a roomful of deformed angels, and the old Ukrainian, and thinking that some journeys we never return from. I know she gets some comfort, and maybe a sense of purpose, from this longing. Perhaps they are her paths, but deep down I don't think my own life has changed. People come, people go. I expect nothing more.

~

Then one night I saw Moira on television talking about a book she had recently published. She smiled and tossed her hair like a television model, but when the interviewer asked her about the story, she gave him a wide-eyed gaze and became attractive, like the woman I remembered. She had the same wide-eyed look when she explained that the book was a "futuristic thriller" which dealt with a rash of mysterious deaths. A female detective who drinks and smokes too much realizes that the outbreak affects only diabetics. She discovers that a young, misguided fanatic named Guppy has hacked his way into the site of an important pharmaceutical company and reprogrammed some information, so people who were supposed to receive insulin from genetically modified potatoes got some other drug instead.

I spotted Moira on television several times after, no longer talking only of her book but answering many, many complicated questions about the field Zoravar had willed to me. A few times I dragged my chair closer to the television and stupidly shouted out the correct answers, but her own responses always made me feel proud. I'm sure Zoravar too would have approved when she told the interviewer that genetic uniformity could lead to disease wipeouts, or that biotechnology was the most important development of the last century. She was invited to places like Seattle and Washington, and Quebec in Canada, to talk about Frankenfoods and pharm animals and the lobbying influence of big pharmaceutical companies. Sometimes she would be asked some provocative question, and after she had replied angrily, she would lean back against her chair as if exhausted and I would remember our nights in her bare apartment.

Once, during a short interview with a pleasant, grandmotherly woman, Moira said she would be returning to Brooklyn in a few days to deliver a lecture at the university. That week my mind was in a bad state. Some nights I went to bed determined to meet her, but in the morning I was just as determined to avoid her. Silly thoughts crowded my head while I was returning from my courses at the college. I wished I had never spotted her on television. What right did she have, coming back to Brooklyn? People come, people go. That was the way of the world. Why couldn't she understand this?

It was only at the last minute that I decided to attend her lecture. I would sit at the back and sneak out quietly before either she or Edward spotted me. How stupid! Maybe she would not even recognize me. As the bus approached the university, I tried to understand my nervousness. She would be talking about an area that interested me, but I knew that I was excited to see her again.

When I entered the small lecture hall filled with young men and women with bulky knapsacks, I realized it would be impossible to conceal myself in the crowd. I placed my cane beneath the chair and tried to hide behind the young man who kept shifting from side to side in his seat.

~

Afterwards, Moira told me, "You wouldn't believe how often I thought of you, Zoravar." There were new lines at the sides of her eyes and tiny wrinkles on her upper lip. "I knew we would meet again. Don't ask me how . . . I just knew."

"Your gift?" I asked her.

When I saw her wide-eyed look and amused expression, my heart melted.

"What gift?"

I turned to the young man who had asked the question. He was slim and very tall, and serious-looking behind his large square glasses. I thought he was one of the students, but Moira said, "Oh, I'm sorry, Zoravar. This is Max."

"Max?" I almost said "Guppy," and I noticed Moira staring at me as if she was trying to read my mind. Her gift. Yet she had never seen through my one big lie.

The young man didn't give me a chance to reply to his question, because he walked away abruptly towards a group of students. I could not hear what he was saying, but the students were nodding at his every word. A young woman with small, sharp features reached into her knapsack and withdrew a blue notebook. Max scribbled something in the notebook and returned it to the woman. Moira glanced quickly at him and said, "I need a smoke." She asked two young men who were putting away their tape recorders, "Is there a café nearby?"

One of the young men said, "Straight down the hall to the left. Just opposite the bookstore."

She turned to me. "Do you have a few minutes, Zoravar?"

"Oh yes," I said, maybe too quickly.

"So how's your back?"

"Much better."

She remained silent while we were walking. I guessed she had nothing else to say, but in the café she lit a cigarette, puffed out little thimbles of smoke and said, "I've thought of you so often, Zoravar, but . . . "

"Yes?" She seemed unwilling to complete her sentence, so I said, "Life goes on."

She nodded sadly and I felt she had misunderstood. "I owe you a big debt."

I almost said, "You owe the debt to Zoravar," and smiled at how she would have been confused by that. She stubbed out her cigarette on the table's edge, tapped the glowing ash with her shoe and lit another. Her silver bracelet with tiny hearts slipped down her wrist. I noticed that she was serious and nervous, like the evening she had told me she was leaving.

She said that my interest in biotechnology had sparked her own enthusiasm. In a sense I had pointed out her path. Even the book which had given her the leverage (this is the word she used) to fight for the cause had come from me. Her shoe was still tapping the scattered ashes. She glanced down and told me that in the beginning she felt like a fraud. But as invitations to lectures and interviews poured in, she realized that her appearance was an asset. Newspapers and magazines and television producers sought her out. She didn't wear glasses taped in the middle and didn't have quirky mannerisms or a wild-eyed appearance. Her publisher had even mentioned that she was a "comfortable package." She rolled her eyes and giggled like a schoolgirl who has mistakenly said something mischievous. And with this amused look on her face she said that I shouldn't misunderstand, because she occasionally felt as though she were speaking my thoughts and stating my position.

"What position?" I was about to ask, when I heard footsteps and saw Max coming towards us. He noisily dragged across a chair from a nearby table. When he sat between us, I noticed that Moira was no longer smiling.

Max pinched the cigarette away from between Moira's fingers and threw it to the floor. His hands were long and bony, and when he crouched forward on the table, he looked like a scraggy bird. He told Moira that a group of demonstrators was arriving from England. He made this sound very important, but at the same time acted as if he didn't care at all. I noticed he was glancing around at the few students filing in and out of the café. Some of them smiled at him, but he remained serious. I guess he was important. "So what do you do?" he asked me.

At first I didn't realize he was speaking to me, because he was staring straight ahead at the two young men smoking at the table before us. I told him, "I'm a gardener."

He glanced swiftly at Moira, who was smiling. "Are you involved with the movement?" he asked impatiently.

"What movement?"

He turned slightly, crossed his legs and looked squarely at me. "What did you say?"

I repeated my own question. I expected that he would be annoyed, but he hoisted his knapsack onto the table and took out three stapled sheets. At the top of the first sheet I saw the name, Max Shivani, in bold letters, and just beneath, *Pandora's Box: A Twenty-First-Century Model.* Out of courtesy I asked him, "Did you write this?"

He gazed around and refocused on the stapled sheets, and said very loudly, "I am an anarchist." The two young men at the table ahead glanced over at us.

"Zoravar was a professor in Armenia," Moira said quickly. "He was the head of the biotech department."

"We need people like you." Max drummed a long finger on the topmost sheet and read in a disgusted manner, "Rats fed GM food rapidly developed abnormal organ development." His finger crawled down a few paragraphs. "In the 1980s, pigs which had received human genes to spur their growth developed into cross-eyed, lethargic, arthritic, impotent animals." He seemed momentarily distracted by Moira's laughter, and he tapped his finger on another paragraph but did not continue reading. His eyes were huge and round behind the thick lenses of his glasses.

The smoke from the table ahead drifted across. Max got up suddenly and the sheets fell to the floor. He strode across to the doorway at the end of the café, withdrew a puffer from his trouser pocket, tilted his head upwards and inhaled. From a distance he appeared younger, maybe in his mid-twenties.

"I will be here for the week," Moira said quickly. "Do you think we could meet before I leave?"

"Where are you going?"

"Detroit."

"Your home now?"

"No, no. Just for a few days. Then I will be travelling to British Columbia in Canada. I have joined the ranks of the homeless." She said this in a flat voice as if it was a joke, so I smiled. "So? I really would like to meet you again." She glanced at Max, who was still inhaling from his puffer. "Alone."

"Here?" I asked her.

I don't know what I was expecting her to say. She noticed Max walking back towards us. "Yes. I need your help."

~

On the way back, some of the uneasiness of the past week returned. In the apartment, I took out Zoravar's book from the uneven wooden shelf to the left of the bed, and flipped through the pages. I got out my folder with my notes from the college. But I couldn't concentrate. I paced up and down and repeated uselessly, "Control, Saren, control." Late in the night, I started a letter to Zoravar and Leila. When I reread the letter, it sounded as if I was boasting. I crumpled it into a ball and flung it to the floor.

The next evening, I waited for Ani at the table. Bagrat came instead. He seemed startled to see me there. I heard him fidgeting about in the kitchen. Maybe he was waiting for me to leave. Finally, he sat by the table, crunched into a slice of rye bread, swallowed and cleared his throat. The few strands of upright hair on his head shook with each bite. A crumb at the side of his lip looked like a tiny bandage fastened among the grey stubble.

"Where's Ani?"

He jumped. "How for should I know? Why you ask me?"

We had rarely spoken to each other since I had returned to Panos's house, and although his reply reminded me of my early days in Brooklyn, he sounded more frightened than anything. "Whole day you fookin' read, read, read. Of what use? Eh?" He nibbled at his bread. "You never hear anything."

That was true. Locked in my basement, I had lost track of their quarrelling. He got up, but sat down immediately and pressed his hands against his cheeks. "Whole night long she walk up and down, up and down. Why she not go back to Armenia? Why for she make life miserable for me?" When he heard the front door clicking open, he rushed up the stairs, his pants flapping against his thin legs.

"Was that Bagrat?" Ani asked when she came into the kitchen.

"Yes."

She dropped her book on the table and asked casually, "So were you two having a conversation?"

"He seemed upset."

She sat on the chair Bagrat had rushed away from and breathed out loudly as if she was tired. "So how's your night course?"

"I will be finished in a little while."

"That's good, Saren. Now you can get a proper job." She glanced quickly at my cane and added, "But you can stay here for as long as you like. You seem much better now, though. You don't use your cane as often."

"The tablets you recommended," I told her. Even though she was seated at the opposite end of the table, I imagined I got a whiff of her warm cow smell. The top button of her blouse was unfastened. I glanced away quickly and my gaze fell on her book, *The Loyal Millet: A History of Armenia*.

"It's about the genocide." Then, almost as an afterthought, she said, "I'm thinking of returning to Armenia. Seriously, this time."

"Bagrat would be happy."

"Did he say that? Was that what you and him were discussing?"

"He seemed upset," I repeated.

Now she took the book from the table and, as if she were reading from the back jacket, said, "He thinks Mama's spirit is still in the house. Haunting him. Every night, I hear him twisting and turning in his bed and pacing up and down in his room next to mine. Poor Bagrat. But he got what he deserved." This assessment was uncharacteristic of Ani, and I was glad when she added, "Half of Mama's property. It was all he ever wanted."

When, after about fifteen minutes or so, I got up and went down to the basement, Ani was still sitting silently at the table. At the foot of my bed was the crumpled letter to Zoravar and Leila. Maybe I could get Ani to visit them, though I gathered that her parents had lived in Anatolia, a good distance away.

I took up the letter, smoothed the creases and read.

> Dear Zoravar and Leila,
>
> This is my third year in Brooklyn, but I still think of both of you all the time. I miss your tasty dolmas, Leila, and I remember every detail of your garden, Zoravar. I don't know if you will ever get this letter because I have written many, many others and never got a reply. I suspect that you two must have moved to another village, but I'm writing this just in case.
>
> If you receive this letter, you might notice that my English has considerably improved. This is probably

because I'm doing a few night courses at a college in Brooklyn. You might be surprised at my chosen field. In case either of you guessed biotechnology, then you are absolutely correct. Who would have known, Zoravar, that the seed you planted almost three years ago would blossom in another country and influence so many people

Please don't think I'm joking, Leila, because a woman I met got interested in the field and now she is on American television all the time warning about industrialized agriculture. She is grateful to me, but for the wrong reason, I'm afraid. Sometimes little mistakes that are left unattended grow and grow and grow.

So it was with this woman. When we first met, she concluded that I was an important researcher from Armenia. I felt it was what she wanted to believe and, like the fool I was, I convinced myself that her belief was entirely harmless and that I would never see her again. Besides, I believed that her mistake was pushing her in a suitable direction, and in any case, everyone in America pretends to be someone else. Now I see how stupid these thoughts were, how stupidly I behaved. I hope you can forgive me, Zoravar. I have no intention of usurping your good name. I am and will always be your humble disciple. The woman wants to meet with me this week and I guarantee that I will put the matter to rest. I will let her know that I am nothing more than a simple gardener and housekeeper.

I straightened out the crimps in the letter and wrote the final paragraph.

Apart from this misunderstanding, life in America is not bad. I am still living with Panos's relatives. His poor wife died a while ago, and his son-in-law believes that her spirit is still in the house. Panos's daughter is a very kind woman. She told me today that I could stay here as long as I like. Maybe because I cook all these tasty dishes taught to me by you, Leila, but mostly I believe because I remind her of Armenia. She is constantly reading of our history, then she becomes sad and quiet. She plans to return to Armenia and, with your permission, Leila and Zoravar, I will give her the address to which I am posting this letter. I will now say goodbye to both of you.

PS: please reply if you receive this.
Your friend now and always
Saren

I was reading the letter when Ani came into the room. She sat on the bed and rubbed her hand along the sheet as if she was straightening the folds. I felt she wanted to talk.

"I am writing a letter." She smiled just a bit, and glanced at the letter. "To Zoravar and my wife."

"Do you miss her?"

Although she knew I had a wife in Armenia, I had never mentioned all the details and she had never pressed. Her hand was playing with the folds in the sheet, and she was looking downwards in a way which made her lips fuller and her face less rough than usual. I took a deep breath and prepared to explain as honestly as I could. I told Ani that there were nights when I missed Leila's big, mischievous eyes and the warmness of her breasts and the sweet smell of her neck, but that these longings, though they were sudden and unexpected, came and went quickly. And I was left with scattered memories of the damp sheet and the sticky sweat on our bodies, and most of all, of the idle talk as my back re-adjusted painfully after the activity.

I don't know whether Ani believed what I had said or whether she was just more curious, but I noticed her staring at the letter as if that would reveal some secret about myself. "Please, read it."

"Do you really want me to?" she asked.

"Yes. Please."

She read slowly and paused at the end, where I had written of her family. Then she folded the letter and placed it on the bed between us. "So, do I seem sad and angry?"

"I think . . . when you are reading your books."

"Only then?" She smiled a bit, maybe to encourage me on.

"I only see you when you are reading at the kitchen table."

"Maybe I am always like that. Always sad and angry. And you're the first person who's ever noticed."

She was still smiling, so I made a joke. "I think maybe Bagrat noticed also."

She laughed and got up.

~

Five days later, I met Moira and my new troubles began.

Max, thankfully, was not around, and from Moira's nervy manner I guessed she had made some excuse to leave him behind. She was wearing some kind of khaki shirt and trousers, suede hiking boots and sunglasses which seemed too large for her face. Her hair was scattered over her forehead in unruly ringlets. When I sat at the table in the café, she ordered a large coffee, which came in a Styrofoam cup. She opened her purse, took out a tiny brown capsule, tipped back her head and swallowed the capsule with a drink of coffee.

I had imagined that our meeting might be like two old friends catching up, but immediately, Moira began talking about her research. She told me of large companies which were developing terminator genes and forcing farmers to constantly buy their seeds, and of other companies which were experimenting with transgenic pharm animals to produce nutraceuticals in their milk, and of attempts made to engineer cereals to eliminate trans fatty acids. Her silver bracelets shook and jangled as she was making all these points. When she said in a very bristling manner that people generally assumed there weren't costs to all these aberrations, I was reminded of her many, many television interviews. She said that the virus vectors into which these new genes were spliced could recombine and create deadly new diseases. All of this I knew already, and I had the sudden feeling that she was just recycling some of Max's paranoia when she told me that all this research was for her new book. This book, she explained, was about the natural world being gradually replaced by a genetically contrived universe. She had already chosen a title: *The Second Formation*.

She was looking at me closely when she broke in her speech to light another cigarette. She placed it on the aluminum ashtray and leaned forward, her hands clasped before her. I remained silent and a little frown crossed her face. She took a deep puff from her cigarette and blew out the smoke in tiny tubes. "There's just so much my research can throw up, Zoravar. I've hit the ceiling." I looked at the smoke trailing upwards. "What happens to the soul when genetic manipulation takes place? Are we cannibals if we eat a plant with some engineered human gene?" Maybe it was the way she was waving her hand around or perhaps the tired tone of her voice, but I felt she had asked these questions several times. "Where is all this leading?"

I couldn't answer these questions, but I knew who could. After a while I told her that concerns like those were important because they would force us to think about things other than ourselves.

"Max believes that we are now creating an analogue of the natural world. He thinks we are all guinea pigs in an experiment over which we have no control. He said the appearance of superbugs and the increase in so many diseases is due to the tampered food we are eating. He believes that plants have minuscule amounts of toxic substances, a defence mechanism which kicks in when there is any genetic interference." Mention of Max shook her out of her brief relaxed mood. "I plan to visit India later this year," she said anxiously.

"For a vacation?"

"I wish!" After a while she added, "Do you want to hear a crazy thought?"

I nodded.

She stubbed out her cigarette and said in a hoarse voice, as if she was forcing out a whisper, "People like me . . . and you too, I guess—people like us who move from one place to another—are no different from a vector spliced into an alien organism."

"We're like viruses?"

"Oh, come on, stop smiling. I know it's silly." She seemed flustered. "I was drunk when I thought of it, okay? Anyway, as I was saying, I'm going to India for the book. It's the big thing now."

"What is?" I asked, but I was still thinking of her analogy.

"Genetic piracy." Now her voice became once more television-smooth. "These big companies poaching and patenting crops developed over thousands of years. In India it's a plant called neem. Rice and other grains too."

I thought immediately of Zoravar and his research into *Triticum urartu*, the wild grains located in the Ararat valley, progenitors of the first cultivated wheat in the world.

"But it's so difficult to get any authentic information. The companies of course have kept everything very quiet, and the information on the Net is exaggerated and alarmist—put out by anarchists."

Before I could stop myself, I said, "Like Max?"

"I need some level-headed advice." She shook her Styrofoam cup in a firm manner and I smelled the deep-roasted aroma of the coffee. "You must think—" She seemed uncertain, then she said quickly, "I need your help, Zoravar."

The moment I had dreaded. So many times I had gone over in my mind my confession. And in a moment of complete madness I reached into my coat pocket and withdrew the pipe I had purchased in the antique shop. I had brought it along because it reminded me of Zoravar, whose courage and fortitude I needed today. I tried to steady my hands as I stuffed in the aromatic tobacco from a little tin. I prayed Moira would not notice my nervousness, but all she said was, "I didn't know you smoked, Zoravar, but the pipe suits you."

She finished her coffee and placed the cup at the table's edge, away from her. "I can understand your reluctance. You must think I'm such a fraud. A poacher." The way she said the word, the shape of her lips, seemed childlike and funny. A slight breeze blew her cup to the ground. She bent down, retrieved the cup and held it with both hands. "Max says I'm a biohacker. He's dead set against my going to India. We had another argument last night." She cradled the cup in her lap. I remembered Edward and, stupidly, looked at her face for bruises.

But her sudden nervousness cleared the path for me. I knew I had to confess quickly, before my weakness returned. So, waving around the pipe in my hand like Zoravar, I told her. I told her everything. Maybe as a means of atoning for my fraud, I stressed his brilliance and generosity and charming manner. And throughout, she just twirled the cup in her lap, pinched out pieces of

Styrofoam from the edge and said nothing. I was expecting anger and outrage, but she just looked more confused then ever, like a sad little girl. I wished I could see her eyes behind her sunglasses.

After about ten minutes or so she dusted the Styrofoam off her dress and got up. She glanced at her watch. "Are you busy, Zoravar?" She caught herself and said, "I don't know what I should call you now."

"Saren."

"Is that your real name?" she asked, as if she didn't believe me.

~

While we were waiting for the taxi outside the campus's main office, she asked about my back, about the courses I was doing at the college and especially about Zoravar. I told her, "Without Zoravar's help I would have been nothing. He was . . . " I stumbled for a word.

"Like a father?" Her gift. My eyes burned. I hurried into the taxi, and during the short trip I looked away from her, to the new, expensive cars speeding by. At the adult college, another student had asked if I owned a BMW, and when I shook my head, he had said that all the Armenians he knew drove those cars.

We got out of the taxi at an intersection, where, at the corner, stood a small gift shop with glazed windows. On a revolving wrought iron display near the doorway was a collection of postcards, done perhaps by a local artist. The watercolours looked faded, as if the artist had painted the scenes from an unreliable memory. In one, a young girl was balancing in the middle of a see-saw by stretching her hands on either side. She seemed to be flying, but her white dress was torn at the hem and her cheeks were stained red. In another, a family was leaving Coney Island, and in the backdrop were Ferris wheels and merry-go-rounds and swings and slides.

Moira bought one of each. Afterwards, we went to a cinema across the street. This cinema did not have a wonderful name like the Ambassador or the Palace. The movie featured two American actors, Tom Hanks, with a big nose which seemed to be forcing his face constantly into a smile, and Meg Ryan, who was skinny but had nice enough eyes which looked as if they were inviting some shocking statement, or maybe a warm kiss. It was a senseless movie, but midway, when the woman, Meg Ryan, was uselessly awaiting a friend in a café, Moira began to cry. She leaned her head on my shoulder and I felt her tears. She passed her finger along the back of my neck and through my hair and sniffled out, "Oh, Saddlehead." For a moment I felt unhappy that she would no longer think of me as Zoravar, the esteemed professor of biotechnology. But I had fulfilled the promise made in my letter.

Outside, in the bright, flashing lights of the buildings and taxis, Moira's features seemed to be constantly changing, as if she were before her mirror in the bedroom, applying her makeup. She had not called a taxi, so we stood at the curb for about fifteen minutes or so. She was shifting her weight from foot to foot as if she was exhausted. A bus with tired, sleepy women passed by. Finally, I told her, "I think I should leave now." Even though we were standing just a few feet apart, she raised and waved her hand. Her bracelet glittered. Then she turned and walked away. While I was waiting for the bus, a slight drizzle sprinkled across the buildings, washing the lights so that the surroundings looked faded and fuzzy, like one of the paintings in the gift shop.

Exactly nine weeks and three days later, I took from my mailbox an envelope with an Armenian stamp. It was from Zoravar. He apologized for not replying to any of my letters, and explained that he had been busy with his research. He congratulated me on my interest in his field and on the courses I was doing at the college. America is like that, he wrote—full of opportunities for those who are young and ambitious. He was sure I would have been frustrated and bitter if I had remained in Armenia. Like Leila. She seemed unhappier with each passing day. Zoravar ended his letter with the startling suggestion that America might be the cure for Leila's unhappiness. For about twenty minutes I stared at the card in which he had written his letter before I pushed it into my shirt pocket. I got my cane from the foot of the bed and walked down the street where, almost three years ago, I had been slammed against the hood of a police car and, lower down, where I had spotted the beautiful prostitute who had vanished without a trace, only to reappear a few weeks later as a murder victim in a newspaper. When I got into a bus, the driver, a fat man with spongy-looking welts in his cheeks, seemed impatient with my slowness. I took out the card a few times, but read nothing.

When the bus was almost empty, I got out, by a small park overgrown with wildflowers. Maybe because I was walking faster than usual, or maybe because my mind was in such a turmoil, I stumbled and fell. I raised my head from the concrete pavement and saw my cane about two feet away, but when I attempted to reach for it, my back and shoulders were seized in a painful cramp. I pushed my fingers into one of the cracks in the concrete and tried to lever myself forward. I heard footsteps and, out of the corner of my eye, saw a pair of feet detouring and hurrying away. Finally, I was able to get into a kneeling position. I reached forward carefully until I was able to grasp the tip of the cane.

"You hurt? What you doing down there like a dog? Have I seen you before? Yeah, I think I seen you before." She helped me up, muttering all the while. "I'm sure I've seen you before. You look familiar, but who's counting again? Here, let me help you to the bench. Put your arm around my neck. Hey! Stop squeezing, take it easy. Is that blood? Were you mugged? You gotta be careful in this neighbourhood. Okay, slide down. Here, take your cane. Do you want me to call a taxi? I can't wait, you know. I've already lost a couple of customers, helping you here. You a professor or something? I'm sure I've seen you before. What's that falling out of your shirt pocket? Is the girl flying? It's beautiful. Can I have it for my room? It's okay, you know, if it's important to you."

"No, you can have it." And I gave her the postcard Moira had bought in the small gift shop.

"Hey, there's writing inside here. Don't bother, I won't read it. It's none of my business. Who's Zorro?"

"Zoravar. A friend."

"Yeah? That's nice. Well, I gotta be off now. You sure you gonna be all right? A bus should be around in, I guess, half an hour. Thanks for the card. I know exactly where I will put it. Bye." While she was walking away, she shouted, "Don't go crawling away. Stay where you are. You should be safe."

~

In the beginning I had written to Zoravar every month, and I had received just three replies. Now the situation was reversed. Every two weeks I took a card from the mailbox, and although I was always tempted to throw them away, I read each in my apartment. Every single letter left me more worried and frightened. Zoravar's thoughts about Leila coming to America were no longer simple suggestions but sounded as if the decision had already been made. I felt that each letter was shortening the distance between my old and my new life.

I guess Ani must have noticed the letters in the mailbox, because she began to come regularly to my basement apartment with her talk of Armenia. Just like before. Maybe she expected me to comment on these letters, but I never said a word while she talked about her grandfather who had been rounded up and marched to the desert in Der Zor, and about other relatives who had been murdered by the Turks or had perished in the earthquake. After a while I began to feel sorry for Ani because, from her stories, it seemed as though she had no one left. One night I told her, "People come, people go."

I realized from her expression that she was offended and maybe surprised, because it was the only time I had offered a comment on her talk. She looked at me in amazement, so I told her of my father who disappeared one night, of the parades of uncles, some cruel, some just indifferent to me, of my mother's death soon after I turned twenty-one, of the claims by an uncle to my father's property, of the night, twenty-one days after my mother's funeral, when I was followed from the cinema by four men, beaten and kicked into a drain. But I had fought as well as I could, and a few days later, in the solicitor's tiny office, I noticed the bruises on my uncle's face. I told her of events I had forgotten, and in the end I took a deep breath and said that my wife was preparing to migrate to America.

"That's wonderful, Saren. I've been so worried about you." It was useless to explain. She smiled with a faraway look and said, "See, everything ends happily. Your family is coming to join you here in America and I'm returning to join mine in Armenia."

"But your relatives are all dead. They are just ghosts."

"Not to me, they aren't." She said this in a breezy, casual way, as if it were a normal, reasonable response, but after she had returned upstairs, I thought: What's wrong with these people, splicing into their lives events they can barely remember and people who have long since departed? It was as if they had locked themselves tightly in a room and were listening to voices from another time. Ani, Bagrat, the prostitute with her room of angels—all of them. I wondered how they might have reacted to my assessment. Me, with my cane.

But Moira would have understood.

~

While Ani was making her plans for departure and, far away, Leila was making hers, I tried to spend more of my time studying for my exams, now just two weeks away. Late at night, when my head couldn't hold any more studies, I would turn to the small television in my room. One night, I saw a singer talking to a fat woman who had some of the mannerisms of the television midwife. The singer, with her high cheekbones and mischievous eyes, reminded me of Leila. But she didn't have Leila's plump cheeks and quick smile. The singer said that her name was Cherlyin Sarkissian but everyone called her Cher. I felt that Ani would be interested in hearing about this Armenian singer and decided to mention it, but the next program made me forget all of this. This program had an oldish man with fake-looking hair falling in curls over his forehead. He was saying that people like Timothy McVeigh and those who had sprung up in Waco and many other small towns were antibodies. They were antibodies, he said, to the appearance of foreigners all over America. He seemed set to smile, then he grew serious and said there would soon be a war.

I turned off the television and thought of Moira, who had expressed the same view, more or less. I tried to imagine her in Armenia, walking with Zoravar in his garden and listening to him talk of his research, but the oldish man with long fake hair and tiny eyes and plump lips kept popping into my mind, like one of the genies from the stories told to me years ago by my father. When, a few days later, Ani showed me her ticket, I saw him staring sternly at us. When she packed her suitcases full of silly gifts, when she emerged from her bedroom followed by Bagrat, holding the railing and watching his wife walk down the stairs, when she hugged me and removed from her purse a letter addressed to the library where she and Bagrat worked, when I helped her heave her suitcases into the car—during all this time, I imagined the tiny eyes of the genie staring down at us.

After I re-entered the house, I spotted Bagrat sprinting up and down the stairs as if he were preparing for some competition. "No more ball. No more chain," he laughed out. He noticed my gaze and looked at the ceiling above his head. "What you fookin' staring at?" He looked up again, let loose a loud shriek and fled into his room.

Later in the night, I heard a low wailing cry as if a *nhang* had been set free. Then there were footsteps rushing up and down the stairs. After that I could not sleep. I turned on the television and saw three tall skinny women with gummy smiles running on the beach and splashing water on each other. A phone number flashed on the bottom of the screen, and one of the women walked close to the camera, shook her hair and invited the viewers to call the number for "an intimate encounter." At her back I saw the genie rising from the spray of a wave. I blinked quickly and he disappeared, but when I switched the channel to a show with a noisy crowd heckling a man sitting on the stage with his five wives, I saw the genie again, in the audience.

He soon began popping up on all the television programs and sometimes in the bus and the train. Once or twice I spotted him in the library, where Ani's kind letter had made it possible for me to get a job. Now I too have my own ghost. I had to smile at the thought.

~

At the library, I file books from a trolley onto their proper shelves, and I sort and index the weekly acquisitions. The work is not difficult, and well suited, I think, to my unreliable back. Bagrat works in the office upstairs for just three hours a day. He tries to avoid me, and our only contact is when, at the end of the month, I give him an envelope with four hundred dollars. My rent.

A few days ago, when I was replacing some of the hardcover books on the shelves, I spotted a book of Armenian poetry. I glanced around the table from where I had taken the book, but there were just some high school students gathered around a magazine. I walked around, searching behind the shelves. I could not understand why I was so interested in who the reader might have been.

I kept the book on the trolley, hoping that someone would ask for it. After I had filed away the other books, I took it to my desk and flipped through the pages. A previous reader had underlined some of the stanzas, and next to a poem written by Zabel Assadour I saw, scribbled in pencil: *How can I know who I am if all the coordinates are missing?*

Throughout the journey on the bus I was impatient, and if Bagrat had been at home, he would have been startled to see me rush wildly into the house and pluck Ani's books from the shelf in the living room and search for places where she had written her name and address. But maybe he would have understood if I had told him that the handwriting matched.

I don't pretend to understand what Ani's handwritten note means—though I have a rough idea. Rather, I was excited by the thought that she had left all these little clues behind. Perhaps she had written other notes in books scattered throughout the library, just like the game I had played as a boy, with each secret note leading me closer to the concealed treasure. Most of the time the note was written by my mother, and they usually led me farther and farther away from the house. For the first time I realized that they had been a ruse to occupy me while she was busy with an uncle. Poor Mama.

I read the book of poems late in the night, as a sort of homage to Ani, who had done so much to assist me. And among them I came across one written by Catholicos Mgrdich Khrimian. It began with the lines: *Oh, not for me will be a grave / With cross-marked stone to view / I die upon the field of death / My name will perish too.*

I always believed my father had made up those lines.

~

Coincidences! Ani searched constantly for these little coincidences as if they were her own secret notes pointing to a bigger picture. This morning, I received the news that I have passed my courses at the college and now, this evening, I am here at the airport awaiting the arrival of Leila. I am strangely calm; gone are all the various schemes of escape which had clustered in my mind over the last few weeks. What is the use of fighting against events over which we have no control? Bagrat, for one, seems happy, and the only time I can recall him ever smiling with me was when I told him my wife would soon be joining us.

~

An announcement from a hidden speaker just announced that Leila's flight has been delayed by half an hour. A fidgety little man with worry lines on his forehead and very red lips looks up from the computer screen behind his desk and listens to the announcement. He gazes around and notices me staring and looks away quickly. The flashing message on the screen above his head tells me that Leila will be coming through the gate to the man's right. He dips into his pocket as if he is searching for cigarettes. I suspect he is a bit nervous that I am staring down at him, so I walk down the stairs to a shop selling cigarettes and books and newspapers. On the shelves are magazines with many of the people I have spotted on television during the last three years. I see the midwife, now looking plumper, and the pastry maker and his wife. The woman, Meg Ryan, is also there. She looks a bit worried, like when she was awaiting her friend in the café. I see the Armenian singer too, but in this photograph she appears older and quarrelsome. There are also new faces, mostly young and skinny. A magazine with black-and-white pictures on the cover mentions various prophecies and warns that America is under siege.

Ever since I received Zoravar's letter stating Leila's date and time of arrival, I have been worrying about myself and this new situation. Now I begin to worry for Leila. How will she deal with this new life? Will she lock herself in the old country like Ani, wishing forever to return, or will she be forced into another kind of life, and grow into one of these grumpy, tired women from the trains and buses? How soon will she realize that in this confusing place there are secrets far bigger than any she may have brought?

The hidden speaker announces that her flight has landed. Time passes by so quickly when we are distracted. The man behind the desk seems nervous and angry and worried as he opens the gate and the first of the travellers, a lumpy man and his five lumpy children, all identical-looking, flow out from behind the gate.

Epilogue

Leila has taken control of the house. Everything is now spotlessly clean, and both Bagrat and I are treated to weekly delights of *khabourga*, stuffed lamb flanks, followed by a banquet of desserts. But I think Bagrat is more pleased with these improvements than I am. He smiles at all her fretting and has now begun wearing elegant pants with many zippered pockets rather than his old flapping trousers. For my part I feel more congested with all these changes and all this attention. I have tried to resist, though, and four days after her arrival Leila pointed out that I am no longer the Saren of old. She made this observation the evening I suggested she sleep in Ani's room. I told her that the doctor advised I sleep alone because of my bad back. I think she believed me because of my cane and all the tablets. I suspect she has grown used to this arrangement and might even be secretly thrilled to be occupying Ani's spacious, nicely decorated room.

As I said, Leila remarked that I have changed. I wouldn't have seen these changes if she had not come to America. But she is right.

I feel a bit of confusion and, I must say, some irritation too at her frank manner of saying what is on her mind. Her fussy gestures and loud laughter and expressive speech seem strange and unreal to me now. But it is not an act, I know that: we are an expressive people with rich, meaningful mannerisms. People sometimes misunderstand our intent.

It is impossible to misunderstand Bagrat's intent. Who would have guessed that all this time there was a charming, cultured man hidden away inside the rough, insulting person I have known? Although most of his improvement is directed towards Leila, he is now friendly with me too. A few nights ago he told me that, although he was born in Armenia, he had spent his childhood in Iran before he came to America. So that explains his funny accent. The next day, he revealed he had joined a gym. He flexed his spidery arms and invited me to feel his muscles. Another day, I saw him whirling around madly in the living room. I was concerned and asked him, "The spirits?"

He stopped for a while and with a funny voice said, "Spirits? What fookin' spirits?" before he resumed his dervish dance.

I can say he has been cured.

Leila likes all this attention, Bagrat is happy, and I am left alone. The arrangement is not perfect, but it suits each of us. I suppose I could end here, but the picture would not be complete.

Every two weeks, I take a bus to the park overgrown with wildflowers. I like the disorganized fragrance of the trees and the grass and the flowers, and whenever a stranger sits with me, I avoid any conversation and wait patiently for the intruder to leave.

I have grown used, though, to the smell of stale urine and cat litter in Christiana's place. The first few times I attempted to pry open the window, she fussed about rapists and murderers as if they were all congregated outside her building. I didn't know what she was so afraid of until she showed me her scars. She offered no explanations, and a few minutes later forgot all about it and continued chatting about her popularity. After our act she goes to the bathroom and I hear the splash of water as she is washing herself, and always, unexpectedly, I am touched by the intimacy of that ritual. When she emerges, she goes straight to her shelves and pretends she is straightening and rearranging her angels—a signal that she is finished with me.

I would have it no other way.

One night, as I was leaving Christiana's place, it occurred to me that my father must have been with women like her on the nights he came home singing his drunken songs. So we are alike, as my mother pointed out. This knowledge brings no further curiosity on my part. I accept the fact for what it is. The son can never escape the burdens of the father. I do not make this up. Gago, the old hollow-eyed preacher at the church my mother sometimes dragged me to, repeated it several times, and I always had the feeling that he was glaring at me as he proclaimed his curse.

My other curse, the exams at the college for which I studied so hard, has long been finished. I think the lecturers were pleased with my responses, because they have written to me about doing additional courses in the field. Maybe later, but for now I stay up late at night watching television in my basement. I sometimes imagine that I might see Moira popping up and worrying about the results of some new research, or perhaps announcing another book. But she is far away. The genie is still there in the background, but astonishingly, his attraction has gradually faded ever since I began to notice him in the trains and buses. He has somehow become less real.

So I observe these Americans fighting and quarrelling and making love and winning prizes each night. Everything is a big competition—even in the show with the black midwife, and now a white midwife too, and a bald-headed man with a tight smile and squinched eyes.

He looks like a pirate. But the guests treat these people like the villagers did Gago.

I try to understand Americans from such shows. They are a frank, talkative, inventive, superstitious people. I sometimes believe life is not too complicated for them, because they boil down all their problems and ambitions and fears and hopes into a big colourful ball and roll it playfully before them.

A few nights ago, I was watching the midwife show. She leaned forward on her couch and looked sad and concerned when the guests talked about their unhappy former lives, but when they brightened up and recounted how they had healed themselves through all sorts of crazy acts, the midwife clapped her hands and shouted encouraging words. After the show, I imagined that these guests would brand me as one of those halfway "before" persons anxiously awaiting some wonderful transformation, but I couldn't help thinking that they are no different from me. Or Zoravar. Or Leila. Or Moira. Even Ani. Their attachment is only to themselves. Maybe one day I will get my own big, colourful ball, but in the meantime I am simply Saren, the son of Taron. For so long I imagined I was making some long journey which would make sense when I had reached the end, but now I realize there are no journeys, just imprints in other people's dusty footsteps.

Sometimes, when I look carefully, I think I can see, behind the different expressions, all the old, familiar faces staring at me. Like the old Ukrainian muttering to himself. I mention none of this to either Leila or Bagrat. Maybe if Moira was still around, she would slip into her television voice and say that they are like recombinants but, unlike the eager subjects on the midwife's show, transformed against their wills.

I have received no further postcards with Zoravar's curly handwriting since Leila came to America. Sometimes, I imagine Moira and Zoravar walking silently in his garden, stepping on the dried dates and occasionally stooping to pat an unreliable tongue of moss around one of his grafted plants. The air would be ripe with the fragrance of rotting mazzards and of Zoravar's aromatic tobacco. I see Moira, in the heat, wearing a sheer muslin dress and soft leather sandals. Her hair would be bunched and there would be a sprinkle of perspiration on her neck. This image brings a fresh thought: humidity softens and ripens a woman. Against my will I feel a cut of envy. I will never again have any conversations with Zoravar, waving his pipe and offering advice and encouragement. He must still think of me as Saren the gardener.

This morning, I received my first letter from Ani. It was brought to me by Bagrat and he watched anxiously as I opened the envelope.

"What she say?"

For a minute I was tempted to tell him she was returning. "She is going to Der Zor."

"What she fookin' go there for?" But he was relieved.

This time I couldn't resist. "She is looking for spirits."

I was surprised at how quickly he was transformed into the Bagrat of old. He let loose a small, dry shriek and fled up the stairs.

Laugh Now, Cry Later

Diana flung open the door, clamped her fingers over the jamb and shouted at her husband, "Lalchan, you is nothing but a no-good missogiss."

"Me?" Lalchan whimpered, his toes pinching the carpet and pushing his chair closer to the wall. Braced against the jamb and blocking the light from the small living room, Diana looked like an avenging angel. He probed the word. *Missogiss*. It sounded like a disease, a sore which appeared suddenly on the body. But he had never heard of it before. Maybe it was a French disease. "How you could say I is a missogiss, Dhanmatiya?" He still used her Trinidadian name.

"Because you is a woman-hater."

"But I love women," he said cautiously.

"Then you is nothing but a sexual harasser."

She slammed the door. Lalchan took off his spectacles,

twirled them around, noticed the tiny cracks on the frame and the smudges on the lens. He placed them over his newspaper.

Coming to Canada had been a serious mistake. He had imagined a life of organized comfort: buying a taxi and transporting these polite, well-dressed people here and there, opening an account at the Bank of Montreal, shopping at Canadian Tire and, in his leisurely moments, nibbling at Kraft cheeses and sipping Smirnoff vodka. During the cool, balmy, wintery evenings, the family would sit before the fireplace and his two sons, Prakash and Adesh, still wearing their striped school ties, would nod respectfully and say "Yes, sir" and "Correct, sir" to his advice.

The taxi business had had to be shelved immediately. There were graduating licences and probationary periods and points and concessions and highways which led to another province entirely if you made one minor slip. But above everything, people drove on the wrong side of the road. He had nightmares of suddenly diverting to the accustomed side and knocking down some old man wheeling a trolley of groceries or a young woman pushing a pram with a cute, chubby baby. And appearing from nowhere, a courteous policeman with a pencil and pad: "Sir, you have just killed two innocent Canadian citizens. I'm afraid you will have to spend your life behind bars. Could you step this way, please." Cold tea and hard bread instead of Smirnoff vodka and Kraft cheeses.

In Trinidad, he had been a warden officer, working with six other employees in a small wooden building. The salary was small, but every week there were little bribes: a bag of grapefruit, a fowl (already plucked), a twenty-dollar bill folded neatly in an envelope. Five weeks after his arrival in Canada, long after he had dispensed with his taxi-driving scheme, he had stood at the corner of Jarvis Street and stared at the glassy twenty-storey buildings and, when his neck began to hurt, at the young men and women spilling out from some kind of revolving, circular door. I could spend one day trying to escape from a door like that, he thought. But the young men and women emerged unscathed, clutching their shining briefcases and their laptops. In Trinidad, all he needed were pencils, an eraser and a coil spring book into which he scribbled his calculations.

That marked the end of his active job-seeking period. Every morning, he walked down to the convenience store owned by Indians from India, collected the unemployment newspapers, which were free, and scanned the advertisements. And in his coil spring book which he had brought with him, he would scribble in and, a few days later, cross out the jobs that had briefly interested him. Occasionally, he would flip through the pages and stare at the entries he had made in the warden office.

But while Lalchan languished in the two-bedroom apartment on Ellesmere, his wife, Diana (he tolerated the name only because it reminded him of Diana Rigg from *The Avengers*), took to their new country like a fish to water. She went to seminars and workshops organized by the Migrant Women's Association and the Newcomers Club, and returned brimming with enthusiasm. She cut her long hair, started wearing jeans and makeup at home, and developed a puzzling accent. She began referring to everyone as "these guys."

At first Lalchan tolerated these changes with a watery humour.

"These guys at the workshop say that I should take a computering course. What you think of that, Lal-*lay*?"

"My name is still Lalchan," he said, smiling wearily. "I didn't change to a Frenchman as yet."

"You know what these guys will say to that?"

He was about to say, "These guys could kiss my ass," but changed his mind and asked her, "What, Dhanmatiya?"

"They will say that you still living in you backward little country."

Lalchan could not sustain his humour in the face of these changes, and after a while he began to hate these faceless guys. One afternoon, she returned from a workshop, stared at Lalchan and frowned. She fixed her gaze on him when he went into the kitchen to get his food and throughout the time they were eating. He coughed into his cupped palm and pretended he was reading his unemployment newspaper, but for the rest of the evening he felt her eyes following him around in the apartment. In the night, while he was on top of her, he looked down and caught the whites of her eyes, unflinching and fixated. He leaped off and screamed, "Oh god, Dhanmatiya, what going on with you? Why you watching me so all the time like that?"

She pulled up the sheet and replied coolly, "These guys say that you must always look levelly at other people. Any time you look away is a sign of weakness."

Arguments spun from nowhere. Another evening, she returned from a workshop and snorted disdainfully in her handkerchief. Lalchan prepared himself. During dinner, she told him, speaking slowly, "You making a serious mistake if you think you could keep me in purdah."

In spite of himself he asked her, "In what?"

"In purdah. Cover up from head to toe so nobody else could look at me. Is how these backward people in some Muslim country like to treat women. As if they own them, lock, stock and barrel."

"But I never ask you to cover up, Dhanmatiya. And in any case I is no Muslim."

She continued as if she had not heard him. "From now on I going to let my whole goodness show."

"What you mean by that?" he asked, alarmed now.

"I mean that I alone control my body. I not going to allow anybody to throw hot oil on me just because they didn't get enough dowry."

Lalchan took off his spectacles, placed them in his pocket and walked slowly to his room.

As time passed, he felt that he was being forced to pay for the assorted injustices carried out by all the backward men from all the backward countries. He listened patiently to the lectures on the evils of second-hand smoke and on littering. Yet he had never smoked a cigarette in his life, and he was always neat and orderly.

He couldn't understand any of this. He had always considered himself to be quiet and considerate, and had never been unduly bothered when his friends from Rio Claro mentioned he was living under a "petticoat government." He brought in the money and his wife ran the household, and there was nothing more to it.

In the beginning, he had convinced himself he could accept these changes for the sake of Adesh and Prakash. He and his wife were in their late forties when, eleven months earlier, they had left Trinidad to ensure a brighter future for their children. But no brightness had descended on the children. They were, if anything, worse than their mother. They wanted Nike shoes and jackets and all kinds of basketball paraphernalia, and honked impatiently when Lalchan explained the financial situation. They argued and fought in the small apartment, and called each other morons and dorks and wieners. They bumped balls against the walls and turned the radio to its highest pitch.

One night, Lalchan told his wife, "What these children want is a good slap."

From the darkness he heard, "The effect of that good slap, as you put it, will haunt them for the rest of they life." He regretted mentioning anything because she had recently attended a workshop which touched on hidden memories, and for the next hour or so he listened to her unearthing memories of her uncle Jailal bathing under the standpipe at the side of the road and exposing himself; of her mother, extracting a thorn from her foot, suddenly sinking the needle deep inside; of a neighbour reversing his truck over her favourite doll.

"Tell me when you reach the part where you and Deonarine son use to meet behind the cattle pen." Deonarine's son had been her childhood sweetheart.

She turned over in a huff. "Wait until I reach the part about *you*."

In spite of his anger he was offended. "You mean you forget everything about me already?"

When, a few days later, Diana bought a skipping rope to stimulate her brain cells, Lalchan sat before the table, took in the bumping and banging, listened to the wall shuddering and imagined he was in a waterlogged ship, like the *Titanic*, slowly sinking to the bottom of the ocean.

He tried his best to avoid his family, but the small apartment did not possess the facility for escape. And so he was forced to listen to the demands and the increasingly dire warnings. Prakash and Adesh, no longer interested in basketball, now wanted pucks and helmets and knee pads and cable so they could look at MuchMusic. One afternoon, Adesh returned from school and declared he was joining a rock band and expected an electric guitar for his birthday, five months away. Lalchan missed the two quiet children who, after school, had brought in the two goats, Samlal and Ramlal, and tied them to a post beneath the house. After bathing from the pipe at the side of the step, they went upstairs and did their home lesson quietly in the living room. The next morning, they packed their geometry and algebra and literature books in their canvas bags and trooped straight off to their school, half a mile away.

Now there were no bulging book bags, and no books either—just binders emblazoned with stickers and names written with liquid paper. Jess. Mel. Shawn. Brian. Snuggles. *Snuggles!* Once, he had opened a binder thrown carelessly on the table and scanned the empty pages until he saw on the last page, neatly written, the words of a rap song. He was shocked by the violent images. He tore off the page, crumpled it into a ball and pushed it in his pocket.

When he and Diana were discussing the move to Canada, they had agreed it was necessary because of the increasing crime, the smutty calypsos and the delinquency of many schoolchildren. He realized that it was useless pointing this out to Diana. His few cautionary utterances were rebuffed with talk about "giving the children they own space" and allowing them "to find they inner self."

It was the outer selves of his family which worried him the most. He tried to prepare himself for all eventualities, but it was difficult. On a Tuesday afternoon, his wife returned from a workshop, took one look at him and broke down into laughter. He was encouraged when he heard her tittering in the kitchen; perhaps something good had come from this session. Then he heard her screaming gleefully in the bathroom, and during dinner she giggled between each bite.

"Tell me," he asked in a tired voice, "did these guys say that laughing all the time for no apparent reason is a good thing somehow?"

"That's good, Lal-lay," she said, chuckling. "Is the best cure for stress." And she burst into a horrible, ringing shriek.

That was when he coined the phrase "Laugh now, cry later." He muttered it while his wife was doing aerobics in the kitchen, while his children were banging against the walls and sometimes when he was alone in the apartment, scanning the unemployment newspapers. He recited it silently, like a mantra, when his children renewed their demands for CDs and guitars, and when his wife warned him that he should not expect she would change her religion just to please him, nor was she prepared to engage in extramarital sex with corrupt politicians for him to get a promotion or to make some extra money. His fingers spun as if he were counting invisible beads when she notified him that she was not a prostitute and that he should be ashamed of thinking along those lines. When she left, he opened his eyes and between clenched teeth whispered, "Laugh now, cry later."

He began taking long walks outside, but he was bothered by the idea that all the other walkers—people returning from work, old men shuffling along with their canes, women hurrying after children, teenagers crossing the streets—saw him as an oil-throwing, litter-mongering, chain-smoking fundamentalist who, according to his mood, wanted his wife either to cover from head to toe or to have sex with important officials to procure some unspecified favour. And, his jaw like a vise, he would hiss, "All of allyou: Laugh now, cry later."

But the tainted image of himself swelled. What if it was true? What if there were men like himself, backward men from backward countries, who would fit this picture? He began to scan the black, and yellow, and off-white, and brown faces. Was it possible? One evening, while he was purchasing chicken from Knob Hill Farms, he absent-mindedly asked the butcher, a black man, "You will allow you wife to sex another man for some extra cash?" The butcher asked him what he had just said and Lalchan repeated the question.

"Look, haul you mangy little ass from here"—the butcher raised his cleaver—"before I split you in two."

The next day, he asked the owner of the convenience store if he had ever thrown hot oil on his wife. He walked away while the owner was telephoning the police.

But the idea could not be discarded. He studied the foreigners on the streets, and those dismounting from buses, for little signs: burns, abrasions, hidden scars. He paid attention to the newspapers they held, the brown envelopes, the parcels—anything that could be casually tossed on the sidewalks. When there were larger groups, he watched for evidence of surreptitious bartering. Once, he followed a heavily veiled woman for two blocks.

His mission—he had begun to view it that way—obsessed him. When he returned from his walks, he would cloak himself from the anarchy (the word somehow thrilled him) and mutter, "Laugh now, cry later." Then he would prepare for the next day's foray.

His queries were generally met with puzzled stares, but there were a few narrow escapes. Sitting next to a scruffy-looking Sri Lankan with red, sleepy eyes, he leaned over and peeped in the man's bag. A crumpled cap, a tattered book and a lunch box. No fuses, plastic caps or electrical wires. The Sri Lankan, discomfited by this stranger examining his bag so intently, quickly took out his book and pulled the zipper shut. Another day, he trailed a group of black youths to the cinema. He waited outside for half an hour and, hearing no gunshots, walked away. A huge Sikh glared menacingly at him when he asked if the Sikh had ever beheaded or quartered anyone with his sword.

But he did not give up, and one day his persistence led to an unexpected benefit. He had gone into the Super Loonies store to purchase a pair of cheap reading glasses when he spotted a short man, brown but with Chinese features, examining a packet of razor blades. The man was passing his fingers over the retractable blades with a strange gleeful expression. When he moved to the section displaying picture hangers, telephone extension cords and an assortment of screwdrivers and pliers, Lalchan followed him. The man took down some of the screwdrivers from the wall and spun them in his hand. He did the same with the pliers, smiling all the while. Lalchan thought of opium dens and intricate Chinese tortures. The man, grinning wildly, turned to Lalchan. "Cheap. No good. Made in Taiwan."

Lalchan didn't get the joke. Maybe, he thought, the grinning man operated some kind of sweatshop in Taiwan, exploiting poverty-stricken peasants and innocent children. He seized the opportunity. "Do you pay your workers next to nothing? Minimum wage?"

"Yes, sure. Minimum wage." He withdrew his card from his pocket. "Call me."

In the night, Lalchan twirled the card, sniffed the paper and stared at the gold-embossed letters: *Paulo Malvidas, Unit 45, Brock Road, Markham.* He barely heard his wife reminding him that she was not going to jump into the pyre if he was suddenly struck dead or Adesh's strident reminder that his birthday was three months away. He was not even aware of the perplexed glances he drew at the dinner table when, without warning, he intoned, "Laugh now, cry later."

The next day, he took the bus to Unit 45, Brock Road and was hired at Mr. Malvidas's garment factory at the rate of six dollars and forty cents an hour. When he was offered the job, he did not immediately understand. Mr. Malvidas led him through the warehouse where six women who might have been his relatives were stitching dresses and frocks. The room was abuzz with screaming, whining machines and Lalchan did not hear a word Mr. Malvidas said. Finally, he ushered him into a smaller room with just one worker, a chubby, smiling woman with big gleaming teeth, and spoke vaguely about Quality Control and Inspection Routines. He said QC and made it seem important.

When Lalchan turned up for work, the woman, Rosalie, explained that all he had to do was check the pleats, the hems and the stitches for uniformity. He had some difficulty understanding because she spoke in a slow, hesitant manner, pausing between words, staring at the ceiling and wagging her head. But within one week he had settled comfortably into his new job. He was ideally suited to the work: his penchant for tidiness ensured no defective dress or frock slipped by. Mr. Malvidas came every evening just before the shift's end, grinned, rubbed his palms and made jokes which were incomprehensible to Lalchan. Rosalie was usually quiet during these brief visits, but when Mr. Malvidas was gone, she would wag her head and giggle as if she were recalling his jokes. When, still giggling, she looked at Lalchan, he felt obliged to force a wan smile.

Lalchan found that he enjoyed working with her. He liked the mounds of fat that jiggled around her waist when she bent over, her perfectly round face, the way she wagged her head and stared at the ceiling when she was searching for a word, and the syrupy aroma of coconut oil that he sniffed during their coffee breaks.

When Diana stopped cooking in the mornings because some research had established a connection between carbon monoxide poisoning and infertility among women in an East Asian country, Rosalie offered Lalchan bits of gingery meat and water chestnuts from her container. And while Lalchan munched slowly, she wagged her head and revealed the details of her life. He nodded and said, "Yes, I see," although he was able to distinguish only a few facts. She had arrived from the Philippines four months ago. She found it difficult to understand the Canadian accent. Mr. Malvidas and all the other workers were from the Philippines. She was a devout Roman Catholic. Her husband apparently was not, because he had deserted her fifteen years ago. She sent down one hundred dollars each month to her three children, who were living with their grandmother.

"You are very lucky," Lalchan said when she mentioned her children.

She looked at him, puzzled. Maybe he did not understand. "Three boys. Eighteen, nineteen, twenty."

She was worried about her English and occasionally Lalchan would hear her uttering a word, but when he turned to her, he saw her reading from a dog-eared dictionary. Sometimes, she practised on him.

"Toe-run-toe."

"Tranno. Say Tranno."

He enjoyed this new role he was thrust into. He explained that the dictionary was misleading. "Say masheen, not mac-hine. Is a tool, not somebody from Scotland." And another day, "Say guys. Say it like *guise*, not goys. For example, these blasted guys always minding other people business."

He became expansive, experimenting with and sometimes modifying the Canadian accent. He stopped to listen to conversations on the streets, and he practised at home what he had picked up. When Adesh and Prakash erupted into an argument about which Spice Girl was the most attractive, he emerged from his room smiling. "Whatsa matter with you guys? Quarrelling twenty-four seven. That's not the way to go, buddies. That's a complete no-no." And when Diana mentioned that he was mistaken if he believed he could use sex to coerce her into submission, he raised a hand and rocked his neck. "Talk to the hand, girlfriend. What-*everrr.*" He greeted the other workers in the factory lavishly. "Morning, guys. Nice day today, ay. Gotta run though. QC, you know. Catch ya later."

Rosalie's English—or a version of it—improved steadily under Lalchan's diligent tutoring. One evening, she was able to invite him over for dinner without once staring at the ceiling and wagging her head. She lived about half an hour from the factory, and Lalchan was immediately impressed by the small, tidy apartment with the bare furnishings enlivened by pictures of Canadian landscape arrayed on the walls. A cream-coloured couch sat atop an intricately patterned rug. "Only a few furniture," she apologized.

Furniture don't argue all the time, he thought. "It look nice." She went into a room and Lalchan broke off a leaf from a potted plant and kneaded it. Mint. Then another scent, the familiar aroma of coconut oil, but stronger, more oily somehow. When he turned around, he saw Rosalie naked on the couch. Her fat, glistening body excited him. He tore off his clothes and fell on her. And slipped straight off. He climbed on her again, trying to gain some kind of traction. Her arms and shoulders were too slippery, so he gripped the sharp edge of the couch. He left the apartment one hour later, smelling of coconut oil and aloe vera, his right elbow sore from crushing against the rug, but he felt light and satisfied.

When he received his first paycheque at the end of the month, he opened an account at the Bank of Montreal, got a nice blue bank card and withdrew one hundred dollars. He took the one hundred dollars into Canadian Tire and emerged two hours later with a pair of silicone earplugs, a metal prong used to warm coffee, a toaster, an elbow pad, and a leather portfolio with innumerable flaps and pockets.

He continued tutoring Rosalie, energetically applauding all her improvements: "Way to go, Rosalie," or "Super duper." He went to her apartment twice a month.

He bought Adesh a guitar, not an electric model but a Castillan version with plastic strings. "Gotta practise on this first, buddy. Learn the rhythm and"—he recalled a phrase he had heard on the bus—"all that yada yada yada."

On his fiftieth birthday, he returned home with a bottle of Smirnoff vodka in one hand and packets of Kraft cheese in the other. And with his astonished family gathered around the table, he munched and sipped and muttered, "Laugh now, cry later. Yada, yada, yada."

Swami Pankaj

For most of his life, Pankaj lived with the dream that when he retired from his job as a farmer—the most popular farmer in Trinidad, he liked to boast—he would move to somewhere in the Himalayas region and spend the rest of his days meditating. Those who knew of this ambition had already, as a kind of preparation, begun calling him Swami or Swami Pankaj.

My wife and two teenaged daughters were not so sympathetic. I could see that they were annoyed by Pankaj's constant complaints and by his gloomy, mystical moments. I could not blame them: they didn't know Pankaj in Trinidad. They didn't know him planting his cabbage and *pakchoi* and *bodi* on a piece of land less than a lot wide, and selling the produce for a penny or two in a wooden stall in front of his house. They didn't know him saving and saving, expanding his farm to one acre, then five, then one hundred. They didn't know him winning the Farmer of the Year award, year after year, and university students visiting his farm and mentioning him in all their papers and write-ups.

My memory of Pankaj in Trinidad is more of the later period, when he was already recognized for the techniques he had developed to get rid of the red beetles which had ruined nearly all the coconut plantations in the island, and for counteracting the papaya mosaic virus which had left the papaw trees of neighbouring farmers useless and diseased. Pankaj's coconut and papaw trees were always healthy, lustrous and laden with fruit. The other farmers paid sly visits to his farm, carefully noting the chemicals he used and the way he would throw everything in a steel drum, fold up his sleeves, push his hand in the drum and carefully mix the yellowish liquid. Graduate students from the Tropical College of Agriculture in St. Augustine also came with their notepads and pens, but Pankaj resisted them all—resisted even the officials from the Ministry of Agriculture who descended on his plantation with letters authorizing them to collect data for their reports. They too left disappointed, stumbling back into their shiny new cars and complaining about "peasant mentality."

In the meantime, Pankaj's estate flourished, and year after year he won the Farmer of the Year award.

I lived about five miles away from Pankaj, and on Friday evenings after work I would stop at his estate and fill my car trunk with pineapple and papaw. I would comment on the size and texture and taste of his fruits, but I never asked any questions. That pleased him a lot. Sometimes he would tell me, "Look, take a few extra papaw. Is the best thing for digestion." At other times, if he was in the mood, he would mention that he was thinking of selling his estate and moving to the Himalayas. Although I would say, "Yes, Swami," or "I see your point, Swami," I never really fell for that Himalayas business. He looked happy enough in Trinidad, and his estate was booming.

So I was surprised, after all those years, to receive the letter from my brother stating that Pankaj was moving to Canada and needed someone to stay with for a few days. Pankaj stayed with us for exactly eleven days, then rented a one-bedroom apartment for two months, and finally purchased a small semi-detached just one block away from where I lived in Brampton. Then, in a most unexpected turn, he started driving a cab with the Omni Cab Company, owned by a short, fat man from India. I think he liked the idea that, although we worked for different companies, we were both taxi drivers.

In Trinidad, I had never asked him many questions, but when he was newly arrived in Canada, I was curious about what had caused him to leave and end up here.

And his replies were always satisfactory. He told me that he was forced to postpone his swami ambition because of an illness he had developed in Trinidad. The doctors could not properly diagnose his illness, but they revealed that it was most likely from years of exposure to chemicals. They felt that he could be treated better in Canada or America. He chose Brampton because one of the ministry officials, a graduate of some university in Ontario, mentioned that parts of Canada were becoming just like India, with Indian businesses and Indians walking all over the place. The ministry official spoke about Brampton. Even Pankaj's job as a driver for Omni Cab Company fitted in, because the company was owned by an Indian. Pankaj made it absolutely clear that this Canadian phase was only a stepping stone to the Himalayas.

In some respects Canada agreed with him, and he often mentioned to me that his doctors had given him the right advice. He stopped wheezing, no longer suffered from short breath, and didn't feel as tired and dizzy as before. More than the treatment he was getting here, he felt that it was the nice, clean, cold Canadian air.

But he was not happy. Every time he visited us, I would see that. I knew that he had taken the job as a cab driver not—as my wife believed—because he had overstepped his ambition and purchased an expensive house, or because he needed money to pay for the medical treatment he was receiving, but rather because Pankaj was not the kind of person to be idle for too long, and, more importantly, because the company was owned by an Indian. From India. Maybe somewhere around the Himalayas. But things were not working out. The owner, according to Pankaj, was a cheap, money-hungry scamp, as far removed from a swami as one could imagine. There were too many rules. Pankaj didn't like that. Pankaj argued frequently with the owner. The owner didn't like *that*.

One Sunday, when he was off-duty, he took me for a ride in his cab. We went to Niagara, where there were miles and miles of apple and grape and plum farms. While he was driving, he kept staring at the fruit trees. "That is how farms should be," he told me. "Well organize and maintain. Not like the little garden and them we had back in Trinidad, with everything mash-up and mix-up together. Look how neat and clean everything is. No disease, no rotten tree, no waste."

He looked so happy during the trip, I asked him, "Why don't you open up a farm right here in Canada?"

He shook his head. "The doctors advise me against it. They tell me to keep away from that line of work."

"Well, at least you have the cab job."

Mentioning that was a mistake. He told me very bluntly that the owner was a jackass of the highest order. After a while he cheered up. "But I feeling better now. I might be able to leave soon."

"Leave the cab company?"

He continued driving as if he didn't hear. Then he said, "Leave for the Himalayas."

As Pankaj's dissatisfaction with the owner increased, he began speaking more and more about his swami ambition. He avoided the topic of his recent life in Trinidad, except to tell me once that his wife had died two years ago and that none of his children—little jackasses, he called them—wanted to leave for Canada with him. Understanding his reluctance, I didn't press him.

He needed no prodding to talk about the Himalayas. During his visits he showered us with stories of ordinary men and women who had journeyed to the mountains and, after ten or twenty years of meditating, developed a number of mystical abilities. Swamis who could eat fire, swamis who could sleep on nails, swamis who could survive for months on nothing but air. He mentioned several of these swamis by name, as if he knew them personally.

Whenever these accounts unfolded, I would see my wife frowning and wait for my two teenaged daughters to leave in a huff. After one visit the elder told me, "That man is absolutely crazy, Daddy. We shouldn't have him around visiting."

How could I explain? How could I make them understand that twelve years ago, just before I left for Canada, I, like so many others, had been gripped by the idea that a simple man, not college- or university-educated, could develop techniques to counteract plant diseases that had puzzled so many? As it was, I felt his desperation; I suffered with him.

I knew that they were angry when he began visiting us, not in his everyday shirt and pants, but in salmon-coloured kurtas and dhotis. And I knew that they were angry when, unexpectedly, his manner of speaking began to change, to fit more with his image of a swami. Once, while we were strolling through the park, he pointed to some seagulls and told me, "Those birdijis are so wery wery lucky. Not a single care in the entire uniwerse." At that time he had already started speaking in the singsong way of Indians from the sub-continent. Then he told me about a swami who was levitating when he encountered a flock of birds. The swami, who understood their language, overheard them saying that it was so strange that a creature without wings or feathers could fly. And he told them that when you know you can do something, then that thing becomes possible—just by knowing you can do it. But the slightest doubt that came in his mind, he explained, would cause him to drop on his head like a stone.

I may have been the only person sympathetic to this transformation that had taken hold of Pankaj. He was fired from his job with the Omni Cab Company when, during an argument, he told the owner that he would be reborn as a hippo in his next life. I had to smile when Pankaj related that, but he was in a serious mood. "All the signs are coming together. It is getting wery close now." Then he told me a story about a swami who could distinguish different kinds of personalities just by sniffing at the owners. "Just one smell"—he shot up his index finger—"and this swami would know all that there was to know."

I suppose that I had become used to Pankaj's talk about swamis and the Himalayas and I didn't pay any extra attention to him then. But less than a week later, he called me over the phone and said that there was "a matter" he wanted to discuss. He asked if I could come over.

I put on my coat and boots. I didn't tell my wife and daughters where I was going. The day was pleasant enough, not very cold, so I decided to walk the block. While I was walking to his house and enjoying the cool air which was responsible for Pankaj's recovery, I wondered about his "matter" and whether he had decided to return to Trinidad, now that his problems with wheezing and short breath and giddiness were gone.

When I saw the sign on his lawn, I felt that my suspicions were correct. Pankaj didn't really have a lawn, though, because the majority of his yard was occupied by parallel rows of purple and red and yellow flowers. They were of all shapes, some like bells, others stars and a couple like tiny hearts. And in the middle of all this was a sign: HOUSE FOR SALE.

I knocked on the door. Pankaj was in grey pyjamas and fluffy slippers. "Please do come in," he said, acting surprised, as if he was not expecting me, and shaking his head from side to side. As usual I was struck by the number of plants he had managed to fit into his living room. They hung from walls, climbed over shelves, twisted around lamps, peeped from behind chairs. Pankaj was pleased by my staring. "My only wice." And like so many times before, he lectured me on the names and properties of every single plant: African violet, philodendron, Boston fern, English ivy, caladium, tropicals. Midway through his lecture, he stopped. "It is now yours."

He had been talking about a guava plant which he had sneaked in his suitcase when he left Trinidad. I remembered that it was his favourite plant. "But I can't."

"Oh, don't be saying such and such a thing." He removed the pot from the centre table, pressed the leaves against his nose and then held out his hands. "Here. Take it."

"Thank you, Pankaj." I felt uncomfortable with this unexpected gift.

"No need for all this thanking business." He waved his hand. "You can be taking any one that you like."

"Oh no, no. This is okay. I am not really a plant lover."

Pankaj looked at me sternly. "I am knowing a plant lover when I see one."

I tried to change the subject. "Are you leaving for Trinidad?" He looked hurt. I thought he was going to cry. "The sign on the lawn . . . "

Pankaj got up, took a deep breath and clasped his hands behind his back. "I am sailing for India."

"Sailing? In a ship?"

I felt that I was saying all the wrong things. I decided to keep quiet. I looked at Pankaj, still standing with his hands clasped behind his back. His eyes, halfway closed, were gazing at the wall. I followed the direction of his gaze and observed the framed picture of a swami whose eyes were also halfway closed. They seemed to be halfway gazing at each other. It was a touching scene in a way. I felt that it was time to leave.

"His name is Swami Purohananda. He is the smelling swami."

I remembered Pankaj's story. And the swami with his eyes halfway closed, with a little smile on his face, really seemed to be smelling something. It looked like a pleasant scent.

"My favourite swami. I am always recalling something that he said. Would you like to hear the werse?"

"Sure, Pankaj."

"Wherever we go, we leave a piece of ourself."

"That's very profound, Pankaj."

He unclasped his hands and turned around. "We are forever leaving smells. Good smells. Bad smells. In-between smells. They remain behind. Did you know that?"

I shook my head.

"I wonder what smell I left behind in Trinidad?"

I began to smile, but then I realized that Pankaj was not speaking to himself; he wanted an answer. "Pine and papaw." That didn't seem to satisfy him. "And chemicals." I tried to remember the name of some weedicide or fungicide. "Benlate. Gramazone." He was getting slightly angry with me. "And some sort of swami smell. Like incense and ghee and pitch pine wood." It only made him angrier.

"And what good would that sort of smell do in Trinidad? Anybody will appreciate it? All these jackasses who try to trick me into telling them how only my papaw tree and only my coconut tree never get any disease?" I had heard the boast before, but this time Pankaj continued. "They thought they was smart, but I was smarter. All the little trick they would come with. But I never tell a soul. Not even my own worthless children. You know why?"

"Why, Pankaj?"

"Is because nobody ever help me. They laugh at my little backyard garden, they laugh when I expand to five acres, they laugh when I say I going to plant one hundred acres total. But they stop laughing when only my tree remain healthy. And all the time, they was expecting me to fail." I realized then that Pankaj was no longer speaking like a swami or even an ordinary Indian from India. "They expect me to fail because I was too small. I was stepping outa my shoes. 'What wrong with that kiss-meass Pankaj,' they used to say. 'He think he is some damn French Creole or what, with all this plantation stupidness? Take care he don't bring in a few slaves to work in the estate just now.' And the rest of them used to laugh gil-gil and say that they only waiting for him to end up with his foot in the air like a dead cockroach." He came and sat next to me. "But they never understand me. None of them." He gazed at the guava plant in my hands. I felt that I should give it back to him. "I was the enemy, not because I do harm to anybody, but because I didn't fail. They couldn't understand that. And that is why I never tell none of them that the only way to avoid the papaw mosaic disease was to cut off the top of the plant when it was only one foot high. Then cut off all the secondary branch when they spring up. Excepting one. And that one branch never get the disease. It take me years to discover that. Day and night, night and day, I was trying something different. It was the same with the coconut trees. Day and night, night and day. But I never give up. And then I discover that the only thing that could keep away the red beetle what used to live in the heart of the tree was to mix up some garden salt with Aldrex and car oil, tie everything in a piece of sugar bag and put it in the centre of all the leaf.

Right in the heart. Kill the beetle one time and keep away all the others. Just two time a year. And no disease again. So simple-simple and nobody ever think of it before me—none of them university people with they thick notebook and none of them government people who was afraid to dirty up they clean shoes in the mud."

It took a while to realize that Pankaj was actually revealing his secret to me, the secret he had held for all these years. It was too much.

"I could tell you something?" He leaned close to the guava plant. "Sometimes I feel that it was really all the bad-mind that used to get me sick, not the chemicals and them." He was talking softly, and his lips were moving but not his teeth. I felt worried for him.

"You think this is a good move that you are making, Pankaj? Going to India?" He leaned back on the sofa. I saw that he was looking once more at the framed picture of the swami. I pressed on. "I mean, Canada seems to agree with you."

For a minute or so he remained silent, his eyes never leaving the picture. Then he said, "If you don't have any dreams, you might as well give up."

"But you've established yourself here. The house. Your health."

"Is why I never ever give up," he continued, as if he didn't hear me. "Because my dream was no little-children-stupidness that disappear at the first sign of any problems.

That only make it stronger. I walking around with it inside me all these years." And Pankaj told me a story about a swami dedicated to discovering the true meaning of life. From city to city this swami travelled, from shrine to shrine. Sometimes he spent months in the jungle before he reached another city. He saw famines, floods, miracles, kings, beggars and saints. But he kept on walking, searching, searching. Then one night, when he was asleep under a banyan tree, some dacoits killed him and stripped him of the little clothing he had.

I waited for Pankaj to complete his story, but he was staring at the picture again. I got up. There was something I had to ask. I didn't know how my voice would sound. "Why did you tell me your secret, Pankaj?" He looked as if he didn't understand. "The secret about the papaw and coconut trees."

He remained serious, then a little smile came on his face. "Because of your smell."

"My smell?"

He nodded. "Your smell tell me that you is a honest person. A honest person who too frighten to see the dream hide away in the back of his mind." He was still smiling. He may have been joking, but my eyes began to burn. I had to leave.

"Thank you, Swami." I hurried to the door.

A little more than a week later, Pankaj left for India, and I never got the chance to ask him about this swami who had been searching for the true meaning of life. But sometimes, on the weekends, I take little drives to Niagara to admire the rows of pears and plums and grapes. And looking at them, I imagine Pankaj sitting alone in some cave, his eyes halfway closed and a little smile on his face.

Escape to Etobicoke

Dear Harold:

It's now exactly two months since I moved to Islington. Does the name ring a bell? Remember the poem in primary school about a mad dog that had bitten an Englishman? I believe the last line may have been, "And it was the dog that died." Well, this is a different Islington. There are no mad dogs here, and the only Englishmen are those from humid, dust-ridden countries.

The letter you posted to my old address was rerouted by my relatives there to this apartment. I stayed with them for eleven months and two weeks. They are the kind of migrant you see in movies or read about in books: Husband working night shift in a factory, wife working day shift in a packaging plant. Proud of their labour, ennobled by their sacrifices and humbled by their good fortune. They were both teachers in Trinidad.

They rarely spoke to each other or to me. When I stayed with them, I used to think that newcomers, from a lack of practice, might soon lose the gift of speech, but then their two children, who were away at summer camp, returned and I saw how they wielded their accent like a weapon, frightening their poor parents. Still, I feel that the fright is a necessary prelude to the pride. I watched them cowering before their shrill, garrulous children, afraid of what they were seeing and comforted by what they couldn't understand.

Progress. It was the only word they spoke and the only thing on their minds. Over here the word is not what we know it to be. New, ingenious definitions have been crafted: an act of involuntary suffering; a moratorium on pleasure; a postponement of life.

I know all of this sounds rather ungrateful and it has occurred to me that my assessment may be unfair. For all I know, they may be able to see things that I cannot. These same obsequious teenagers may grow into doctors or lawyers and engineers. Still obsequious, but rich. And their parents might be no different from those who, a hundred or so years ago, were forced into the same sacrifices. Different land, same illusions.

But they depressed me with their tight, pungent dreams, and for half the time I stayed there I was planning my escape. I went out, studied the other foreigners, tried to start conversations and discovered that there was another kind of migrant—those who continually nourish their wounds, tear away the scabs and offer their bruises for inspection. Such an elaborate preparation for sympathy, yet offended when it was given.

There were nights when I thought only of returning. I can't tell you the number of times I mentally packed my bags and headed back to Trinidad. But I couldn't return. I had burnt my bridges: resigned from my job at *The Gleaner*, told my friends goodbye, accepted their congratulations, made foolish promises.

I could easily have panicked. Then, as so often happens in times of desperation, salvation was granted. Granted by Marsha, the mother of the child I was tutoring. English lessons. Can you imagine that? Me with my thick West Indian accent, barely able to pronounce Etobicoke, an English tutor? But the mother was grateful that anyone, even at a price, was willing to direct some attention to her son, who, as it turned out, was as dense as a slab of concrete. She brought me to this place, spoke to the superintendent and acted as my guarantor. She brings her son twice a week, on Saturdays and Sundays, and while I'm struggling with him, she arranges the food she brought, in the cupboard. She believes her son is suffering from an attention deficit disorder, which may be true, because he fidgets and stares all over the room while I am tutoring him. It is very distracting. The mother also believes that I eat badly, which is why, I suppose, she brings her weekly gifts of food. She is worried about me. I am worried about her son. The world is filled with worried people.

Marsha looks exactly how you would expect a Marsha to look—nice hair, good teeth, large, sympathetic eyes, prominent chin, and a bit of fat revealed only in the dimples at the sides of the lips and in the softness of the neck. Attractiveness and plainness positioned so closely that a simple shift of the face, a confession of light on some feature or a shadowing of another, could propel her in either direction.

I know what you are expecting to hear, Harold, but I'm not a poet or a writer: self-delusion is not part of my armoury. If the opportunity presented itself, I did not view it as an opportunity. To me she is simply the mother of the child I am tutoring. My bread and butter.

I still remember what I told you and Sandra at the airport's bar. That the world is what we make of it, our lives not just the excess of another person's dreams. I know that Sandra was deeply offended and hurt, but I thought it profound then. In any case, I was drunk from the beers and hours from leaving Trinidad.

I didn't know what I would find. In Trinidad, the only Canadians we knew were the exchange teachers who taught us at Mon Repos Secondary and the Presbyterian missionaries who came from Nova Scotia. I didn't know what to make of them; they could have been paler, plumper, quieter Americans. And now, so many years later, after one year in Canada, I'm in no better position to answer the question you posed, so innocently, in your letter.

To put it simply, I just don't know. Despite what we in Trinidad thought, they are not Americans. I could say that Americans are malignant and Canadians benign, but I could be wrong. Small societies, bound to their disgust and envy of bigger, newer things are easier to understand. Big countries are more elusive with their secrets.

I have realized, too, that we judge people from the perspective of our own distress and assign qualities which they may not really possess. Do you remember the mansion we passed in Charlieville on our way to work and the rumours that we shared, adding our own fanciful touch? A refugee in

Canada, about to be kicked out, he won millions in a lotto. A repentant Canadian government offered him immediate citizenship if he remained with his new wealth. But he had suffered too much, we said, been humiliated too often. So he took his money, returned to Trinidad and built his mansion. The rumours became more than rumours: they clarified our vision, offered superiority.

I'm hardly ever out these days. I leave once a week to buy my groceries, and occasionally I go to a free reading at the Harbourfront or at the University of Toronto Bookstore. A little over a month ago I went to a reading by a very young writer who had published his first book. He read with bristling anger. The words fell like fire from his mouth. The audience was riveted. At the end of his reading they rose and applauded. An old woman standing next to me wiped her eyes. Afterwards, in the train, I too felt like crying, because his writing was so horrible. But he had read so passionately that I wished it were otherwise. A week later I attended another reading, this one by a woman who was from either India or Pakistan. She also was an angry reader, but her anger was misdirected, scalloped, I saw her losing her audience. She became angrier, and in the end it was all she had left.

Whenever I go to these readings, I feel

extremely guilty, and for the next few days I submit a number of applications to various newspapers. So far I haven't received any replies, and I worry that my little savings will run out before I get a job. Marsha advised me to apply for the position of supply teacher, but that too led nowhere.

And so the days tumble over one another, while I, alone in my apartment, think of a well-respected journalist who inexplicably left everything behind and I try to understand the reasons for his migration. I have come closer, I think, to understanding Sandra's bitterness about my sudden departure, but nothing else.

I have analyzed my life here and I have concluded that it's inertia, not boredom, that punishes me. Boredom, you see, is a quality that we invite into our lives; it suggests that there are other things we can do if we choose. It's an aristocratic affectation resulting not so much from laziness as from a disregard for everything and everyone. But inertia is different. It stifles and paralyzes, and it draws your weakness around you like a dead fog that thickens each day.

In these situations, little distractions take on a romance of their own. I stopped shaving. Every morning I saw a lunatic staring at me. The beard itched and tickled, but because it reminded me of someone I felt I hated, it could not be removed.

Every day, I questioned the mirror. Three weeks later, while I was purchasing my groceries, I saw the young man, bearded, who had laughed when I spoke the name of a Trinidadian ground provision. I shaved that night. Small things rub me the wrong way. Romance dies easily in such situations.

So I spend my time waiting, not sure what I'm waiting for. In the stillness of the night my appliances throb with the power of the alive. When I concentrate, I can hear the amplified heartbeat of the clock, the belch of water filling the toilet tank, the phlegmatic wheezing of the fan, the groaning of the fridge. I could think I'm in a sanatorium, but my own breathing is melodious. Cavorting, trilling birds rise from my nasal passages, crickets and grasshoppers from my throat. They have enlivened my suffocation, given music to my congestion. Maybe romance is not dead after all.

Meanwhile, time passes and I have done nothing. I am conscious of every day that goes by, all the scattered hours and minutes. In Trinidad, I, you, wrote our articles about government corruption, the complicity of the police in the drug trade, the bribery, nepotism and inefficiency which had embedded themselves in our culture. Our dreams were modest; we didn't change the world, but we knew who we were and what we were doing. And we made enemies, the one sign of progress in Trinidad.

Over here, in my apartment in Islington (I still can't think of the name without remembering the Englishman), I look at television and I see wealthy and powerful men and women with gleaming teeth speaking of the new world they are creating, and I see those excluded, fretting with an effete indignation. I watch the other face of progress and I understand how unsophisticated and backward we, with our false notions of morality, are. I remember a time when the days were whole and the nights glistened with drunken discoveries. I remember when we closed the village bars and, on our way home, half-jokingly discussed all we had spoken of that evening, dismissed our concern for the dispossessed as the conceit of the colonial, but in the morning, shadowed by the guilt of our sudden sobriety, we wrote our minds. It was hypocrisy, but it was sincere. I remember those times and I seethe at my own powerlessness, because I am now denied even this modest conceit. I am an interloper in this place, Harold. Not because of colour or culture or accent or anything like that, but really because I am unnecessary. I am not needed. It is a horrible discovery.

On my grocery days, I observe men and women and children chatting and cycling and driving and smiling with perfect teeth, and I think that their lives will be exactly what they expect them to be.

Sometimes I'm afraid that I might grow into one of those strange, prying old men, the kind that you see in bus stops and on street corners, unconcerned about their appearance, their sharp, oily eyes slicing everything before them. I can see you shaking your head and smiling while you are reading this, but I have changed in ways that I never thought possible. Innocence can be punctured in a single minute or it can be eroded day by day, until you are no longer sure whether it's there or not.

I know that I have not answered your question, and I wish that I could have ended this letter on a more positive note, but I must finish here. In a few minutes Marsha will arrive with her son and I must again be the diligent tutor, at ease with the world and smiling at my minor misfortunes.

She really told me that, using these exact words, smiling radiantly with her perfect teeth to show me it could be done. Perhaps there's the answer to your question. Canadians are people with perfect smiles.

Yours truly
Robert

The Diary of a Down-courage Domestic

"Look, don't make me kick up you little tail good and proper, you hear me?" And that was the end of that interview. Case close. End of text. And me walking out from the office like me foot on fire. Was all I could do to prevent meself from grabbing that *marasme* little boy from the employment agency and wringing out he turkey neck.

Just imagine, he had the boldfaceness to ask me what I will do if the boss start putting the moves on me. On me! A fifty-five-year-old woman with grandchildren as big as he self. And as if that wasn't enough, he hit me with this one: What I will do if the boss say is me who cause the whole *commess*? That was me who was doing the encouraging part? And to cream it off, if he report that I always coming to work toxicated?

My crosses! The things that I have to put up with since I land here three months ago. Is as if everybody want to take a bite from poor Irma. But every rope have a end, and I feel it fast approaching the time when something will have to give.

I can't tell you the amount of time I chook up in me basement, wringing me ears for leaving Trinidad. Granted, things was hard on the job side the last two-three years. Granted, the party I support all me life get move out and a new Indian people party take over. Granted all that, but still Trinidad was me home where I born and grow up and, on top of everything, where I was among me own. Don't mind all the little knocks I pass through, I never ever feel like I was a stranger or a outsider.

And I always had Paul to fall back on.

Paul. I really does miss him, and I wish we did have the money for the two of we to come up here instead of me alone. Sometimes I does think that maybe he should have come up first instead of me. With all he fancy talk and long-long words, he would have put these boldface people in they place in no time. I know he is only a carpenter, but he mind was always set on schoolteachering. Paul, poor thing, never had the money.

I keep all the letters he write me and the copy of them that I post down to him. And in the night, when me head spinning, I does take them out from the box and read them over and over again.

To tell the truth, they make me more down-courage than anything, but is the last link I have with Paul and with Trinidad and, toobesides, is the onliest record I have of this madness I passing through. Something like a diary, you could say. The diary of a down-courage domestic.

This is how it all startup.

Dear Paul,

Well, I in the white people country at last. I write the white people country, but you will surprise at the amount of black-skin people it have all over the place. But they look like some different brand, because none of them smiling at you or stopping to chat or anything. Even Joycie too change. Maybe is the cold weather it have up here. That is the onliest explanation. I stay by she for three days until I get this underground place where I writing this letter from. The people here does call it basement. This one own by a Chinee who don't talk much English, and that suit me fine. I only just unpack me clothes this morning, and by tomorrow I want to start hunting about for a work. Joycie say it have plenty scope for domestics, which is servants, and she give me a list with addresses of place to go. She say the most important thing they looking for is experience. Thank god I have plenty of that, because is nine children I mind until they get big man and woman.

I hope that you keeping well and not hanging out too much with Alphonso, because as I tired tell you, he is nothing but trouble. Give me regards to everybody, and if anybody mention me, tell them that I ask especially for them.

Irma

PS expect that by the next letter I go have a work.

My dearest Irma

I is feeling very bereaved since you departed these shores. The children do drop in now and again, but it is really Alphonso who is the most consolationing. He is still addicted to gambling, but he has sweared a solemn oath that he is attempting to supervise his drinking. I cannot lie to you Irma I make him swear on the bible that he will only take two drinks per day.

I is abundantly relieved that you have located a place to rent and that job prospects is on the rosy side. You seems to be doing fine in yonder northern climes my dearest Irma and my only worries is that some rich whiteman will try to turn your head. I know that I is only a humble carpenter with a schoolteacher conceal somewhere inside, but I always had your best interest at heart Irma. Please remember that. I think of you permanently and I pray you do similarly and likewise. The only thing what gives me courage in these trying times is the good book. I read two pages for Alphonso last night and I would have read more but he had to depart to Rankin bars for his last instalment of alcohol per day.

Your lonely husband
Paul

Dear Paul

I really had to laugh when I read you letter about some white man twisting me head. Was the last time I laugh for the last two weeks. The onliest thing these people interested in here is money and I is the last of the apostles where that concern. Remember, is only two thousand I come up here with and to tell the truth, I don't know how long that go last.

I visit all these places what Joycie recommend, but is like I bouncing me head on a wall. She didn't lie when she talk about experience, but what she forget to tell me is really Canadian experience alone what count. All these employment agency people telling me the same thing. And the hurtful part is how they does watch me from head to toe, like if I just land from the moon. Skinny little children with they mother milk still on they face, telling me I have to upgrade meself if I want to land a work. Upgrade, like if I is a old motor car. But is me and me alone up here, and I have no choice but to take they bad-mind advice. I already make a appointment to a place what does cater for newly arrive people and train them how to apply for work and how to answer question and what clothes to wear and other stupidness like that. God willing, something will work out.

I hope you keeping you distance from Alphonso. You say that he swear on the bible that he will cut down on the drinking, but as far as I concern, the only thing Alphonso could do better than drink is lie. Watch him careful and don't let him lead you astray.

Irma

My lovely Irma,

I is exceedingly sorry to hear of your present difficulty jobwise, but I knows you is a strong woman Irma and you will find some way to overcome present difficulties. You have always persevered to the utmost on the face of calamities and I rest assured you will do same now. My only concern is that some rich whiteman will attempt to exploit your circumstances for his, and I stress for his, alone benefits.

Every day is lonelier than the last and I am grateful to Alphonso for all his visitations. I know you never approved of him Irma, but I can testify to the fullest that he is endeavouring to try to reform his drinking and gambling. He has given up whe-whe and cockfighting and only partake of legal gambling now. But he is trying, and everything take time.

Work is very slow these days and I is just managing to keep body and soul together. Sometimes I think I should just put away all my carpentering implements and take up preachering, which is not different from school-teachering when you think of it. We know ourself only through our loneliness Irma and I realize it must be far worse for you up yonder, but remember every sky has a silver lining, a pot of gold and a light at the end of the tunnel.

Thinking of you permanently
Paul

Dear Paul,

Today make it exactly one month since I in Canada and I can't see that light you write about yet. It look like the pot empty long time, because any side I turn, is more downcouragement I getting. This week I visit two job counselling people and the two of them tell me the same thing. That nobody will hire me as a domestic unless I get licence and certificate. Just like a motor car, as I write before. If I did know that I was going to pass through this headache, I would have never step out from Trinidad, but it too late for that now.

Maybe you should really come a preacher Paul, as you write in the letter, and put in a good word for me with the man upstairs. And don't worry about these rich whitemen and them, because is only young boys barely older than Philbert I does bounce up in these job place. Nashy-nashy little children advising me on this and that. You could imagine that? I feel that one of these days I will let loose and put one of them in he place good and proper, but for the time being I holding me patience.

I hope Alphonso not asking you for any money borrow to gamble and buy rum with. He always had a way to get around you Paul, and with me gone I know he must be up to all he scheme. Be careful is all I could say.

Irma

My so dearest Irma,

Every day my heart get more heavier by the minute and second. If only I had the money Irma, I would migrate to you tonight before you fall in some rich whiteman trap, but I is scraping to make ends combine. It look like nobody want a honest carpenter no more. More and more I is thinking of the preachering venture. Alphonso too think it is a worthwhile experiment and I agree wholeheartedly with him. His drinking is almost nil now and it is only the gambling which is a sore point. I tried to endeavour to talk him out of it Irma, but he contradict me by saying that every man is entitled to one vice. And Irma I cannot lie to you, because you always had the gift. Is true. I did factually loan him a very small sum one evening for his lotto habit. He promised sincerely to repay me at the month-end and I shall hold him true to his word. Please write soon dear and don't let present difficulties cause you to lose faith in your lonely Paul and in the lord.

Your aching Paul

Dear Paul,

I sorry that I take so long to write this time Paul, but I sign up for a two-month course to train me how to apply for job and how to handle interview. These people here really start getting on my nerves. I don't know how everybody else from Jamaica and Sri Lanka and Somalia does take it, but the counselling people does act as if the whole bunch of we is little children who don't know b from bullfoot. I had was to put one of them in he place two-three days ago. He was getting impatient with some poor woman from Sri Lanka who could hardly talk English, when he just ups and say, "Madam, in my country we address others with courtesy and civility. Now would you please await your turn." I know you always tell me that I too short-tempered Paul, but this time I couldn't control myself. I get up from the chair one time and tell him, "*My* country? What my country you talking about? You have a deed or a piece of paper to show me that this is *your* country?" He face get red as if he damn vex with me, but if he did only know how close I was from picking him up and flinging him out of the tall building we was in. If he did only know. Just before the session end, the head counselling man who, thank god, is not some little pissing tail boy but a jacket and tie mister, apologize to the group of we and try to patch up everything. But the Sri Lankan woman never show up since.

So Alphonso catch you again? Was bound to happen with me gone. But I hope you learn a lesson Paul. I did always know that he would have try to milk you as much as he could, but is up to you and you alone to put a stop to that. Just remember that it take the two of we nearly four years to scrape up for me to come to Canada. Take care.

Irma

My sweet, sweet syrup Irma,

These words is dripping from my pen like *laglee* my dearest Irma, and I feel like the nib is excavating my heart. I know how much trouble you is encountering and I being so far away cannot render necessary assistance. But take heart Irma, at least you have Mr. Jacket and Tie who seems prominently important and rich to give consolation to your harsh moments. I have nobody save and except Alphonso, who praise the lord still see fit to drop in every now and again.

It appear that my ministrations is successful and I can quote with assurance that he is a change soul. He only get intoxicated on the weekend now. I is working on his other vice, but it is difficult because all over the place now there is lotto and whe-whe and pick-two gambling machines. But a good apprentice preacher never put his hat down Irma, and I trying with renewed vigour and strategy. He promised to repay me the other tiny sum by month-end too and rest assured I will insist whole heartedly that such sums be accrued to me.

I know there is temptations in Canada too, especially with all these rich consoling jacket and tie officials and I is so distantly grounded that I worry day and night. Please don't forget your only and lonely husband.

Forever and ever yours truly
Paul

Dear Paul,

I know that a good two weeks pass since I get your last letter, but I just didn't have the time to write before. Partly every day I out hunting for a work and in the nights I still doing the course for newly arrive people. These last few days we was doing something call role-playing and is roll playing in truth because everybody had was to lay down on the floor and roll from one end of the room to the next. You could imagine that? A big two-hundred-pound woman like me rolling all over the place. The head counselling mister say was for we to break down we inhibitions and get more confidence. So far the only thing it breaking down is me bone and them. The little *mingpilling* boy who buff up the Sri Lankan woman does keep he distance, but every now and then I does see him watching me cuteye. But I don't have he to study cause it have more important thing in me mind now.

Every single day and night I does worry about how the little money I have running out on food and rent, and sometimes I does feel real down-courage. That is why I putting up with all these employer who does watch me as if I have no business walking in they place asking for work and all this role-playing nonsense too. At least when the course finish this week I will have a certificate what the head counselling mister say will put me in a better position. Me mind still set on the domestic work, but right now I will take anything I get.

So Alphonso still chiselling you? I don't know what to tell you Paul. Cause is only you who could put up a resistance to all he schemes. I too far away. The most I could do is warn you that when dog accustom sucking egg, they go never change. Never. Mark my word. All that talk about stop drinking and paying back money is just wind. I know he is you cousin and thing, but all Alphonso interested in is bamboozling you out of you money.

Nothing good will ever come out from that scamp. Take heed.

Irma

And that was the story for the last three months. I don't know how Paul managing with Alphonso back in Trinidad, but I have me plate too full to take on that extra worries. Every day, I does hit the street looking, looking for a work, and in the evening I does phone up these people who advertise for domestics in the papers. I don't know if is me Trinidad twang or what, but I just can't make no headway. Right now I only have money to last for one month again, and god alone know what will happen then. Maybe I will go back to Trinidad because, to tell the truth, I getting real fed up of some of these people here. I know fully well that not all skin teeth is laugh, but it does really grind me when everybody talking so nice and polite but deep-deep down they only seeing me as a uneducated woman what spring up from some backward place. And that does really get me pressure up.

Go back to Trinidad and fix up that chiselling Alphonso good and proper. And at least I will be with Paul again, because I can't lie, the last few days I really miss him.

Anyways, tomorrow I will hit the street again.

~

Look how things does work out, eh. The good lord does really test all of we to see how far we could walk without stumbling. Just when me money about to run out and when every last drop of patience in me body melt away, I get the letter from Paul in the mail this morning. I did always in the back of me mind know that the lord had a purpose for everybody. Even no-good scamps like Alphonso.

> My cherished item Irma,
>
> Excitement is boiling and stewing in the interior of me, dearest Irma, because I have found the light and the pot. And I have nobody but Alphonso to thank. The very said Alphonso who I had extended the bounty of my generousness to so many numerous times. As proof herewith I enclose a brand new shiny one hundred Canadian bill.

Enjoy it my dear. Buy a dress. New shoes. Jewellery too. Because there is more where that originated I can assure you.

By this juncture you must be wondering my dearest Irma if your Paul has lost some of his grey matter, but nothing could be farther from the truth. Let me expashiate forthwith and with due haste. Yesterday morning my cousin chum and fellow Samaritan asked me for a loan and in spite of my solemn oath and promise to the contrary the good lord in his strange and mysterious ways stepped in and lo he softeneth my heart. In consequence and subsequently I did in fact see fit to loan him fifty dollars. And I must confess that you too played a part in wavering my fortitude Irma, because Alphonso insisted and reiterated with excitement that he had dreamed you that night for the first and only time in his livelihood. It was some sort of sign of the highest order.

Anyways to cut a long story short he proceeded to bet the fifty procured from myself together with another fifty of his own to a grand total of one hundred dollars on number thirty-one in the Play-whe. And number thirty-one as luck, chance and destiny would have it turned out to be the winning number. This morning Alphonso told me the fortunate news.

And it was Alphonso too good soul and Christian that he is who come up with the suggestion because as he quoted, he knew how much pine away I feeling for you. No sooner said than done and the two of us together journeyed to Astral Travel Agency and purchased two tickets for Canada. Yes my dear I in accompaniment with Alphonso will be arriving in Canada this weekend to be forever and ever amen with you and furthermore to put a stop to you rolling about on the floor with any Mr. Jacket and Tie.

Your soon to be reunited husband
Paul

Aja

For the first twenty-one years of my life, I soak up every bit of advice my grandfather, or Aja, as we call him, throw my way. He was a big, powerful man, nearly two hundred pounds, and even though in the late stage his diabetes had cause him to be hook up in the settee or in the puja room most of the time, whenever he bark, every single body in the house use to quake.

At one time it had nearly twelve of us living in the house at the same time: me, my mother and father and two younger sisters, Tara and Renuka, my uncle Uttam and his wife Cookie and their two show-offy daughters, and my other uncle, Ramu, and his wife Babsy. They, thank god, had no children, and two-three times I hear my mother saying that Babsy was something like Gautam.

Gautam was the cow that, no matter how much bull we bring to service her, could never get full. Once, when Ramu suggest that we sell her off, Aja tell him in Hindi that it was exactly the kind of suggestion that a one-stones *gaddahar* or a donkey will make. That put a stop to any talk about selling away Gautam, but in the evening I use to see Ramu, who job it was to tie her out, attacking the poor animal with a guava switch and screaming, "You damn useless old *dwine*. Take that in you ass." *Switch! Switch!*

Ramu was drunk most of the time, though never in front of Aja, and when he wasn't beating Gautam, he was beating Babsy. Which was surprising to me, because his wife was nearly twice his size and I was sure she could rumfle him up if she had a mind. But she was a peace-able woman, and a few times I would spot her staring out from the window in the last room which they live in, combing her long hair with a fine-teeth comb.

When Ramu get knock down with Partap lorry, I thought that he would quieten down now that he was broko-foot, but he just get worse, and sometimes for the whole day he use to be hopping around in the room, chasing Babsy with his crook stick.

When I fail my common entrance exam, he tell Ma that my head was full with *bagasse*, the cane trash, and that I would end up driving taxi just like my father.

Because my father was the oldest brother, we had the front room right next to Cookie and Uttam and their two girls, Shauna and Sherry. My mother never tell me this, but I think she was shame that I had to drop out from school while Shauna and Sherry was both going to the convent college in San Fernando. After Ramu get broko-foot, it was my job to see about Gautam, and every morning after I tie her out, I would bathe with the cold rainwater from the copper and bring a little basket of zinnia and hibiscus flowers in the puja room for Aja. Once, I hear my father saying that he might buy two more cow for me to mind.

Aja use to sleep in the puja room, and every morning when I bring the flowers, I would notice all the gods line up on the chiss. He alone was allow to open the chiss, and he had the key between the beads in his mala. I think Aja was please by my bringing flowers and seeing about Gautam, because I notice that he was not as quarrelsome with me as he was with everybody else. Mostly, he would give me advice about this and that. One morning, he point to his chest and say, "Is what you have here that count." Then he point to his head. "Not up here."

I was really glad when Cookie and Uttam went to live in San Fernando near to the convent college because I get their empty room. But Aja was mad like hell, and he warn them not to come back when trouble take them. But no trouble never take them, and whenever they come back to visit, Shauna and Sherry would complain about how it getting dark and how they don't like to travel in the nighttime. One evening, Ramu say, "What happen, it don't have enough man in the village for allyou." Babsy say, "Mmm-mmm," with her nose, which she always do when she feeling worried or helpless. They never visit after that except for a few Christmas and Divali days.

Not too long after, Ramu pass away. One night, just before he die, I see him in the bed with his head on Babsy lap. She was massaging his forehead and saying something in a soft voice. I was surprise because I never see them like that before.

With Ramu gone, the house get much quieter. Aja too cool down, maybe because he had nobody to quarrel with again, but one morning in the puja room he tell me, "The worse punishment a father could ever face is to bury his own son." After a while he say in a quiet voice, like if he talking the himself, "God does be testing we every step of the way."

In a strange way I too miss Ramu, but the quietness was good for my sister Tara because she was writing the common entrance that year, and it was my mother hope that she pass for the convent college. My father didn't know if we could afford it, though. I know that he was thinking he was a ordinary taxi driver and not a regular bus driver for the government like Uttam. Because of that, I was glad when I get the work in Chin Lee sawmill to cut down tree with Joe and Blades from the

Tortuga forest and winch it up in the Bedford truck and canhook the log down in the sawmill. After that, I would pack away the pieces of scantling in the slab heap and shovel out the wet sawdust from the pit below the band saw. But every morning, I would still tie out Gautam, bathe in the copper water and bring a basket of flowers for the puja room

As time pass, Aja diabetes get worser and worser, until it reach the point where he couldn't move around on his own. Then it was my job to do the puja for him, and after I come back from work, I would support him to the toilet or to the settee which was in the gallery. One night, after I bring him back from the settee to his bed, he say that I was getting real strong from my sawmill work, and he start talking about when Ajee was still alive and when he was a worker in Portillo cocoa estate. While he was saying that, I remember something that old Sonny, who use to operate the band saw, tell me—about how Aja was one of the strongest man in the village long-time and how he use to put a hundred-pound bag of cocoa on each shoulder and walk nearly half-mile to the estate house.

I believe I was the only person to really talk with Aja, because my father didn't return from his taxi driving until late in the night and, according to the custom, it would have been disrespectful for my mother or Babsy to carry on any conversation with their father-in-law. Then Tara pass the common entrance for St. Stephen's College, which was not as high-class as the convent college but still good enough to give a bundle of home lesson.

As Aja get more weaker, he start talking more and more about his young days, when Ajee was still living. And after every talk he would give me advice. Sometimes I use to think that he was frighten about losing all his power and control, but everything he say I take note of. Keep away from drinking and smoking and people with plenty bad-mind. Drink a cup of *dahee*, the bitter yogurt, every morning and a cup of ginger tea every night. Never start anything on a Tuesday, because it will fail; choose Thursday and Saturday instead. Sleep with your head facing the east. Watch out for anybody with a black spot in they tongue because anything they say about you will stick. Careful with *maljou*, the evil eye. And his favourite: never leave the house if anybody sneeze. That last one was the worse, because my little sister Renuka was always getting the cold, and sometimes I had to hurry out from the house a hour or so before my sawmill work just so I wouldn't hear her sneeze. One such morning I take out my temper on Renuka, and Aja must have hear me because, when I was carrying him to the toilet, he say, "You mustn't let a little cold get you upset." Still, I was losing a whole day salary.

Then Renuka too pass for St. Stephen's College and start leaving for school the same time with me, so I didn't have that problem again. Three years after, Tara pass five subjects in the Cambridge and get a job in the post office about a three-quarter mile from where we live. By that time Aja was stick up in bed for nearly the whole day, opening his mouth wide and breathing heavy. I use to change his clothes and feed him every morning, and I believe Babsy use to feed him for the rest of the day.

One night, he was breathing heavier than normal. I was cracking his fingers, which he always like me to do, when he pull away his hand and rest it on the mala around his neck. He ask me to take it off. Then he tell me to open the chiss. I was surprise, because I had never ever see what was in the inside of it. The chiss, which was make of solid steel, was smelling of *googool* and *hing* and clove, and it was pack with yellow paper tie up in rubber band. From the bed Aja ask me to open the drawer in the bottom and take out the brass box. I bring the box for him and he take out a brown envelope and put it on his chest. "Count it," he tell me. The envelope was full of money. Six thousand in all. Then Aja say, "Take it. Is yours." I didn't know what to say. I just start shaking my head, but Aja put the envelope in my hand. "I had this for you all the time. Take it." I begin to cry because it was so unexpected and also because I thought it mean that Aja was going to die soon.

I didn't tell anybody, and that whole night I was waking in bed wondering what I was going to do with the money. I thought of buying a plot of land and planting a small garden. I thought of going to a private school and learning some trade. And I thought of something that Tara always talk about—how ordinary people from the village, uneducated like me, migrate up to America and Canada to pick apple, and how every month-end they does post down a letter full of foreign money for they family. That was too much, but as the night progress, more and more I thinking of these people picking apple. Uneducated just like me. Sending back a envelope fat with money. Red, juicy apple. Slipping up a tree and pulling out a few apple. So simple!

The next day, in the sawmill, I mention this apple-picking business to Sonny, casual like, as if I not really interested. It turn out that Sonny brother was a apple picker. And Babooram brother and three of Deolal son. So much people, right next to me, and I never even suspect it before. The idea grow.

In the evening, I mention it to Tara and she burst out laughing, but by then my mind had seize up with the idea. In the night, I tell it to Aja and, even though I was worried that he would get vex with me, he say, "*I* use to pick cocoa. *You* want to pick apple. What is the difference?" Then he smile at me. "You just carrying on you grandfather tradition, not so?"

"Yes, Aja," was all I could say.

My mother and father was a different matter. They

put up all kind of objection about how the place will be too cold and I don't know anybody over there and supposing the plane crash and thing like that. Then I mention Sonny and Babooram brother and Deolal son and they quieten down a bit.

Tara and Renuka was excited for me, and after two-three months pass, I notice that my mother wasn't objecting too much, and that she and all was getting a little bit excited. When I get my visa and work permit, she start fussing about the kind of things I will end up eating in Canada and about these foreign girls she see on *Melrose Place* and *The Young and the Restless*. When Renuka and Tara hear that, they start to giggle up and scream, "Ooh. White chick and thing." And, "Take care you don't fall down from these apple tree, watching these chicks whole day." And Renuka say, "Braps," and pretend she fall on the floor.

All the time, I was excited about going to Canada, but the day before I was suppose to leave, I was more frighten than any time in my life. My mother had cook *dhalpuri* and chicken and *phooloorie* and fry rice, and Tara and Renuka get deck off in nice frilly dress, maybe because they know that Shauna and Sherry was coming that evening. When Uncle Uttam and his family reach, I was surprise at how big Shauna and Sherry, who I didn't see for more than two years, had get. Seeing them, my mind flash back on how they use to run around the house in merino and old home-clothes. But that day they was wearing jeans and jersey decorate up with singers' pictures, and the way they was talking and sitting down and wearing dark shades make me feel a little shy. At first they didn't talk much, but when they hear that I going to pick apple, they get more talkative and start giving me advice about all sort of thing. I notice, too, as they get in a more talkative and laughing mood, Tara and Renuka get more and more quieter. But all the time, my mind was on this crazy thing that I was doing.

After we finish eat, I rush up to the puja room, but Aja did look as if he was sleeping. So I stand up before all the gods line up on the chiss and beg them not to forget me even though I will be so far away. As I was about to leave, Aja open his eye a little bit and ask me to crack his fingers for him. *Crack. Crack. Crack.* The noise was so hard. Then Aja, as if he could read my mind, say, "*Beta* everywhere have good and bad. Good people, bad people. Good friend, bad friend. Good habit, bad habit. Is up to you to make the choice. You alone have to choose the road you going to travel on. Nobody could do that for you." Then he pull me to him and say, "My life nearly over. Yours now starting. Go and pick you apple and them." And the way he was talking, with his eye soft and watery like I never see it before, I had this feeling that I would never see Aja again.

~

The strangest thing about coming to Canada was how easy this whole apple-picking business had look back in Trinidad. Just slip up a little tree, grapple onto a few apple, full them in a basket and slip down. So easy. These red, juicy, sweet apples. Picking them would be a joy, so different from cutting down tree from the Tortuga forest and loading and canhooking and shovelling wet sawdust whole day. And in the back of my mind I had this idea that in a little while I would be able to send down an envelope fat with money, and Tara would rush home and show Renuka and my mother and father and Aja. Just like Sonny and Babooram brother and Deolal three son.

The funny thing is that I couldn't find no apple farm at all. Back in Trinidad, any time I think of apple, I think of Canada, but I spend nearly one whole month looking for apple farm. I take the bus and the train and travel through the length and breadth of Toronto, and all that I see was people walking fast-fast and these sort of tall building that King Kong did climb up on. But no apple farm.

Every evening, after all the travelling, I would stop off by Shop and Save, which was walking distance from the apartment where I was renting, and buy my milk and bread and cheese. And I would stare at the apple section—watch them, try to figure out how much they weigh, how far they travel, where they come from and where they going. If only they could talk. A few times

I hold them up against my face, hoping it would have some fine writing with the name of a farm, but the only thing print out was *McIntosh*.

One evening, while I was gazing at some newly unload apples with the soft green paper still underneath, a big fat Creole lady who was packing things in a nearby shelf come up to me and say, "But ay-ay, young man, what you have with these apple and them? Is a good time now I noticing you watching-watching these apples like if they have some special secret. Why you don't buy one and done."

Even though this lady was talking in Trinidadian, I was too shame to tell her, so I remain quiet.

Then her voice sort of change. "What happen, young man? Like you hard up or what? Look, take a apple and I will pay for it." She pull out a nice juicy one with a McIntosh print and hold it up for me.

I shake my head. "I don't want no apple. I just want to work in a apple farm."

The Creole lady watch me from head to toe as if I mad. She take a big breath, like when these crappo fulling up, and tell me point-blank to forget this nonsense. And without me asking her anything, she say that we foreign people does land up in Canada with our mind seize up on one thing, and only when the pressure start that we begin to understand that we have to take what we get. Then she take another crappo breath and say that she too had come up hoping to land work as a domestic, and how for months she looking and looking until she find this job packing away things on the shelf.

Then she look at me from head to toe again. "A young, strong boy like you shouldn't have so much trouble finding a work." She pull in her lower lip and press down her top teeth against it as if she was thinking about something. "You from Trinidad, you say?"

I hadn't mention that, but I tell her yes.

"You just around the same age as Philbert, you know. He is my son." She smile a little bit. "Big and strong just like you. He working as a mechanic at Massy. You ever been there?"

I shake my head.

The Creole lady put one hand inside a pocket of the green overall that she was wearing and say, "Hmm-hmm." Then she too start staring at the apples. Finally, she tell me, "You know what, young man? I could talk to the manager mister here if you want. They always looking for people to work in the warehouse in the back. Is only six dollars a hour, which is why nobody don't stay too long, but is better than nothing."

Six dollars! That was twenty-four Trinidadian dollars. I could see the fat envelope already!

"Wait here." She come back about twenty minutes later with a big smile. "You could start tomorrow."

Fat-fat envelope!

"They does ask for reference and thing, but I tell him that I know you for years back in Trinidad." She take up a cardboard box from the floor and start arranging tins of tomato soup on a shelf. And while she was neatening them in a row, she say something that I will never forget. "You see how things does work out, young man? Back in Trinidad, we Creole and Indian killing each other all the time. But over here we have no choice but to get along."

That was how I start working at Shop and Save. Don't mind the three other men working in the warehouse use to always complain about the small pay and how hard the work was, to me it wasn't even as half as hard as when I was in the sawmill. And plus that, a good few of the box that I had to off-load from the truck and stack up for the forklift had apple in them. In fact, the first letter that I write after I get the job, I mention how I unpacking apple. And I promise that the next letter will have some money in it.

My shift was from nine to three, which add up to thirty-six dollars a day and two hundred and fifty-two dollars a week. Nearly eleven hundred Trinidad dollars—the amount that I would take a month to make in the sawmill.

The Creole lady was working in the evening shift, so the only time we would meet was when I leaving and I bounce her up coming to work. We didn't have much time to chat, but she would always ask me how things going and then talk a little bit about her husband and some other lazy, good-for-nothing person who was living with them. Plus that, the three men from the warehouse wasn't like the workers at the sawmill, who use to be talking and shouting and making joke all the time. Mostly, they was quiet and vex-looking, like how Uncle Uttam use to look just before he and Cookie and Shauna and Sherry move to San Fernando. But that didn't bother me much, because the most important thing was I had a reasonable job and I was making enough money. Not too much, but after I use up six hundred dollars for rent and four hundred for food and other things, I still had an extra hundred to post down every month. That was four hundred Trinidad dollars, nearly the same amount that Tara was making in the post office. Things was really going good.

Then one evening, I get a letter from Renuka telling me that Aja had take a turn for the worse. According to the letter, he was now in the bed all the time, and whenever he want anything, he would shout and curse in Hindi. And if nobody didn't come in time, he would take the cup and plate from the bed and dash it on the wall. Plus that, he was always saying that everybody just waiting for him to dead.

Two weeks later, I get another letter saying that he pass away. He was sitting in the bed brushing his teeth when he just fall back with the toothbrush still in his hand. All throughout that letter Renuka stress that he didn't suffer and that he die real peaceable. And I was thinking that maybe he didn't suffer at that exact minute, but what about before?

It was something I had try not to think about when I was leaving Trinidad and for the seven months that I spend in Canada. Who carrying him to the toilet? Who putting flowers in the puja room? Who cracking his fingers while he talking about Ajee and his young days in Portillo estate?

When I get that letter, the first thing that stick in my mind was to go back to Trinidad for the cremation, even though Renuka had write that it wouldn't make much sense because everything would be over by the time I reach. For nearly the whole night I thinking and thinking, and in the end what change my mind was not Renuka advice but the feeling that Aja wouldn't want it so. God does be testing we every step of the way.

I remember all the other heaps of advice he use to give me, all the things that I forget when I reach in Canada. And I realize that in this place I was nothing like the person I was in Trinidad. I had become somebody else. That night, I beg Aja to forgive me and I pray for his soul to born in a good, happy body.

In the weeks that follow, I start doing all the things that Aja had advise me to do. I didn't have to worry about anybody sneezing in the morning because I was living alone, or about the evil eye, because hardly anybody ever watch me. But I change my bed to face the east, I start eating yogurt, which was in these little jars at Shop and Save, and drinking ginger tea every night. And every morning, I would stand before the gods that Aja had give me when I was leaving and which I had arrange on top of my bedroom table, and say my mantra and *bhajan*, and pray for no harm to fall on my family in Trinidad.

But as time pass, I realize that the loneliness I had feel the night I read Renuka letter just keep getting worse and worser. It was as if, with Aja gone, something get take away from my life. The whole picture was spoil in Trinidad. As hard as I try, I couldn't imagine the house without him in the bed or in the settee. And because of that, I find myself thinking more and more about how things use to be when I was growing up. Then, the house was always full of people, and later on, it still had Tara and Renuka to make jokes with. I remember how Babsy hug me the night that I was leaving Trinidad and start crying and saying that I was like a son to her. The strange thing is that I didn't think much about Ramu chasing Babsy with the crook stick, or about Shauna and Sherry sometimes saying that their mother didn't want them to play with we, but only about the good, happy times. And about the sawmill too, where, even though I had no really close friends, I still had the feeling that I could talk to anybody when I had the mind to.

In Canada, the only person I would talk to for five minutes or so was the Creole lady, but even then I would mostly listen rather than do any talking my own self. I decide against telling her about Aja because she too had her bundle of worries. And it strike me that maybe these other vex-looking men from the warehouse had their own pressure to think about. Maybe wife or children or some other Canadian worries.

As the place start getting colder and colder, I find myself missing all that I remember about Trinidad. And because the place was so cold, even the five minutes' chat with the Creole lady get cut down to just "Hello" and "Make sure you dress proper for this winter, eh, young man. It does be hell." One night, while I was hurrying to my apartment with my hands push deep inside the coat, I remember something Aja had tell me. "You mustn't let a little cold get you upset." And with these small pieces of snow falling on top of me like soft white cornflakes, I remember something else he had say: that the worse thing in this world is loneliness. Is like a rope around you neck that getting tighter every day.

And so, many thousands of miles away, after all this time, I get the feeling that maybe Aja had been preparing me all the while. Preparing me for this time in my life. And I know then that the first thing that I had to do was get rid of this rope.

I decide that I would be friendly to everybody from then on. That was a hard thing to do because I was a naturally quiet person, and even in elementary school, before I drop out, I never went down by the creek during recess with the other boys or remain by the junction after school to chat and lime. It was the same story in the sawmill, although that was really because the other workers use to go by Dilpaul bar every evening and I had to rush home to bring in Gautam and see about Aja. One evening, the Creole lady tell me, "You know something, young man? The only difference between you and Philbert is that he does talk like if he eat parrot bottom, and you does talk like if you have to pay for every word." Then she say, "A young, good-looking boy like you shouldn't be so quiet-quiet all the time. These Canadian girls don't like no *coonoo-moonoo* boys, you know." When she see how shame I was looking, she burst out laughing, which make me laugh a little bit too.

The next day, at work, I put on a big smile to show everybody how friendly I was. But as the day progress, it was difficult to keep this smile in place and, plus that, I notice the other workers looking at me suspicious-suspicious like if I plan to thief something. At the end of the shift, while I was taking out my overalls, I tell one of the other workers, whose name was Tom, that I enjoy the day today. I didn't really mean that, it was just conversation. Tom open his mouth like if he going to say something, but he didn't tell me nothing. And when he collect his bag from the locker, I hear him using four-letter words and grumbling to himself.

During that whole week, I keep on smiling and telling the other workers how I enjoying the work so much. It was the sort of thing that, back in Trinidad, would make everybody know that you was real friendly, but here it was having the opposite effect. Finally, a worker name either Bob or Bill, with a belly like a big pot, tell me, "Look, I don't know what your game is, but just lay off. Okay?"

But I wasn't about to give up. I was determined to slip off this rope from around my neck. Canada was a big place, full of thousands and thousands of people. And I discover that from my balcony in the fourth floor I could see a whole heap of people walking in and walking out from the building all the time—people who was living in the same building with me. In Trinidad, that would have make we family. And so, every evening after I finish work and bathe and eat, I would watch over from the balcony at the different people coming in and going out. That was when I first discover Anne.

Anne was not her real name, but the way she used to be wearing these tight wrangler jeans and walking with her foot wide apart, like if she was a horseback rider and still feeling the animal between her leg, remind me of a comic book lady name Annie-something. That

Anne was a real gunslinger, but this one was mostly in a hurry, coming in and out of the building with a green canvassy bag hanging from her shoulder. Every evening at half past four she would leave, and two hours later I would spot her coming from the bus stop with her wide-apart walk. I don't know why I decide on Anne except to say that she remind me of Sonny daughter, who use to bring his lunch in the sawmill sometimes. The same long black hair, the same roundish face, the same smooth, rolling walk. And Sonny daughter, whenever she was giving her father the carrier full with rice and *bodi* and chicken, would watch me fast-fast, and other times, when her father was busy and she had left the food on the old table and was leaving, she would spin around real quick with her hair making a circle in the air and catch me looking at her. Then she would smile and continue walking slow. One day I had give Jairam, who was living near to her, a little note saying that the food she bring for her father does smell real sweet. It was a stupid note but was all that I could think of. And it was a good thing, too, because Jairam had read the note, and for weeks after, whenever we near to each other, he would pretend to be breathing hard and he would say things like, "Mmm, this smell sweet," and point his nose in the air and ask me if I smelling anything. I don't think he ever give her the note, and I was too shame after that to ever watch at her.

I was determine that nothing wouldn't go wrong this time. The Creole lady had said that these Canadian girls didn't like *coonoo-moonoo* boys, so the most important thing was that I had to act bold. That was the first step. But as I was thinking about the other steps, I realized that it was not so easy as all that. What I would write in the note? I didn't even know her name and what floor she was living in. And how I would pass this note to her? The only thing that keep me from giving up this idea was the rope that Aja had told me about, getting tighter every day.

The next evening, at about six o'clock, I went by the letter box downstairs, where I know she must pass, and pretend that I was opening my box and looking for letters. I believe I open and close my box about seven or eight time before I spot her from the glass door. My heart start to pound real fast when she walk through the door and open her own box. It had a small brown envelope in it, which she open and read right there. I pretend that I couldn't find the correct key in my bunch to close back the box, and was fidgeting with the bunch while she was reading her letter. And I was watching her closely out of the corner of my eye. She was around the same size like Sonny daughter, maybe a little bit taller. And she had the same nice roundish body. Not fat. Not skinny either. Her tight wrangler jeans had two small rips by the knees in the style of these Canadians, and

I thought for sure that the knees must be feeling cold from walking outside. Just then, she slam the door of the box and climb up the steps. I too slam my door shut and wait for about quarter-minute or so, then rush up the step. I had just enough time to see her going inside a door down in the end of the hall. I walk down the hall as though I was living in that floor until I reach the door she had gone in. Number 23.

That was step one. And now the difficult part: to write the note. I know that I couldn't write no stupidness like in the note I had write in Trinidad because this was a different country and I was sure that she was more educated than Sonny daughter, who never went to college or anything. I start picking my brains, trying to think of something that Anne might fancy. I tried to remember all these shows on television that my mother used to watch, and all the different things these foreign girls had like the boyfriends to do. Carrying them to restaurants. Bringing them flowers and chocolate and bottles of wine. Inviting them to concert or to the cinema. Buying jewellery for them. And I realize that I couldn't do none of these things because, first of all, I didn't have the money and, plus that, I didn't have the courage. It would have to be just a note.

In the end, I get the idea not from *Melrose Place* and *The Young and the Restless* but from a Indian movie where Rajendra Kumar had spin around Saira Banu in a flower field and sing out that he was like a hummingbird thiefing nectar and that she was his special flower. And that is what I write in the note.

It is only after things happen that you realize what you should have really do and see all the mistake that you made. It was a big mistake putting my room number in the note, and a bigger one signing my name at the bottom in big fancy letters like Teacher Soogrim in Elswick school. Maybe I should have just write a little note first and see how she would react and then follow on from there. But it was too late for that—she had already pass on the note.

The superintendent had the note in her hand, and from where I was sitting opposite her by the table in her office, I could make out my fancy handwriting, plain and bold like in Teacher Soogrim blackboard. Her other hand was tapping on the table with the fingers like a crab preparing to attack. And I find myself looking at this crab on the table moving closer to me than at her face while she was saying how this was a respectable building and the only trouble they ever had was schoolchildren scraping car and thiefing a few tire and writing rudeness inside the elevator. The way she was mentioning all these things make what I do look like a first-rate crime, as if I had murder somebody. Suddenly, she stop talking about all these other thing and ask me point-blank why I write the note. I keep on looking at the crab on the table. She ask me if I was interested in this girl, whose name was not Anne but some hard-to-pronounce name like Miss Sickle-ho-wisk or something. I thought of saying no, but she had the note in her hand. In any case, she didn't give me a chance to answer, because she continue talking on about these different kinds of perverts like rapists and molesters who does choose out a victim and stork them all over the place. And all these storkers could pass for ordinary people, looking quiet and decent—just like me. At that point I was feeling to rush out from the office and pack all my thing and find some other building to live in. Then she ask me if I ever talk to this Miss Sickle-ho-wisk. I shake my head. And she say that maybe that was what I should done, because I wasn't bad to look at, in her exact words. At that, I look up at her and notice that she was not vex-looking again but was smiling with her thin lip and brushing her cheek with the note.

The thought cross my mind that maybe she was trying to trap me or something, so I remain quiet. And she continue on about how lonely it must be for me in this country and that she too understand how that does feel. She ask if I have any girlfriend and I shake my head again. And that set her off on another long talk about living alone and not having no friends to talk with and spending the whole evening watching television by yourself and eating unhealthy food. She mention that how she had join some gym or the other but had to drop out because all the other gym people was show-offy girls twenty years younger than her. And I was thinking that maybe Miss Sickle-ho-wisk was one of these girls and that was why the superintendent wasn't feeling sorry for her again.

On and on she went, talking faster now, then talking slower, making it hard to follow her conversation. And all the time, I had me head bend, wondering what madness had cause me to write that note, and waiting for the superintendent to finish so that I could rush back to my room and beg all the gods line up on the table to forgive me for what I do.

I didn't notice when the superintendent get up from the chair and come and sit on the edge of the table before me. It was only when I hear a scratch-scratch sound that I look up and see her scraping her cheek with the note and looking at me. Then she tell me that it didn't make any sense wasting my time on girls like Miss Sickle-ho-wisk, who would only get me in trouble. And she would hate to see that happen to a fine, decent young man, her exact words. She rest the tip of her tongue on her upper lip as if she was waiting for me to say something.

I freeze. I couldn't say nothing. Because right at that very minute I see a round, black spot underneath the end of her tongue. I run out from the office straight to my room and lock the door tight.

I still working at the warehouse in Shop and Save, but now, instead of trying to be friendly all the time or putting on a false smile, I do my work quietly and try to finish as much as I could. Just like how I imagine Aja use to be in Portillo estate. And it look like people over here like this sort of behaviour, because not too long ago the manager tell me that if I get my forklift licence, he would let me operate it and I would get two dollars an hour more.

I still post down one hundred dollars every month, which is a good thing because Tara no longer working in the post office again. Now she going to the Technical Institute in San Fernando, doing some computer course. And she too in every letter that she write always mentioning how she would like to come up to Canada. I suppose she thinking about working here and posting down one hundred dollars a month. Then it will be Renuka turn. I never tell her what she should do in my letters except once, when I write that she alone could choose the road that she want to travel on.

I still think about Aja a lot, and sometimes I wish that he was still alive and I could talk with him. I would tell him about the Creole lady who I visit once in her apartment in Mississauga, and how she and her husband remind me of Ramu and Babsy, with one so fat and the other one so thin. I wouldn't tell him about Miss Sickle-ho-wisk, who I still see coming and going in the evening, or about the superintendent who does always make it her business to stop and chat whenever she spot me. But I would tell him that I finally understand what he had mean. Is we self who does put the rope around we neck and only we could take it off. I will tell him that, just like when he was working in Portillo estate, I do what I have to do and never worry about anything else.

Miss Blinky and Duckie

Jan. Week one.

It was Miss Blinky's idea that I keep a journal. She said that it was the best way to organize my thoughts. Miss Blinky believes in organizing. She always files away her notes in different-colour folders in her cabinet, and whenever Mr. Dukchuk spreads his coat on the chair, she rearranges it so that the sleeves are equal. When he goes to the cupboard to make his coffee, she places a napkin on the table for his cup. All of us in the multi-exceptionality class know that the only way to get her annoyed is by scattering our books on the table or throwing paper on the floor. But most of the time she is pleasant to us. Even though she is only the teaching assistant, she makes sure that we understand everything we are taught. Just last week she spent a lot of time explaining the real meaning of phrases like "skating on thin ice" and "turning green with envy."

Some of the other students say that she treats us like little children, but me, I like the way her eyes get soft when she smiles, and the pink and yellow sweaters that she is always wearing, and her nice warm smell when she is leaning over the table to explain something to me. I have to say, though, that not all the students are happy to be in this class. I feel for sure that Jermaine, who lived in Antigua until he came to Canada about two years ago, hates being here. And maybe Doug too, who hates the entire school and all the teachers. Doug would rather be with his grandfather fishing by the cottage near Lake Simcoe.

In the beginning, I too didn't like the idea of being in this class. I suppose that I felt like Jermaine, that I had no right to be in a class for dumb students. Because that is what the other students think of us in this class. Dumb.

I am more comfortable now. At least I am not in any class again where the other students can make fun of my accent or whisper things about me. That was why I stopped saying anything in the other class. If I kept my mouth shut, they couldn't laugh at me again.

Here it is different. Miss Blinky does not tolerate that sort of behaviour. Whenever she is annoyed, her top lip gets thin and presses against her lower lip. It is enough to make us stop whatever we are doing. If she is really annoyed, she looks at us in a serious way and says, "That's a complete no-no." Most of the time she tells that to Jermaine. I don't think that Jermaine cares. I feel that one of these days he is going to end up in some serious kind of trouble.

~

Jan. Week two.

Today makes it exactly one month since I am in this class and about four months since I left Trinidad. This week we had an exploration session. That is what Mr. Dukchuk called it. He explained what we were supposed to do and then went back as usual to his table to read. It was left to Miss Blinky to carry out this exploration session with us. She asked each of us to talk about some happy experience in our childhood. Doug talked about the time he went sailing with his grandfather in the ocean. Perry, a tall, shy boy with spots on his face, talked about his Dalmatian puppy named Alia. Jermaine, not standing like the rest of us when it was our turn, told us about a fight with three other boys at his old school. At the end of the fight, one of the boys ended up in the hospital and Jermaine was suspended. When Jermaine was saying this, I could see Miss Blinky's top lip getting thinner and thinner. Most of the other students talked about birthdays and summer vacations and Christmas celebrations. When it was Martha's turn, she began to cry. Miss Blinky put her arms around Martha and told her that it was okay. Mr. Dukchuk looked up from his book and smiled at her.

I was the last person to talk. All throughout the time that the other students were relating their happy experiences, I was running through my own childhood days. I thought of the months that I lived with my mother and the months that I lived with my father. And, when they made up, the times that I lived with both of them. But these times never lasted very long and after that it was always back to only one of them. And then to the other. I also remembered the year just before I came to Canada, the year that the three of us lived in the same house. It was the longest period that we were ever together, and I had great hopes that we would be able to live like all the other families. Then my mother decided to leave for Canada. I thought of mentioning this to the class, but I changed my mind. The happiness didn't lead to anything. It had shown me that all my hopes were useless and stupid.

I didn't know what to say. Although I wouldn't have minded Miss Blinky putting her arms around me, I didn't want to cause her any further distress. In the end, I talked about my first week in Canada and how excited I was. Everybody believed me. Miss Blinky smiled in her soft, warm way and Mr. Dukchuk nodded his head at her.

~

Jan. Week three.

Yesterday we were given little blocks of wood to make into different shapes. I could have finished my shapes in about five minutes, but I was careful not to let anyone discover that. It was the same with the crossword puzzles, with words like bat and cat and rat, and colouring fruits in their correct shades and learning nursery-rhyme songs about spiders. I never wanted to be sent back to the other class, so I always put on a big pretence.

While we were working on our patterns, Mr. Dukchuk came and stood next to Miss Blinky. He said, "Great stuff, Miss Blinky. The kids seem to be enjoying this."

"Aren't they great?" she told him, pressing her two hands against the front of her yellow sweater.

"Yes, yes," Mr. Dukchuk said, chewing his big moustache. "Everyone's improved since you came here." He moved a little closer to her.

Miss Blinky said, "Oh," and she blushed.

For the rest of the day, while Miss Blinky was bending over the table to help some student or when she was arranging her folders in the cabinet, I saw Mr. Dukchuk staring at her and chewing his moustache.

In the afternoon, when I was putting my stuff in my locker, Jermaine asked me where I was from. I told him Trinidad. He said that I looked as if I came from some island near Hawaii. One of these people that you see on TV with spears, running around naked. I had to laugh at that. I explained that my parents had Chinese and African and European and Carib blood in them. But I didn't tell him that some of the boys from the school in Trinidad used to call me "no-where-ian." He opened his locker and asked me, "Do you know why I am in this class with all these other morons?"

I shook my head, although I already knew what he was going to say. "Cause I'm black, man. That's why." He slammed the locker door shut. "Is why I was always in trouble in my old school."

"Don't you like it here?" I asked him.

"Like it here?" he said in a loud voice. "Do you like it here?"

I thought for a while. "I prefer it to my last class."

"Why?"

"Because the work is easier."

That seemed to satisfy him. "Colouring apple tree and pear tree," he said, laughing now. He put on his coat and left, still laughing. Maybe I was wrong about him. We could be good friends after all.

~

Jan. Week four.

Martha did not come to school on Monday and Tuesday. Miss Blinky was very worried. Mr. Dukchuk did his best to calm her down. He told her that it was nothing serious, probably just the flu. But Miss Blinky remained worried. On Tuesday afternoon, while she was going through her folders in the cabinet, Mr. Dukchuk came by her and placed his hand on the open drawer next to hers. He told her that he had phoned Martha's foster parents and they had informed him that Martha just needed some rest.

"The poor girl," Miss Blinky said. "The things she has been through."

Mr. Dukchuk put his hands on top of Miss Blinky's and said, "She's improved a bit now. We just have to keep on trying."

Miss Blinky took a deep breath and closed her eyes. When she opened them, she watched Mr. Dukchuk's hands on hers. Maybe she didn't notice them before. She looked up at Mr. Dukchuk and her eyes were blinking fast.

"She will be in school tomorrow," Mr. Dukchuk told her, removing his hand and putting it inside his pants pocket. When he went back to his table, Miss Blinky's eyes were still winking faster than usual.

After school was dismissed, I asked Jermaine, who was in this class longer than I, if he had ever spoken to Martha. I was thinking of the conversation between Miss Blinky and Mr. Dukchuk. Jermaine said that as far as he remembered, Martha never talked with anyone.

I asked him why.

He took out his coat from his locker and told me that she had been abused by an uncle she was living with when her parents separated.

"What kind of abuse?" I asked him.

He grinned at me and said, "C'mon, you're a big boy now. Nice young thing—old drunkard uncle. That's a dangerous combination." He laughed out loud.

That night, I wanted to tell my mother what I had discovered about our class, that everyone I knew came from divorced parents. Martha, Jermaine, Doug, Perry, me, and maybe even all the other students. In the end I didn't tell her about my discovery. Instead, I asked her if my father will ever be coming to live in Canada. She looked very surprised. She asked me if I wasn't happy.

I thought of the answer I should give her, then I said that I was okay.

Nowadays, I have to lie so much to everyone.

When Martha came to school on Wednesday, the first thing that Miss Blinky did was hug her. For the entire day Miss Blinky was by Martha's table, helping her cut out and paste pictures of different animals onto a sheet of drawing paper. While Martha was writing the description of these animals beneath the pictures, she had her head bent low over the table and her hair kept covering her eyes. I think that her shoulders were shaking sometimes.

On Thursday, Mr. Dukchuk gave her a box of chocolates. Martha opened the box carefully and took out one of the chocolates. She gazed at it, then put one in her mouth. Miss Blinky looked at Mr. Dukchuk and smiled. While Martha was eating the chocolates, Miss Blinky went by Mr. Dukchuk's table and told him, "That was a great idea, Mr. Dukchuk. Whatever made you think of it?"

Mr. Dukchuk looked pleased. He said, "Everyone has a soft spot, Miss Blinky."

On Friday, Mr. Dukchuk brought another box of chocolates, but not for Martha.

~

Feb. Week one.

This week Mr. Dukchuk did not spend much time by his table. Instead, he was mostly by Miss Blinky's side, with his arms clasped behind his back and looking at what we were doing. I never realized before that his nose was so big. Miss Blinky too looked different. Her face was redder than usual, and her lips were not pressed together but a little open. Every morning, he brought her a box of chocolates.

One morning she told him, "You are spoiling me, Mr. Dukchuk."

"Now why would I do that, Miss Blinky?" He smiled as if he had made a joke.

On another day, while Miss Blinky was correcting the spelling in a paragraph Doug had written about a weekend at his grandfather's cottage, Mr. Dukchuk asked her, "Have you ever been to cottage country, Miss Blinky?"

Miss Blinky told him that the last time was when she was a teenager.

Mr. Dukchuk asked her if it was one of those wild teenage parties with lots of beer and fooling around. "You must have been quite a handful then, eh?" he told her.

She covered her mouth with her fingers. "Oh no," she said from behind her fingers. "Whatever gave you that idea?"

"Come on, Miss Blinky. Don't tell me that you never did the light fandango."

"I don't understand, Mr. Dukchuk."

"The light fantastic. It's an old expression, Miss Blinky. Parties, dancing, letting loose."

"I will have you know, Mr. Dukchuk, that I was always a respectable woman." She tossed her hair and both of them laughed. This is so unlike Miss Blinky.

This week too, Martha was more at ease. Not laughing or talking with anybody, but not with her head bent over the table either. In the afternoon, I saw that she was getting a bit impatient while she was making her patterns with blocks and I was afraid that she would become depressed like the last week, so I went to her table and moved some of the blocks to their correct positions. But I did not say anything to her.

After school, Jermaine told me, "Putting the moves, eh?"

"What moves?" I asked him. He did not explain.

But he said, "Have you ever noticed what's been going on between Mr. Dukchuk and Miss Blinky?"

I felt that it was safer to pretend that I hadn't. I shook my head.

"C'mon," he said. "It's been going on for the whole week. This afternoon he invited her to his cottage."

"Mr. Dukchuk? He invited her?"

"Well, not exactly," he said. "But he mentioned that he had a cottage by some lake."

"So? That don't mean . . ."

"Listen. He said that he had been neglecting this cottage for too long. And it is so romantic in the evening when the sun hit the lake water that it can make you do really crazy things." He was laughing when he said this, but then he became serious. "They think that just because we are from the dumb children class, we can't understand anything. But they can't fool me. I have too much experience." It sounded like Jermaine was boasting.

~

Feb. Week two.

This was a totally unbelievable week. First of all, Mr. Dukchuk stopped calling Miss Blinky by her last name. He started calling her Miss Emma. I didn't even know that was her first name.

"Why, that's a lovely dress, Miss Emma," he told her, passing a finger on the material by her hip. But the biggest surprise was yet to come.

"And is it only the dress that's lovely, Mr. Duckie?"

Mr. Duckie! I couldn't believe it.

As the week progressed, I couldn't help remembering what Jermaine told me a few days ago, about Mr. Dukchuk and Miss Blinky saying these things to each other because they felt that we couldn't suspect anything, just because we were in a dumb children class. But at other times I thought that maybe they were just in love and didn't care about anything else. Even as I write this, it seems amazing. Mr. Dukchuk and Miss Blinky in love. Or rather Miss Emma and Mr. Duckie.

I don't know if anyone besides Jermaine and myself know what is happening. Maybe Perry, because on Wednesday, when we had indoor recess on account of the coldness, he went by Mr. Dukchuk's table with a math problem he couldn't solve. Mr. Dukchuk and Miss Blinky were sitting very near to each other and whispering. I don't think they saw Perry. When he returned to his desk with his problem still not solved, he was looking very embarrassed. For the rest of the week, whenever he noticed Mr. Dukchuk and Miss Blinky together, whispering to each other, he had that same expression on his face. A few times I wanted to ask him what he had heard, but he is too shy and nervous-looking. He might just get more embarrassed.

Martha also looks at Mr. Dukchuk and Miss Blinky when they are chatting, but I feel that it is because Miss

Blinky is not by her desk as often as before. Martha doesn't like working with blocks or anything dealing with patterns, and she gets discouraged easily. Two times during the week, I went over by her desk and put her blocks in the correct places. I wanted to help her more often, but during those two times I saw Jermaine grinning at me and I know what was going through his mind.

Jermaine looks like he is enjoying this class for the first time. Instead of always looking angry, he is now usually grinning, especially after he comes back from wherever Mr. Dukchuk and Miss Blinky are chatting. I think that they are surprised by Jermaine's new interest in his school work, and maybe pleased too. Because one morning, just after he came back from Mr. Dukchuk's table with a story he had written about superheroes, I saw Mr. Dukchuk and Miss Blinky looking at Jermaine and nodding their heads. Mr. Dukchuk's moustache was curving upwards and Miss Blinky's eyes were looking a little sleepy. Jermaine had his head down on his desk, and from the way his shoulders were moving quickly, I knew that he was laughing. I'm sure that Mr. Dukchuk and Miss Blinky would not be so pleased if they knew why.

After school, he told me, "Just now everybody in the class will have to get pet names like Duckie and Missem." Then he broke out laughing.

"Who is Missem?" I asked him.

"Miss Blinky, man. Didn't you hear Duckie calling her that all week?" He could barely complete the sentence.

"Maybe it's Miss M," I told him. "For Miss Emma."

"So what's the difference," he said. "It sounds like Missem to me." Then he looked at me and said, "Hey, wait a minute. Maybe that is really your pet name for Martha. Miss M." After that, he couldn't control himself. His cheeks filled up with air and he put his head inside his locker and laughed and laughed. For a minute I wanted to slam the locker door against his head, but then I too started to laugh. Then he pulled back his head from the locker and I saw that he wasn't laughing again. "These people can get away with anything," he said in a serious voice.

"You mean just because they are teachers?" I asked him.

He looked as though he was going to tell me something, but all he said was, "Never mind." Then he walked off.

Even though Jermaine is from an island not far from where I grew up, I feel that I can't really understand him.

~

Feb. Week three.

I can't believe what Jermaine did today. For almost the whole week he was in a bad mood. I don't think that he even noticed Miss Blinky's different hairstyle or the new orange-colour suede jacket that Mr. Dukchuk came to class in. He didn't pretend as usual that he wanted Mr. Dukchuk or Miss Blinky to correct his work just so that he could hear what they were whispering to each other. Most of the time he spent drawing either aliens or horror creatures with his black marker, but once he drew a scene with a sea and coconut trees and someone skipping with a rope.

One morning, when Jermaine was drawing one of his aliens, Miss Blinky told him, "Hmm, another one of your comic book characters? What are you going to call it?" I noticed then that, even though Miss Blinky didn't walk around the class as much as before, instead spending most of the time by Mr. Dukchuk's table, she still had her nice friendly voice.

Jermaine shrugged his shoulders, but when Miss Blinky moved away, he said in a soft voice, "Jermaine."

For the whole week he didn't talk to me, and I too never tried to start any conversation because of how angry he was. But this evening, while he was trying to fit all the drawings he had done from the week in his locker, he told me, "It's getting crowded in here."

I was a bit surprised that he had spoken. I told him, "Maybe you should clear out some of the old stuff."

He pushed the pile of drawing paper between two stacks of comics and said, "Listen, man, I never throw anything away, okay." Then he forced the locker door shut. "So how are things going with Missem?" he asked me in a less angry voice.

I remembered Miss Blinky leaning over Mr. Dukchuk's table this morning, with her elbows against the top and Mr. Dukchuk saying something to her. While he was talking, she had a bit of hair from her new hairstyle between her fingers and she was brushing her lips with it. Once or twice she opened her lips and passed her tongue over the bit of hair.

With that in my mind I told Jermaine, "Things are progressing fast between them."

He looked at me with a faraway look. "I meant your Missem," he said. "Miss Martha."

"Oh." I felt a little ashamed. "She doesn't like to make any patterns, so I help her." I tried to change the topic. "Duckie and Missem seem to be having a good time." I used their pet names hoping that he not be in a bad mood again.

"Yeah. Having a good time. Going to his cottage. Buying expensive clothes. Everybody's having a good time." I didn't know what to say. Then he told me, "Betcha I can put a stop to that." He opened his locker, took out a purple marker and went to Miss Blinky's filing cabinet. And in big block letters he wrote, *Miss Blinky is a whore*. He closed his locker, threw the marker in the recycling bin and left. I was frightened.

Walking home from school, at home in my room, I

was still frightened. I knew it was a very serious thing that he had done, and plus that, I was the only witness. I believe that if my mother was at home when I came from school, I would have told her, but she is working on the evening and night shift at a delicatessen and I am always asleep when she comes home, plus she is asleep in the mornings when I leave for school. It's now 9:30 in the night as I am writing this, and I believe that even though she will be home tomorrow, because she doesn't work on Saturdays, I will not mention anything to her. I hope that the custodian rubs off what Jermaine wrote before either Miss Blinky or Mr. Dukchuk gets a chance to see it.

~

Feb. Week four.

Keeping this journal has been the biggest mistake of my life. Almost three months ago Miss Blinky told the class that it was a good way to organize our thoughts, and I believed her. I should have done like the rest of the class and just write only three or four lines every week. But I believed Miss Blinky. And now it has caused me nothing but trouble. I don't know if I will write anything more when this journal is complete.

On Monday morning, I went to school later than usual. I was hoping that by the time I reached the classroom, the words on Miss Blinky's filing cabinet would have been erased and everything would be normal, but I made a serious mistake.

The minute I entered the class, I realized that trouble was just around the corner. Mr. Dukchuk and Miss Blinky were standing before the blackboard, and to their side was the custodian. I glanced at the filing cabinet and saw that what Jermaine had written was still there. All the students in the class were looking straight at Mr. Dukchuk and Miss Blinky and the custodian. They all looked scared. Even Jermaine.

"You are a bit late this morning, Adrian," Mr. Dukchuk told me, looking at the clock on the wall. All the eyes in the room looked towards me.

I had to fumble for an answer. I told him, "Yes, Mr. Dukchuk, I got up a little late this morning."

"Did you?" Mr. Dukchuk asked. "You've never been late before. Is this the first time for you?"

"I think so, Mr. Dukchuk," I said in a soft voice.

I couldn't believe this. They thought I had done it. While I walked to my desk, I felt that my feet were weighed down with lead. I knew that everyone was watching me. When I sat down, I looked straight at Miss Blinky. She had the same expression like the time when she was leaning over Mr. Dukchuk's table with her lips little open, but now her eyes were different. They looked sad and angry at the same time. And confused too. I felt sorry for her. I believed I may have smiled to show her how sorry I was for her.

Mr. Dukchuk stepped forward closer to us. His

hands were not in his pants pocket as they usually were when he was speaking to the class, but were stiff and straight by his sides. And when he spoke, the voice sounded like it was coming from his nose. I could tell that he was very angry. He told us that this crime was tasteless and it could not go unpunished. He used the word *crime*. He spoke about his own school days, when the students were given the strap for any sign of disobedience. Everything worked smoothly then. There were no special education classes like this one. Students had to shape up or ship out. Teachers demanded respect, and the classes knew that and behaved accordingly.

While he was talking, I saw the custodian nodding his head and Miss Blinky looking sadder and sadder. After about fifteen minutes of talking about his own school days, Mr. Dukchuk said that he was going to give the culprit the opportunity to confess. Then he moved back until he was standing in the line with Miss Blinky and the custodian.

He looked at the clock on the wall and said that we had five minutes.

We all glanced at each other, but no one spoke. The class was very quiet and I could hear the ticking of the clock. Miss Blinky kept staring at the clock, but Mr. Dukchuk and the custodian looked at each of us one at a time. I never knew that the clock was so loud. Miss Blinky said, "We have only one minute left." Her voice sounded scattered and up and down.

Then Mr. Dukchuk marched out of the classroom. We all waited. Everyone was taking little glances at each other. Finally, Mr. Dukchuk returned with the Principal, Mr. Hessey. The Principal looked angry to have been disturbed. He said that he was not going to tolerate that kind of behaviour in his school, and that he was shocked and disappointed. He asked Mr. Dukchuk for the class register. And holding the red folder in which Mr. Dukchuk recorded our daily attendance, he asked all of us the question. He started with Doug. "Mr. Agernethy, did you write 'Miss Blinky is a whore' on the filing cabinet?"

"No, Mr. Hessey."

Every time he asked the question, I saw Miss Blinky's eyes opening and shutting really fast. But the answer was always the same. When it was Jermaine's turn, I held my breath, but Jermaine answered almost as if he was bored. "No, Mr. Hessey. I didn't do it."

I was nervous when my name was called, but I looked at Miss Blinky and some of my nervousness disappeared. "No, Mr. Hessey, I did not write it," I told him.

Then there was just Martha and Doug and Brian left.

"Miss Timins, did you write 'Miss Blinky is a whore' on the filing cabinet?"

Martha had her head down, looking at the desktop. She did not answer. Mr. Hessey tapped the register with his thumb as if he was impatient. He repeated the question. And Martha began to cry. She placed her head on the desktop. Mr. Hessey gave Mr. Dukchuk the register and left. He didn't even bother to ask Doug and Brian anything. The custodian left too.

When I looked at Miss Blinky's face, it seemed as if she also wanted to cry. Mr. Dukchuk went to his table and sat with his chin resting against the palm of his left hand. He was staring at Martha. Miss Blinky was looking out of the window, maybe at the leaves on the trees covered with snow. The custodian returned with a wet cloth and erased the words from the filing cabinet.

Mr. Dukchuk's and Miss Blinky's staring continued for a long while. I wondered if we were going to spend the entire morning like that. Then Mr. Dukchuk went to the blackboard and wrote: *Math pg 97. Questions 1–7.* He didn't say anything to us.

When he went to his table, Miss Blinky moved a chair from by his cupboard and sat next to him. My desk is near to Mr. Dukchuk's table, so I could always hear whatever they are saying, unless they are whispering. But Mr. Dukchuk was too angry to whisper. He told her that for some time now he had been having doubts about these special programs. He believed that it was time to bring back some old-fashioned discipline. He talked about our ingratitude, after all they had done for us. Especially Martha. He couldn't understand what caused her to do such a thing. Miss Blinky told him that she knew. Mr. Dukchuk looked surprised. "Do you?"

Miss Blinky nodded slowly. There was a far-off look in her eyes. She told Mr. Dukchuk that it was because she had been neglecting Martha during the last few weeks and Martha had responded to her hurt in the only way that she knew.

Mr. Dukchuk chewed his moustache and said, "Hmm." After a while he said, "Whatever the reason, her response was not appropriate. I am going to schedule a conference with her foster parents later this week to determine the best course of action."

That didn't please Miss Blinky. "I feel somehow responsible," she told him.

Mr. Dukchuk looked at her. "Rationalizing is always imperfect when it's clouded by guilt, Miss Blinky."

"Guilt, Mr. Dukchuk? Now isn't that a funny word to use." She got up and went to her own table at the opposite end of the classroom. For the entire morning she sat there. And for the entire morning Martha cried.

In the afternoon, during the first period, Mr. Hessey came into the class and told Mr. Dukchuk that he had spoken to Martha's foster parents and that they were very concerned. He said that he had scheduled a meeting for Wednesday lunchtime.

When Mr. Hessey left, Mr. Dukchuk wrote on the blackboard: *Create the following shapes—squares, rectangles, polygons, hexagons, and decagons.* Miss Blinky opened the first drawer of the filing cabinet and took out the blocks. She asked for a volunteer to distribute the blocks. I raised my hand. Miss Blinky gave me the blue plastic bin with the blocks and I went from desk to desk. When I went to Martha's desk, I saw a piece of paper covered by her palm. There was some writing on the paper. I placed the blocks at the end of the table, knowing that she would have to remove her palm from on top of the paper. When she moved her hand to get the blocks, I saw what she had written. *They said I did it too. That it was my fault.*

And I knew what I had to do.

I waited for Jermaine after school, but maybe he was avoiding me, because he didn't even go to his locker. He had taken out his coat during the afternoon recess.

That night, I wished that I could have talked with my mother and told her what was going on and ask her for advice, but she did not come home until I was asleep. In the morning, when I left, she was still sleeping.

I left very early for school. Miss Blinky looked surprised to see me. "Well, aren't you the early bird this morning, Adrian."

I didn't want to waste any time. I didn't want to change my mind. I went straight away to her table and told her, "Miss Blinky, Martha did not write anything on your filing cabinet."

She got up. "How do you know that, Adrian?" I noticed that she was not wearing one of her new sweaters and that she had curled her hair in the old style.

"Because . . . " I hesitated. ". . . because I know who wrote it." She looked at me, waiting. I took a deep breath and with the air still in my mouth I told her, "Jermaine did it."

"How do you know that?" she asked me in a suddenly serious voice.

I felt like someone else was talking to Miss Blinky and that I was just listening. "I saw him writing it."

"But he said that he did not write it," she told me.

"I know," I said, feeling suddenly miserable and hopeless.

"It's your word against his, then."

"Yes," was all I said.

"Mr. Dukchuk believes that Martha all but confessed."

"She was just crying." I remembered what I had seen on the piece of paper on Martha's table the day before, and without thinking I told Miss Blinky, "I have proof."

"What sort of proof?" she asked in a confused voice.

And at that moment I realized my mistake.

Miss Blinky would have to see everything. It was too late to pull back. "My journal," I said in a weak voice.

"Can I see it?" I stood before her. She repeated the question. Then I went into my backpack and took out my journal and gave it to her. With the journal in her hand she said, "I will have to show this to Mr. Dukchuk and the Principal." She went to her table and began to read. I stood before her table.

She read slowly, from the beginning to the end, never once looking up. When she was finished, she closed the journal and placed her fingers on her forehead. Perry and Doug came and went to their seats. They told her "Good morning," but she did not answer. Then she opened the journal once more and began to read. She crossed out how I spelled *delicatessen* and wrote the correct spelling. She put punctuation marks and circled all the words that were spelled wrong. Then, without looking at me, she gave me back the journal.

When Mr. Dukchuk came, she called me and we went to his table. She told him that I had seen Jermaine writing the words on the filing cabinet, but she didn't mention anything about the journal. Mr. Dukchuk chewed his moustache. While the three of us were together, Jermaine entered the class, and from the expression on his face and the way he was clenching his hands, I could tell that he knew what I had done.

Jermaine barely had time to put his books on the table. Mr. Dukchuk went to him and the two of them left the class, with Jermaine walking in a kind of way to look as if he didn't care. They were away for most of the morning, returning just before the bell rang for lunch. In the meantime Miss Blinky sat by Martha's desk and spoke softly with her. I couldn't hear what she was saying.

During the lunch break, in the playing field, I saw Jermaine walking towards me. He had his backpack with him, so I knew that he was being sent home. For a little while I wondered if he was going to hit me. I prepared myself.

But Jermaine's mood was different. His eyes were wet. "I thought you was my friend, man. The only friend that I ever had."

I really didn't know what to say. "I'm still your friend," I told him.

"Yeah? And that is why you reported me? You know how happy you made the Principal and Mr. Dukchuk and even Miss Blinky?"

"Happy about what?" I asked him.

He placed his hands against the straps of his backpack. "Happy about what?" His fingers tightened on the straps. "Happy that a stupid blackboy with no future did it. Happy that their own little Martha is innocent. Happy to think that they could continue to think the way they always think. Is the same story over and over." Then he walked off. And I thought: but you really did it.

In the night, I waited for my mother. When she came home about twelve or so and I was still awake, she asked me if I didn't have school the next day. She told me to go to bed and said that she was very tired. Looking at her, I saw that she was really very tired. I went to bed.

On Wednesday morning, Mr. Hessey called me into his office and said how proud he was of me. He said that although several of the teachers had complained about us, he never lost hope. At first I thought he was talking about the children from the multi-exceptionality class, but he had said "several teachers," and we only have two.

In a respectful voice I asked him, "Complained about who, sir?"

He looked a little embarrassed. But he did not answer. Instead, he repeated the part about how he never lost hope.

When I left his office, I was more ashamed than ever about what I had done. I didn't want to face Jermaine again.

But I did. When I came into the class, I saw him cleaning out his locker. Mr. Dukchuk was at his side. Everyone was looking at him. He stuffed everything in his backpack. All his comics and his drawings. Just before he left, I saw him looking at Miss Blinky as if he wanted to say something, but he just walked away.

The bell for recess rang a few minutes later and I went into the playing field. I saw Jermaine standing by the swing. I realized that he was waiting for me. I walked towards him and he went and sat on one of the swings. I sat on the other one. With his toes, he rocked his swing.

"I'm sorry," I told him.

"I know why you did it. You was just protecting your little love, Missem." He laughed.

I was relieved. I laughed too.

He pushed his swing off with his feet. He began swinging faster and faster, higher and higher.

"Be careful," I told him.

"Careful about what? I'm accustomed to this." But he stopped. "I'm going back to Antigua."

"Why?" I asked him. I felt the coldness from around me coming into the air I was breathing and inside my body.

His voice was flat and sort of sprinkly, like loonies falling on the floor. "Cause these people I'm living with had said that if I get suspended one more time, they will ship me back straight away. That I didn't deserve to be with them."

I felt horrible to have caused something like that. He must have seen the expression on my face, because he said, "Don't worry about it, man. It's for the best. I never liked staying with my uncle anyways. Six of us in a little two-bedroom apartment and every evening the only talk I could hear about was the extra expense I was causing and how I was turning out just like my father and how it was a mistake sending for me to Canada." He began to swing again, but slower this time. "At least now I will get a chance to see my mother and father." I saw that there was something else he wanted to say, then he said it. "If they want to see me." He planted his feet on the ground, got off the swing and told me, "Take care, man. Things are never easy."

In the night, when my mother came home, I was still awake on my bed. I heard her opening the fridge and then pulling the chair by the table. I wanted to ask her if we would return to Trinidad if I got suspended. Return to Trinidad with all three of us living like a family. I heard the cup falling in the sink and a few minutes later the sound that she made tossing on the bed, maybe for an hour or two, before she fell asleep.

The Book of Ifs and Buts

We became friends, Pegu and I, under the most unusual of circumstances. He claimed he was a deadly assassin trained in the ancient art of *hakula*, which, he explained happily, involved fastening pieces of rope around selected parts of the body until all circulation had stopped. As he related the complicated manner of binding and constricting, and stressed the agonizing pain of the *hakulee*, it was only with the greatest of effort that I prevented myself from laughing.

The first time I saw Pegu at Skit's Coffeeshop on Harwood Avenue, I was at the lowest ebb of my career as a writer for the fantasy imprint Perils and Illusions. To use the exact words of my editor, Mr. Borfus, "Your stories have become too flat and ordinary, my boy. They show your inexperience. They lack aftertaste. Take your last story, for instance."

"I worked for three months on that story, Mr. Borfus."

Mr. Borfus rocked back on his chair as if he had not heard me. "Russian cosmonaut spends three years in spacelab. Breaks record and becomes a national hero. Meanwhile, elections in Russia. Candidates, as expected, all corrupt and reprehensible. Some idiot proposes cosmonaut and, *voilà*, he is elected as president. Learns of results but refuses to return to earth. Prefers sanity of space instead. Hee, hee, hee. What's the point?"

"Stated like that, there is no point, Mr. Borfus. However, I tried to convey the idea that to a desperate people, his distance and unavailability made him a reluctant god unprepared to embrace the burdens of others. He just wanted to be left alone, like our own gods."

Mr. Borfus had pointed a stubby finger at me. "Listen, boy. Don't go blaspheming here. I want something that strains the imagination. Give me an entity whose past is shrouded in mystery. An unlikely, menacing—"

"With all due respect, sir, I'm not a comic book writer and what you are proposing—"

"My boy. All I am asking for is a simple story. Don't bother me with facts or reality. The world is bad enough as it is. No one wants to hear any more of it, and if they do, they go to the newspapers." He seemed to expand with every breath. I expected him, with his finger lodged deep in his nostril, to rise to the ceiling at any minute.

"My stories are little slices of life, sir. They are funny and sad and poignant. They are more than they appear to be."

"Hee, hee, hee. In case you haven't noticed, this is a fantasy imprint. We don't publish poetry journals crawling with sour, man-hating women, and itty-bitty boys yearning for their childhood and their mommies. Imagine a solitary person walking alone in the night. Imagine a streak of lightning suddenly brightening the sky. Now think of that solitary traveller as your reader and the lightning as your story. It provides details to the shadows, it illuminates the surroundings, but when it is gone, it is gone. Simple as that. *Now* write a story that will make me forget my fat wife, my mortgage, my ungrateful children, my inexperienced writers, my sinking magazine." As I was about to leave, he added, "A story is just a story, my boy. Nothing more, nothing less."

From then on, every afternoon, armed with notepad, cigarettes and coffee, I would sit in a darkened corner at Skit's and try to conjure up Mr. Borfus's amazing being. It was useless. My mind would be as dry in the coffee shop as it had been during the morning in my apartment. I thought stupidly that the space, the chatter, the movement would help me, but I had arrived too late at this game: all of Mr. Borfus's awesome entities had already been created, most of them decades ago. Super strength, invincibility, X-ray vision, were all there before me in the dozen or so comics I had bought from The Ten Ton comic book store. Mutants, replicants, metahumans, all flew around, jumped from buildings or just stared arrogantly from the yellow pages.

Finally, I tossed the comics aside and began to examine the faces of the other customers at Skit's, hoping for some errant spark. Teenaged girls from Exeter High drifted in and out with their purchases of gum, cigarettes and condoms. Teenaged boys strolled around, not buying anything. An old, bespectacled man saw me smoking and asked why I was not at school, even though I was twenty-seven years old. A middle-aged woman, maybe from some Caribbean island, slapped her noisy son, and when the boy began to sob and squirm, glanced around furtively and hugged him. One evening, a man in his late forties dragged a wooden box just outside Skit's, placed a chair on the box, climbed on top, opened his guitar case and began singing. His voice was smooth and mellow, and he sang his country and western tunes with genuine sadness. A woman dropped a loonie in the opened guitar case. A couple stopped before him and stared. A young man did a little jig and continued on his way. Two hours later, the singer put down his guitar, collected the five or six coins thrown in the case, replaced the guitar and walked away. I felt the sadness of this talented man. But my sympathy was presumptuous; it implied that I was different from, or better than, him.

That afternoon, long after he had left, I saw my profession in a new, diminished light.

The next day, I spotted Pegu, looking like a huge egg, with his moustache, stiff and waxed, curling upwards in a neat little semicircle. From a distance it looked as if a scorpion was emerging from his nostril. He was staring straight ahead, not flinching from my gaze, not blinking in embarrassment. I had no idea how long he had been staring or whether this examination had been conducted, unknown to me, on other days.

It was like that every day for the next week and a half. I changed my table, I sat at different angles from him, I looked up suddenly and forcefully, but he just continued his scrutiny, as if I were invisible. Then, one day, he was not at the coffee shop. My first thought was that he had been hauled away by the police for some criminal act, and at that moment I realized that Pegu looked like a comic book representation of drug smugglers and money launderers.

I didn't give him much thought for the rest of the afternoon, but in the evening, when I opened the door to my apartment, I heard a well-modulated voice saying, "It was most foolhardy to leave your door unshuttered." I jumped. The voice had come from the direction of the couch. Hurriedly, I switched on the light and saw Pegu sitting on the couch, with a square travelling bag next to him.

Before I had the chance to say or do anything, he continued, "I would like to advise you at this juncture that escape is entirely out of the question. On another matter, I have had the time to appraise the contents of your refrigerator, and far from me being a nitpicker, I must nevertheless comment on the lack of nutritional ingredients contained therein." He patted his puffy stomach. "Carbohydrates set me off rather badly. Flatulence, you know. Same with milk."

"What are you doing here?"

He emitted a prolonged sigh as if the question distressed him. "In due course." He must have seen me looking towards the telephone on top of the bookcase, for he added, "A most unreliable thought. I would give it no further attention if I were you." He patted his lumpy bag. "The contents are quite frightening, you know."

I walked towards the table. He was still patting and stroking his bag. "What do you have in there?"

"All the necessary tools. Oh, and my gingko tablets." He reached into the bag and produced a green bottle about four inches high. He shook it and the tablets clattered. Looking at the bottle, perhaps reading the label, he recited, "It's derived from the *ginkgo biloba* tree, and I, for one, can testify to its miraculous qualities. Among other benefits, it improves blood circulation to the brain, relieves chronic ringing in the ear, enhances one's mood and sociability—"

"What else is there in the bag?"

He replaced his bottle solemnly. "All the necessary tools."

"Well, everything works fine, so you can bloody well leave."

He pulled the zipper shut. "My dear boy," he said, his whiskers quivering, his face red, "let me assure you that you will not inveigle yourself out of this situation by making snide remarks. In fact you will only exacerbate your already perilous situation. You enquired about the contents of my satchel. Well, let me confess at this point that my reticence sprang only from a desire not to unnecessarily alarm you. Is that understood?"

I looked at the telephone. It was only about eight feet away. "So what do you have there? A bomb?"

"I should say not. I have always been offended by the image of scalded flesh scattering and flying in all directions." I went by the table. He was sitting upright on the couch, his bag next to him, his alert eyes fixed on me. The telephone was now only about four feet away. "My appraisal of your cupboard has alerted me to the fact that we have rations for just one week. It's rather fortuitous in the present circumstance that I brought my tonics."

"Would you stop speaking like that. And what exactly is it that you want?"

Pegu acted as though he did not hear me. "You can repose there." He motioned to the foot of the table.

"You should now go to your room and get your sleeping paraphernalia. I myself will make do with the couch." While I was walking to the bedroom, he said, "Not that I want to unnecessarily alarm you, but I should caution that your apartment is heavily booby-trapped. Oh, and would you be so kind as to fetch me a glass of water?"

I brought the water to him and went into the bedroom. When I returned, Pegu was already stretched out on the couch, his shoes still on his feet and his hat still on his head. He was curled up against his bag like a child clutching a special pillow, but he had partially unzipped the bag and placed a hand inside. At the foot of the couch was the glass of water with his teeth.

While I was spreading my blanket on the floor, I thought of snatching his bag, but then I remembered him saying that the apartment was heavily booby-trapped. What sort of traps did he lay? I wondered. As was my habit just before I went to bed, I reached into my pocket for my cigarettes, lit one and inhaled deeply. From the couch I heard a wheezing sound, like a dog suffocating. Hurriedly, I stubbed out the cigarette. For an hour or so I shifted from side to side and listened for any creaking on the couch or footsteps. I heard a low droning sound. At first I thought that he was snoring, but when I recognized the song he was humming, I sprang up. "Where did you learn that song?"

"'O land of sheep and flowing meadows'? I have always known it."

So had I. It was the national anthem of Carobenos. Every single Carobenosian knew it by heart. "Are you from Carobenos?"

"Oh, fie and Adam's apple, and all the time I was trying to disguise my accent." He made a great attempt at sounding disappointed, and even though I could not see his face in the dark, I had this feeling that he was smiling.

"Why?"

"Why what?"

"Why are you here? In my apartment?"

He began once more to hum "O land of sheep and flowing meadows."

I was left with even more questions. Could he have been sent by my uncle, Slavo, to check up on my progress in Canada? I had, after all, stopped writing almost a year ago. I quickly discounted that theory. Not even old Slavo was that interfering to send, at such great expense, a lunatic to spy on me. Was he, then, one of those drug barons of whom, as a boy growing up in the village of Caruna, I had heard so much? Those shadowy men who operated as teachers, priests, police officers and politicians. Yet if that was the case, how did I end up becoming involved?

Pegu, as if he sensed my thoughts, said, "In the morrow, all shall be explained."

For the rest of the rest of the night, I drifted in and out of a tiring sleep. Sometimes I thought that it was all a dream, but then I would feel the hard floor beneath my blanket and see this huge egg on my couch.

When I awoke in the morning, I noticed that the couch was empty. My first impulse was to rush to the door. Then I heard the sharp tinkle of a cup hitting a saucer. I looked up and saw Pegu sitting before the table. "Breakfast is ready," he said jovially. "Please pardon the intrusion, but I have commandeered some of the ingredients from your refrigerator and concocted a rather tasty broth."

"I'm not hungry. Is it okay if I use the toilet?"

"Oh, by all means. Go, go." He removed his hand from the bag and waved it at me. "Go have a bath. Refresh yourself. It's a beautiful morning, isn't it? I'm sure the birds are trilling outside. It's such a pity we cannot open the windows. Ah, well." He sipped from his glass.

When I returned, Pegu had already finished half of his broth. With his mouth full, he pushed a plate towards me. "I'm not hungry."

"The malady of youth," he said, chewing in short, quick snaps.

For the rest of the meal, I sat opposite him listening to his chewing and watching his whiskers jump every time he opened his mouth. He was hatless and, with his curly hair parted in the centre and plastered down on his scalp, he looked perfectly round. There was an odd scraping sound beneath the table, and I suspected that his feet, not quite reaching the floor, were swinging and grating against the hardwood. His fingers too were very short. They looked like the river slugs I, as a boy in the village of Caruna, had pried loose from beneath the rocks and stones.

"You should try the broth, you know. It's rather delicious. I have boosted the flavour with some of my special tonics." He motioned to his bag. "I never travel anywhere without them."

"And is that all you have in there?" I asked. He just smiled and continued chewing and purring. "I normally leave at this time for my job."

"I see. And what, pray tell, is your job?"

"I'm a writer."

Immediately, he stopped chewing. "A writer? I had no idea. Are you certain?"

"I have no reason to lie."

"You certainly don't look like any writer to me." He inspected me, frowning. "Your face is too unlined and your eyes don't have the requisite amount of suffering. And where do you leave to go?"

"The coffee shop. You already know that, don't you?"

"What's wrong with this place that you have here?" He pushed a finger in his mouth and dislodged a piece of broccoli.

"I need inspiration."

"Then you are an abject failure." He examined the bit of broccoli.

"Well, excuse me, but there are a few dozen people who would disagree with you," I lied. "I have had a number of stories published."

He cast a quick glance at me. I could not tell whether he was impressed. "What do you write about?"

"Fantasy."

"Explain, please. What do you mean by 'fantasy'?"

"Time travel, alternative realities, space-time continuums, wormholes, amazing beings . . ."

"I see. A comic book writer. I'm familiar with the trash."

"I write for an imprint called Perils and Illusions."

He pushed away his plate and wiped his mouth with the back of his palm. "Perils and Illusions. It sounds rather like a comic book to me."

"Listen, you, my stories are aimed at adults, not children. I try to show the possibilities that exist for each of us, the future we can grasp if we unshackle our minds from—" I stopped suddenly, realizing how bogus and pompous I was sounding. And it was no wonder: I had simply been recycling one of Mr. Borfus's lectures.

But Pegu's moustache was twitching erratically. "Yes? Do continue."

"There's nothing more."

I pulled out my pack of cigarettes and immediately Pegu started his suffocating, wheezing sound. I was about to ask him if I could open the window to smoke when I noticed the strained, solemn look on his face. At first I thought that he was really allergic to tobacco smoke, but then he told me, "As a writer yourself, and notwithstanding the type of writer, I am certain that you would agree most abundantly that words are sacred tools which can either relax the tautness of our souls—act as a balm, if you will—or damage our vitals."

"I'm really not interested—"

"True writers are like chiropractors: they crack our minds and adjust our souls." He remained silent for a while, his hands now clasped over his chin, the index fingers springing up and flicking his whiskers from time to time. I grasped the edge of the table, thinking that if I gave a sudden push, he would be struck flat on the chest and tumble backwards. At that moment he made a hurried snort, as if he were clearing his nose. "Sadly, not all writers are up to their noble task. Regrettably, some of them cannot see, or do not care about, the harm that they bring, the distress that they create. Have you by chance ever heard of *The Book of Ifs and Buts*?"

"I can't say that I have."

"Be more specific. You can't say or you won't say?"

"I have never heard of the book. Are you satisfied?"

"Are you certain?"

Some of my irritation rose to the surface. "Look, I have no interest in your stupid book."

"Never heard of it and yet you cannot escape the consequences." With that, he went to the couch, opened his bag, peered inside, withdrew an old dog-eared notebook and began writing. He must have seen me staring. "I must record everything that transpires. My account must be complete, specific and precise."

"Really?"

He ignored my sarcasm. "For the Guardians. Don't tell me you do not know of them either?"

I felt I was being forced into his game, but I said, "Actually, I don't." He continued scribbling, every now and again moistening the pencil with his tongue. "Well? Would you mind explaining who these Guardians are?"

"They are the elders. The keepers of the flame. And by the way, it was they who discovered—or should I say rediscovered?—*The Book of Ifs and Buts*. Are you sure you have not heard of them? It's most strange."

I felt that I would get nothing more from him at that point, and his writing reminded me of my other bit of distress. "Is it all right if I get my notepad from the bookcase?" He looked suspiciously at the telephone and then at me. "I'm working on a story."

He waved his hand. "Go, go. Do not make me a burden. Go write your comics." He erupted in a clattering burst of laughter.

For the rest of the morning, Pegu scribbled in his notebook. Occasionally, I saw him flicking glances at me. Finally, he asked, "What is your story about?"

Remembering his earlier censure, I told him, "It won't interest you."

He dropped his pencil and stretched both hands before him in a mocking bow. "Please. Humour me."

"Okay. It's about an entity who could metamorphose into any creature."

He rolled his eyes and sighed.

After about an hour, I told him, "I would like to get some old copies of Perils and Illusions. I need something to jog my imagination."

He nibbled the end of his pencil as if he were contemplating my request. "I understand. The curse of fourth-rate writers. Those who are less than gifted always take refuge in repetition."

"I am simply attempting to get into the correct mood."

He waved his hand. "Go, go. I need not remind you that the apartment is heavily booby-trapped."

When I returned with my stack of books, I noticed him nibbling his moustache and looking curiously at me. "Can I peruse one of your little stories? Simply for the record, you understand?"

I gave him a story, titled "The Rebirth," about an empath who could inhabit the bodies of others. Then, one day, he entered the body of a woman filled with so much grief that he felt his detachment receding. Although he knew that it was dangerous to remain in one body for too long, he could not leave this grief-stricken woman. He inhabited her in ways he had never done before. And the woman, unable to cope with this intrusion, thinking herself mad, decided to end her life. The empath, frozen in the woman's body, felt everything: being placed in a coffin, the sprinkle of flowers on his chest, the bumpy road to the cemetery, being lowered into the grave, the dirt scattering over the coffin.

Pegu closed the book and took a deep breath. "And what, pray tell, happened to the other body?"

I did not understand.

"The body that this empath of yours had left behind. His real body."

"Well, it may have . . . I think it disintegrated. But the focus of the story was on the woman's body. And the empath's mind. His own body was immaterial."

"I see," he said softly. "Details. The curse of every fourth-rate writer."

"I suppose you would have handled it more professionally."

"Yes, I believe I would. First of all, I would have appropriately disposed of the body in question, and secondly, I would have made this empath of yours a professor. A professor of philosophy and literature."

"How would you have disposed of the body?" I asked anxiously.

"Disposal is never much of a problem. It's very simple, actually, if you know how." I waited for some elaboration, but Pegu began twirling his moustache. Then he drew his bag closer to him and placed a hand on the zipper, looking at his watch at the same time. "It's almost four p.m. Would you care to attempt a broth of some kind?"

We ate silently, Pegu with his bag on his lap and I calculating my escape. When he was finished, he wiped his mouth with the back of his palm. "Presumably, you are familiar with 'O land of sheep and flowing meadows.'" I nodded. "In that case, would you hum a few bars?" He got up, bag in hand. "Over there." He pointed in the direction of the washroom. "Unfortunately, we are forever at the behest of nature." He must have seen the startled look on my face. "A precautionary measure to ensure you do not seize the opportunity to escape whilst I am otherwise occupied."

Pegu went with his bag into the washroom and I, like a total fool, was forced to hum at the door. He was in no hurry, and I had to repeat the song about four or five times. After each rendition, my voice grew shriller. When he emerged, I grabbed his shoulder roughly. "I've had enough of this! What do you want of me, you lunatic?"

He pulled away hurriedly. "Unhand me, or you alone will be responsible for the consequences." He unzipped his bag, his small eyes flickering.

But I was too angry to care about his threat. "Listen, you. This is Canada, not Carobenos. This is a civilized country. We have rules here."

He walked slowly to the couch. "You are no different from him." Astonishingly, his alarm had completely vaporized.

"Different from whom?" I shouted.

"Spurning the land of your birth. Intent only on making trouble."

"Listen, it's you who—"

"The land of the giant tapir, the majestic jaguar, the powerful anaconda. The skies of which are bespeckled by the cocrico, and the scarlet ibis." He spoke carefully, each phrase separated by a long pause, as if he were reciting from a travel brochure he had read a long time ago. "A land preserved against the ravages of progress. And yet it is an uncivilized place, is it not? So different from this new homeland of yours." He settled back on the couch, clasped his hands over the bag on his lap and stared at his fingers. His mood hinted at confession. I waited.

For about five minutes or so, he stared at his fingers, took deep, rasping breaths and shook his head. My anger receded in the face of this lugubrious pose. Finally, he looked up. "You must forgive me, because I too am an empath." Another period of finger-staring followed. "Is your television functioning?"

I pointed to the remote on the side table. He reached over for it, clicked on the set and eventually found a music channel previewing music videos—a rather strange choice for him. He looked at the music videos for fifteen minutes or so. "The world is shrinking." His voice was soft and he seemed to be speaking more to himself. But he looked very subdued, and I thought that it was a good time to nudge him into revealing the reason for his presence.

"What do you want from me? I'm sure you understand how inconvenient it is for me."

He changed the channel. "I always believed that information was but a synonym for knowledge." He flicked to another channel.

"Look, there are many vacant apartments elsewhere."

"Now we try to compress the wisdom of a lifetime into ten minutes."

"I have my deadlines and my editor is very strict."

"Rushing here, rushing there. It is quite obvious that these Americans are trained at birth to express all their knowledge in one long sentence, and they spend the rest of their lives waiting for an opportunity to speak this sentence. The rest of us . . . it is so sad, really . . . the rest of us are rendered obsolete just because we have no sentences."

"I'm sure you've made a terrible mistake and confused me with someone else. If you leave now, I guarantee that I will not report this incident to the police. All will be forgotten."

"The thing that would warm my bunions is a good old-fashioned detective movie. Simple plot. Beginning and ending where they are supposed to be. Good acting. Thunder. Lightning. Soft, sensual rain. Are there any such antiques still circulating?"

I gave up. "Try channel sixty-four."

As luck would have it, there was an old black-and-white detective movie on channel sixty-four. The detective hero was played by, I think, Humphrey Bogart, and whenever he encountered one of the suspects, the sky was shattered by lightning. Pegu settled back on the couch with a satisfied grunt. When it was over, he opened his bag, withdrew a small vial and threw a few drops of some liquid into his mouth. "Sleep beckons." He clacked his tongue.

I had been forced to look at his stupid movie for more than an hour. "At least you can tell me why you are here."

"In the morning." He removed his hat and placed it on the armrest. "Can I have a glass of water?"

I returned with the water. "You said the same thing yesterday."

"It's for my teeth."

"Yesterday, you told me that you would reveal everything today."

"Oh, did I?" He clamped off his teeth. "Please turn off the lights." He pulled his bag up to his chest, closed his eyes and began humming "O land of sheep and flowing meadows."

I arranged my pillow and unravelled my blanket on the floor. "How long do you plan on staying here?"

He began to snore loudly. I knew he was pretending.

That night, I dreamed that I was back in Carobenos, but it was Pegu's Carobenos, not the land I knew. There were giant tapirs and anacondas and jaguars, and hundreds of agoutis and mongooses and small rodents scurrying all over. The sky was dark with birds and insects. Walking unconcerned in the middle of this confusion of animals was a lone figure, gowned like a priest. Then the scene shifted and all the animals were crowded in my apartment, running, crawling, stampeding, trampling my furniture and crushing me to the ground. The gowned figure looked down at me and threw off his hood. It was Pegu. "It's you!" I screamed.

I awoke. Something was crawling over my arm. A cockroach. I flung it off. In the darkness, I saw Pegu standing by the couch.

"Why did you shout?"

"A nightmare." I wiped off the sweat from my face with the end of the blanket. "Can I open the window?"

"If you must. But only an inch, and don't try anything stupid."

I flicked on the light. Pegu made a dash for the couch, grabbed his shirt and held it against his chest. It was a strange show of modesty, but he was the hairiest person I had ever seen. I thought of a sticky egg that had rolled across a dirty floor.

"Well? Are you going to open the window or not?" I unhinged the bolt and pushed the window open. When I turned around, he was buttoning his shirt. "What was your nightmare about?"

"Nothing. I've forgotten it already."

He cleared his throat with a prolonged rattle. "Memories are genetically transferred from one generation to the next. Periodically, they manifest themselves in the form of dreams and—"

"That's interesting. Do you mind if I smoke by the window?"

"My nightmares no longer bother me because I understand that they are simply memories. Hundreds of years ago, one of my ancestors was chased by a huge turkey, another had special feelings for ducks, and a few others ventured out stark naked in the crowded streets." He looked a little unsettled. "I'm afraid there may have been a few loose screws in the assembly line. Some of the older models could have been a bit defective." I was about to tell him that his prognosis was more suited to the current model, when he said, "Smoke if you must. But I should mention that I find the odour of tobacco extremely offensive."

"I will puff the smoke outside."

Eight storeys below, the parking lot, save for a few vehicles, was deserted. I finished the cigarette, aimed for an empty space and flicked away the butt.

"Have you finished corroding your lungs?" He sounded just like Uncle Slavo.

"Do you know Slavo?"

After a while, he said, "I have known many Slavos in my lifetime."

I saw that his bag was open and in his hand were a number of loose pages tied together with a silky-looking twine. "What do you have there?"

"It's funny you should ask, but here before me"—he paused dramatically and took a deep breath—"is the only remaining copy of *The Book of Ifs and Buts*."

"Isn't that the book you were talking about?"

"It's the reason why I am here."

"Can I look at it?"

"Come here." He motioned to the couch. "It is time." With extreme care he undid the knot, separated the first page from the pile and gave it to me.

The writing, done with a thick-nibbed pen, was elaborate, almost ornate, with a flourishing tail at the end of each word. Immediately, I saw why it was named

The Book of Ifs and Buts: there were dozens of *ifs* and *buts* all over the page. When Pegu gave me page two, it was the same thing. And page three and four and five. The book was stuffed with stupid little paragraphs like, "If we shall keep a smile on our face each day, we would appear to be most happy. But who shall trust us then?" And just beneath, "If we look into the stream and see the face of a stranger, we scream and run in fright. But who told us to look into the stream in the first place?"

I began to wonder how a book that was filled with such senseless homilies could bring so much distress to Pegu and his Guardians. I read on. "If snakes could fly, we would always be indoors. But maybe we too would learn to fly."

The book was so stupid and Pegu was looking at me so intently that I had no choice but to tell him, "This is nothing but rubbish. Pure rubbish."

"Rubbish! You dare call it rubbish. Oh, forgive me, please, O great writer of comics who cannot even dispose of a body properly. I forgot how truly talented you are."

"There is no need for insults. I just can't see how this book could be dangerous."

"Oh, you want danger, do you?" He flipped through the pile, pulled out a page and flung it at me. "Maybe this will help."

I read: "If we climb to the highest mountain and appeal to our flock, our cries shall echo throughout the land. But what if the sheep are not listening?"

"*Now* do you see?"

"See what? It's just stupid."

He rolled his eyes upwards and placed his palms over his fat cheeks. He plucked off another page and thrust it in my face. "Here, read this and see if you still don't get it."

I read out the top of the page. "If we free ourselves from attachment and laugh at our misfortunes, we are seen as exalted souls. But what happens when we laugh at the misfortune of others?"

"Now do you still maintain that this is rubbish from the head of a madman? O great writer of comics?" I must have grinned, because he snatched away the page. "If he were still alive, he would have been totally ashamed of you."

"Ashamed of me? Why?"

"Because, you imbecile, you are his great-grandson."

"Who?"

He rolled his eyes once more. "He was the father of the father of your father."

"The person who wrote this?"

"Who else? And stop pretending, please. It's very unbecoming."

"I am sure you are mistaken. My father's family have always been cocoa planters."

"Except him." He jabbed a finger at the pile.

"You are terribly mistaken. If what you are saying is true, I'm sure I would have heard something."

"And who is to say that you have not?"

"Because I haven't. You are completely mistaken."

"I see." He began fastening the silky twine over the pile of pages. "Your name is Philip Effroo and you were born twenty-seven years ago in the village of Caruna in the republic of Carobenos. Your parents died within a year of each other when you were nine. Your mother's death was due to malaria and your father's fatal ailment has never been established; village rumour was equally divided between a curse and a broken heart. Both you and your father's estate passed under the jurisdiction of your mother's brother, Slavo. At the age of seventeen, one year before the estate was to be transferred to you, you were sent to Canada to engage in the study of law, a wish of your dead father. In Canada, you attended Ryerson College and you have since been a writer of some sort, a little detail which you quite sensibly never mentioned to Slavo. As I speak, he is under the impression that you are a bona fide lawyer fleecing the helpless, the poor and the sick."

I got up suddenly and walked to the window. Day was breaking, and in the parking lot a couple was walking briskly to their car. "I don't understand it. I never heard of this ancestor of mine. No one ever told me."

Pegu was looking at me keenly. After a while, he

asked, "Do you sometimes think of Carobenos?"

"Occasionally."

"Have you ever considered returning?"

"There would be no point. Return to what?"

"It is not for me to say. But perhaps to your uncle and your friends. Your inheritance."

"Everything that I have is right here."

He was chewing the end of his whiskers with an odd sucking sound. "Have you informed this uncle of yours about this decision? I'm sure that it would break his heart."

"Slavo? I doubt it. About a year ago, I wrote him a letter stating that I was fed up with Canada and thinking of returning. But it was just the mood of the time."

"I do not understand." He was watching me closely.

"I had just started my job with Mr. Borfus and things weren't working out."

"Are you, then, saying that you would never return?"

"I no longer know the place. I've been here for almost half of my life. What does it matter to you?"

"Oh, absolutely nothing." He remained silent for a while, then he said, "I cannot fault your logic. Because if anything, matters have worsened. Under different circumstances, the government would topple tomorrow."

"Would that be better?"

"It would be more natural. But better? The question cannot be answered. The peasants have fought for so long, they no longer know for what they are fighting. It is only the Guardians."

"I have never heard of these Guardians."

"It's quite the order of things," he said, slipping back into his fraudulent pose. "Their existence is shrouded in mystery for quite obvious reasons. The operatives of the CIA would simply have to get their grubby paws on them. And on this book here." He tapped his bag.

"What interest would they have in such a . . . such a book?"

Pegu got up and put his hands behind his back. He looked like the silhouette of Alfred Hitchcock. "Follow my train of thought if you will. Imagine a people who for three hundred years have resisted the tyranny of their oppressors. The faces of the oppressors may have changed, but never for once did they surrender their will. Now imagine a book written by one of their own, a book filled with profane heresies and blasphemous treacheries, suddenly resurfacing. Now imagine the effect of this eloquent mockery on their spirits."

"Is that what the book is about?"

"You should really abstain from this pretence. It is most unmanly."

"Well, anyway, all of this is of no concern to me."

"Is it not? Let me explain one small matter to you. When *The Book of Ifs and Buts* resurfaced, the Guardians immediately issued an edict that the writer should be punished by death."

"Did anyone bother informing them that the writer had died more than one hundred years ago?"

"I would not be so flippant if I were you. The Guardians made provisions for that."

"I see. Like digging up the bones and crushing them into tiny pieces?"

"Not quite. They made provisions for all existing descendants to be punished by death. As it stands, there is only one."

"Me?"

"Precisely."

"You're joking, of course."

"My dear boy, I can assure you that I did not travel three hundred miles just to engage in jokes."

I was going to explain that Carobenos was more than three thousand miles away, but instead I told him, "But I had nothing to do with the book."

"The edict is irrevocable."

"You are absolutely crazy."

"Say what you will, it is my task to punish you. Now, would you be kind enough to patch together a broth. All this talk has bolstered my appetite."

Pegu devoured the broth with his short, quick snaps. When he was finished, he pushed away his plate, made a few after-clacks as if he were still tasting his meal, and spoke about the weather and his impressions of Canada. Every attempt to draw him into some explanation of the book, my ancestor and his Guardians was rebuffed by some new observation about Canada. He seemed to be in a good mood.

He got up. "Your bookcase is well stocked. Are they all of the comic book variety?"

"They are mostly from my Ryerson days."

He walked over to the bookcase and pulled out a book. "I can tell that this is a worthwhile book from the picture of the author on the back jacket." He examined the jacket. "Canadian, I see."

"Most of my books are by Canadian writers. From the courses at Ryerson."

"And it's a good thing, too." He passed his fingers over the jacket, feeling the texture. "These Americans have nothing left to say. They repackage the same old stuff all the time in shiny new boxes. Lacking substance, they elevate eloquence into some kind of moral virtue."

He was revealing a new side. "I gather that you are not fond of Americans."

"I am a patriot. Ah, here's a worthwhile tome." He plucked out another book and pressed it against his nose, sniffing in approval.

"I would like to look at *The Book of Ifs and Buts*, if it is possible."

I had expected some resistance, but Pegu unzipped his bag and retrieved the pile of papers. He placed it on the bookcase next to his bag. My heart was pounding when I untied the knot. It was so unreal, this predicament more suited to one of my characters.

I started at page one, reading carefully and slowly. I wanted to know this great-grandfather of mine, this ancestor no one had told me about. As I read and reread, what emerged was not Pegu's blasphemer but a playful and witty man. The feeling grew with each page. I am sure I must have smiled when I read, "If the world is an aspect of our imagination, then we all exist in different spaces. But what if we were without imagination: would the world then cease to exist?" And a few pages later, "If we could squeeze milk out of stones, we would have no use for cows. But would the price of milk change?"

Pegu made a soft, coughing sound. "I am glad you find the book so funny. The Guardians will be delighted to learn of your reaction."

"No, no, it is a funny book. Silly and playful."

For a moment he was silent. Then he said in a brusque voice, "I think you are just saying that to save your skin. That is what I think."

"But it is. I'm sure the Guardians are mistaken. Take this passage, for instance." I gave him the page about cows.

"It is as simple as that clock on the wall," he said gruffly. "The price of milk will never decrease. An apology for capitalism if there ever was one."

"Capitalism? That's ridiculous. My great-grandfather

was probably a cattle rancher. Or maybe a shepherd. Where's the one you showed me yesterday?" I looked through the pile, located the page and read aloud, "'If we climb to the highest mountain and appeal to our flock, our cries shall echo throughout the land. But what if the sheep are not listening?' Don't you get it?"

"There is nothing to get. And *your* deceptions will get you nowhere."

"Follow me. Are there not numerous mountains in Carobenos?"

"What if there are?"

"And is not Carobenos the land of sheep and shepherds?"

"Perhaps it is," he said reluctantly.

"Exactly. He was not referring to any freedom fighter or some martyr of the peasants, but to a simple shepherd calling out to his sheep from the mountain."

"But the sheep were not listening . . ."

"Because they were lost. There are hundreds of caverns and gorges in Carobenos. I can't remember how many times I went with my father to look for sheep that had been lost." I turned to another page, then another. "'If words are thoughts that perish as we say them, then we never say what we mean. But if meaning is thought, not spoken, then our words are the fancies of others.'"

"These Guardians—"

"Should retire gracefully."

"That was certainly uncalled for." And he launched into a long defence of the Guardians, stressing their ascetic lifestyle, their reputation for infallibility and the respect they had earned. At the end of it all I was not convinced, and neither was Pegu.

I recalled one of Mr. Borfus's declarations. I wagged my finger and told him sternly, "We expect too much from our stories. We burden them with our own afflictions. A story is just a story. Nothing more, nothing less."

Pegu looked at me in confusion. But that episode marked a turning point in our relationship.

In retrospect, I feel that I should have seen it then, but my suspicion came later, when Pegu had become careless. In the meantime, I read from *The Book of Ifs and Buts*. I tried to engage Pegu in my amusement, but he was no longer interested in the book. Sometimes I felt that I had done him a disservice by removing all the drama, but to tell the truth, most times I believed he no longer cared.

He rummaged through my bookcase, sniffing, reading and nodding in approval. Occasionally, he would place his stubby finger on a back cover and trace the outline of the author's face. Once, he saw me looking at him. "A face tells me everything. It reveals all the secrets that have been packed away over the years." He put down the book and clasped his hands behind his back. "Once, I was smitten by a very beautiful woman. We were conspirators for three years. She sucked me dry. I often dreamed of meeting her."

"You never met her and yet she sucked you dry?"

"She was a writer. Historical romances. In time, I got to know her as if we had lived together. I felt she was writing especially for me, conveying secrets which only I could decipher. Her eyes, her hair . . . she was like a raven caught fire."

"So did you meet her?"

"Her picture was on the cover of every book she wrote. But one day, during a televised interview, I saw her as she really was: an old woman with a malicious face and tiny, pinched eyes. She should have been writing manuals on rehabilitating old couches and chairs rather than historical romances."

"That's very unfair."

"She was an imposter."

I asked him, "Have you ever seen any portraits of my great-grandfather?"

He shook his head. "The Guardians only entrusted me with the book."

"But there might still be some other record."

"It is conceivable. One does not question the Guardians. One just fulfills their wishes." He pulled out another book and pressed it against his nose.

~

For the rest of the afternoon, he occupied himself with my books, frowning at the fantasy magazines and inhaling the texts from Ryerson. Sometimes, I would see him flicking glances at me and I would feel that a revelation was on the way. And here I must make a confession: I was no longer thinking of escape. Although Pegu still had his bag within easy reach, I had concluded that there was nothing in it except *The Book of Ifs and Buts* and his tonics. I could easily overpower him and send him crashing to the floor. After all, I was young and relatively healthy, while Pegu's shape suggested that athleticism was not one of his strong points. In addition, he had had sufficient time to murder me if he so desired. Yet, in spite of all the threats, he had done nothing.

But I was determined to get to the bottom of this whole affair. I was not sure that I believed his story about these Guardians, and that increased my curiousness. Why had he gone to the trouble of locating me in Harwood Avenue, thousands of miles from Carobenos? And, most disturbing, how did he know so much about me? Could he, on that first day, have scrutinized the letters from Slavo which I had placed in a transparent plastic envelope on the last shelf of my bookcase? But the letters looked undisturbed.

In the evening, while we were having dinner, I put the questions to him. He responded to each of my questions with one of his own. He wanted to know how I was able to survive on a writer's income in Canada, and whether I would return to Carobenos if my financial situation became intolerable. I answered all his questions truthfully, hoping to extract some equivalent candidness. I repeated my earlier declaration that I would never return to Carobenos. He wanted to know why. I explained that writers here were not ridiculed and thrown into prisons. Pegu listened silently, nibbling and purring.

That night, while I was on the floor on my blanket, I heard him shifting on the sofa, clearing his throat and grunting. Then he asked me, "If there are so many laws and regulations in the land, how, pray tell, are there so many foreign types? By what means did they all inveigle the government?"

"Many of them are refugees."

"Refugees? Explain, please."

"People escaping from one thing or the other."

"Like what, for instance?"

"Persecution of some sort, I would think."

He remained silent for a while, then he said, "I see."

When I awoke in the morning, Pegu was at the table, his hands propped beneath his chin, a grave expression on his face. He had the same expression when I returned from the bathroom.

"I have suffered."

"Pardon me?"

"I have suffered," he repeated solemnly. I noticed that he had not touched the toast on his plate. And with absolutely no prodding on my part, he launched into the story of his life.

He had been for more than fifteen years a professor of nineteenth-century literature at the University of Carobenos. Then, one day, he received a letter from the administration stating that his courses had been scrapped and that they had no further use for him. The letter explained that it was all part of the modernization of the university and that emphasis would now be placed on twentieth-century literature. "I was deconstructed out of my tenure," he said bitterly. "By the operatives of the CIA."

"Were they involved?" I asked, smiling.

He looked at me angrily. "Only a fool would not see it."

"Well, I don't see it and—"

"Which doesn't surprise me in the least." He wagged a finger at me. "Try to follow me in my train of thought, if that is at all possible. For fifteen years I lectured on the works of writers who dealt with a real world, real men and women, real occurrences. Zorrilla. Gonçalves de Magalhães. *Poetic Sighs and Longings*. Isn't that a beautiful title? Anyway, with one single directive, it all ended. Replaced by what? you may ask. I will tell you. Magical Realism. Surrealism. Avant-gardism. Pishposhism. No better than your comic books."

"The CIA did all of this?"

He began wagging again. "I can state without equivocation that twentieth-century literature and twentieth-century criticism were both the products of the CIA. Created by a horde of fanatical miscreants."

"And why did these miscreants take all this trouble?"

"My dear boy," he said, ignoring my smile and speaking in the accent of a professor from Carobenos, "we can change reality by modifying our perception of it. Likewise, we can subvert truth by changing the way we react to it. They hounded me at every turn. I was dismissed from job after job. But I planned my revenge." He took a deep breath.

"Well?"

"Be patient, please. I wrote a best-seller. More than two hundred copies were sold. It was on the best-selling list for eight months. *Don't Cross my Path*. That was the name of the book. But I had underestimated my enemies. The next book sold thirty-three copies, and the last, just six. And I knew why, too."

"The CIA again?"

"I am certain of it. The publisher said that there was no suspense left because everyone knew beforehand the criminals would be CIA operatives and university officials. I realized then that he too had been bought over. I was fighting a losing battle." He shook his head. "A refugee if ever there was one." And in a low voice he said, "If we look at the stars, we marvel at their brilliance. But in the morning we see just empty sky."

And I knew then. I was certain of it. For the rest of the morning, I thought of my approach and planned my strategy. I realized that I would have to trick him into volunteering information.

At exactly two-fifteen in the afternoon, I asked him in what I hoped was a disinterested voice, "Have you been away from Carobenos for a long time?"

"Not as long as you." He turned a page in the book he was reading.

"Do you have relatives or friends living in Canada?"

"I am confused by too many shadows." He turned to another page.

"But you know your way around? How did you find me here?"

He acted as if he did not hear the questions, but after a few minutes, he closed the book—and I'm uncertain about the effect he was trying to create by doing this—sort of half-closed his eyes and launched into a story about his trip from Carobenos to Canada. He had passed through remote villages, hacked his way through jungles and escaped from a number of ferocious animals. I asked him if it would not have been simpler to come by air. He sighed as if he had not heard. He had also escaped from drug dealers and guerrillas, and for two weeks he had been followed by a determined band of CIA operatives. Finally, he opened his eyes, looked at the ceiling and said, "I have suffered mightily."

That became his tune for the rest of the day. I waited patiently.

I can see now that he must have taken my silence as a kind of sympathetic interest, because his suffering increased with each account. He revealed that he was so soft and plump as a boy that he had been the target of all the perverts in the village. They sent him flowers with suggestive notes, followed him in the streets, shouted their intentions to him. He stopped going out at night, fearful that there was a sodomizer lurking behind every lamp pole. In a very distressed voice he pointed to his chest. "They had a pet name for me. Titties."

At that, I burst out into laughter.

"You dare laugh at my distress, you malapert." He bolted up from the couch.

I thought I would suffocate. I looked at his expression and broke out into laughter again. "Maybe the CIA was behind it all the time."

"I can assure you that it will not be so funny when I *hakula* you." He explained in detail the process involved. At the end of his explanation he said, "If a man is forced to run and hide, he is called a coward. But is not that man really a refugee?"

Then and there, I asked him. "Tell me the truth. Wasn't it you who wrote *The Book of Ifs and Buts*?"

Without saying a word, he took his bag and went into the bathroom. He returned without his bag, but I saw four or five pieces of rope dangling from his hand. "I must do what I must," he said in a resigned voice.

I got up and prepared to fling him to the floor, but Pegu was not interested in me. He sat calmly on a chair and proceeded to tie an ankle against the chair's leg.

"What are you doing?"

"I am *hakularing* myself," he said, fastening the other ankle.

"I thought I was the one supposed to be *hakulared*?"

"Circumstances have changed. It is the only honourable thing to do."

"But how am I going to explain this?" I was concerned now. "What will I tell the police? My landlord?"

"Tell them whatever you want. Now, if you don't mind, I would like some quiet. This is a very complicated procedure."

"Look, maybe you should choose another apartment."

"It is too late. The die is cast. Fond farewell. In my bag you will find a list of all my friends and enemies. Please inform them of my demise." As I was about to rush and untie him, I noticed that he had used up all the rope—two pieces on the ankle, two on his knees and one across his waist—and he still looked remarkably healthy. "The process is very slow. And excruciatingly painful. Now, I would like some time alone during my final moments." Pegu's eyes were closed, so he did not see me smiling, but he must have heard the door opening. "Where are you going?"

"Outside. Didn't you say you wanted some peace?"

"And leave me like this?" He looked at the ceiling. "The world is peopled with callous and uncaring miscreants."

"You asked for some quiet."

"Oh, just come and untie me. Or would you prefer that I die of starvation?"

This account should end here, but it does not. In the year and a half since he first appeared in my apartment, Pegu has applied for refugee status and expects his hearing any day now. But the result is a foregone conclusion. He has prospered here in ways which, I'm not ashamed to say, make me slightly envious. And hard as this is to believe, people invariably find him charming. When I introduced him to Mr. Borfus, I could see that my cranky old editor was immediately impressed—so much so that he offered to serialize *The Book of Ifs and Buts*. It was a hit. Praised by reviewers as "deceptively simple," "filled with practical wisdom" and "a panacea for the age in which we live," it has opened many doors for him. He was invited to discussions on CBC with other writers, read at Harbourfront with Latin American authors, revealed to the hostess of some cooking show that he was preparing a cookbook which he had named *The Book of Beef and Cuts*, and interviewed by Ziggy Lorenc for Book Television. I laughed when I saw him turning on his charm and shifting to his low, fake voice. He now teaches a course on Magical Realism at Ryerson University.

But I should not complain too much. I was finally able to give Mr. Borfus his story, which dealt with a shadowy cult determined to rid the world of individuals with unacceptable views. Writers, journalists, poets and politicians mysteriously disappear. The unlikely hero of the story is a man who, in spite of his great powers, is hypocritical, boastful and physically unattractive. In fact, he is shaped like an egg.

Pegu still visits from time to time, and it might be his way of showing gratitude, although I sometimes feel that it is because he still can't resist playing his games with me.

Despite all my questioning, he has never yet given me a satisfactory explanation for his mysterious appearance in my apartment and all his fanciful stories about old Guardians and CIA miscreants. At these times his mood shifts between vaguely philosophical and deliberately obscure. I must have asked him more than a hundred times whether he was sent by Slavo to persuade me to remain in Canada, or whether this mission was viewed as a means of arranging his own escape from Carobenos, or whether the few days spent in my apartment confirmed his belief that Canada was the place for him.

But he is more forthright in other matters. He has become, unfortunately, an expert on American movies and television programs. A little over a week ago, while we were watching reports of the American presidential campaign, he told me in a sad, superior voice, "Do you see what is happening? This is a news report and we are getting everything but news. Opinions, judgments, evaluations but, tragically, no news." He began wagging his finger at the screen. "But there is going to be a backlash, I can assure you. A most serious backlash. Soon, very soon, the public will grow fatigued of all these layers of artifice, and demand the truth, pure, naked and simple. And that, my boy," he said, turning to me, "will mark the end of make-believe, dreams and nonsense."

He was looking so smug when he made this pronouncement that I told him, "You shouldn't complain so much, because you have been a major beneficiary of all this pish-posh. *The Book of Ifs and Buts*. Your course at Ryerson. All the interviews. I suppose you are going to announce next some nonsense called *The Book of Lifts and Tucks*?"

His mouth opened a bit, making him look contemplative and sinister. He brought his hands together, looked at his fingers, stared dramatically at the ceiling and in a low, crackling voice said, "If a chef is celebrated for concocting a special broth, would we not all flock to his eating place? But if the chef unexpectedly serves another type of broth, would we not fling our bowls at said chef?" And with that, he burst out into a horrible, pleasurable laugh, like a priest who has committed his first enjoyable sin.

The House in Lengua Village

I cannot offer any explanation as to why I returned after resisting for thirty-three years. I was not there when my sister was killed in an accident on the Beetham Highway, I had not gone to my mother's funeral and I had composed a wall of indifference towards the letters my father had, until the last six or seven years, regularly written.

My callousness—it's the word I choose—did not come without its congruent burdens. My life was troubled and unhappy. I frequently sought comparisons with others to convince myself that there was some kind of conformity in suffering, but I could never find a match. In any case, I had no friends, no one I could use to plot my graph. I believe my ugliness (so undefinable to me, so hard to pin down, so difficult to blame a particular feature for) elicited an immediate irritation, perhaps a revulsion, in those who crossed my path. But there were never many such crossers.

I was always alone. Even before my son left for York University to pursue, against my unstated wish, a degree in Social Sciences, I was, in a manner of speaking, alone at home. My wife was intermittently away, sometimes for long periods. In the beginning there had been protracted arguments because of this, but gradually I became too tired to quarrel, too drained to contemplate her whereabouts. During the periods when she was at home, we never, in any way, communicated with each other, and it is not an exaggeration to say that I have no idea how she has aged over the years. Occasionally, during a solitary moment in my bedroom, I would recall a half-smile or eyes wide with wonder, but these memories, discordant, treacherous, perhaps embellished by my loneliness, were never explored because I knew they could only lead to further distress.

The night before I left, I was convinced that in the clear light of day I would understand my mistake and cancel the trip, but in the morning, as I felt the familiar tiredness descend upon me, I knew that it was too late. I ate my buttered toast, washed my plate and called a taxi to take me to the airport.

I was asleep for most of the flight, but I awoke with a feeling of complete dread when the plane touched down at Piarco Airport. I remained in my seat until everyone else had left. Through the window, I could see the other passengers hurrying to the terminal, and in the gallery, their excited relatives and friends pointing and waving.

Thirty-three years ago, looking through the window of the plane, I had seen my sister straining against the iron railing in the same waving gallery, gesturing with one hand then the other, too young to be affected by my father's disappointment or my mother's sadness. My two brothers were chatting with other relatives—cousins, aunts, uncles—some of whom I barely knew. It was a time when migration from Trinidad was uncommon, and everyone wanted to share in the adventure.

Today, no one awaited me. I had not informed anyone of my visit.

"Sir?" The flight attendant was smiling, but I could see that she was irritated. Slowly, I unbuckled my seat belt.

~

In the taxi, I paid the fare quietly, shelving my suspicion that the driver had already assessed me and charged twice the normal amount to take me to Lengua Village. As a means of redressing this bit of practised fraud, perhaps, for half an hour or so he bombarded me with information about the state of politics in the island, the high incidence of drug-related crimes and a cricket match which was being played against a team from New Zealand. I had forgotten the way Trinidadians relate to complete strangers, extending a familiarity which would seem vulgar to many foreigners.

I offered him no encouragement, although I realized that this would be interpreted as a kind of showing-off: the pretentiousness of the returning national who has acquired all the airs of his adopted country. But he must have been accustomed to this treatment, because he stopped chatting and fiddled with the radio, until he found a station with a woman singing a song from an old Indian movie, *Baiju Bawra*.

This song, which I had not heard since I was a boy running through the house or sitting at the kitchen table, was immediately recognizable. I closed my eyes and rested my head against the seat. I felt the memories, shuttered for so long, seeking release, bursting through the years, straining against the walls I had built.

A woman with a distant look in her eyes, singing while she was washing wares, sweeping the floor with her *cocoyea* broom, stitching a torn shirt, preparing breakfast, her voice pleasant and melodious, transforming, to a boy of about twelve or thirteen, some menial task into a happy activity; the boy, twelve or thirteen, holding this image of a happy, contented woman.

But my mother must often have been lonely. My father, who was a county councillor and constantly involved in community affairs, was always off to meetings. Even when he was at home, some villager would drop in and occupy him until late in the night. His advice was solicited for the smallest matters: fixing some part of the road, repairing a house, purchasing a cow.

That was how they lived their lives, without complaints, without arguments, each holding firm to his or her notion of duty—my father to his community, my mother to her children and husband.

Duty. How often I had heard that word. Husband to wife. Wife to husband. Parents to children. Eldest child to parents and siblings. When, at the age of twenty-three, I was preparing to leave for Canada, I knew that they felt betrayed, could not understand this recklessness. But, characteristically, they did not convey their disappointment, though they must have felt that as the eldest child I was forfeiting my responsibility to my brothers and sister. I knew, too, that they had expected me to take ownership of the house in Lengua Village, as my father had done and his father before him.

I mentioned that my father was frequently away, but to us, the children, the house was never a lonely place. There were cricket matches after school in the big front yard, and once a month a mobile unit from the Ministry of Information would arrive with its noisy projector and mildewed screen, and the villagers would be treated to films displaying farming techniques in India and Africa and Malaysia. During those TV-less days, we laughed and clapped at everything, especially the short animated clips.

Sitting in the rear seat of the car, my eyes closed, I was bewildered by this memory of a happy, carefree time of cricket matches and films, and of three boys and a girl running through the house playing games and, when they were tired, listening to the eldest recite a story while he cleared out the soot from a lampshade. This memory, so distant, so unexpected, could have belonged to someone else.

"We almost reach, boss. You had a good sleep?"

I opened my eyes. "Yes." I was grateful that the driver had not disturbed me earlier.

"The place is a little smoky because of the cane fire. Is crop season."

"I remember."

That encouraged him. "Things didn't change much, eh, boss? Country life always remain the same, if you ask me."

Men and women with straw hats and blackened clothes were piling the cane into stacks to be weighed and then taken to the factory, and in a pond, drained down to its deepest basin, three boys were casting a net into the muddy water.

Once, during a trip to San Fernando, with everyone piled inside the blue Consul, my father had pointed to the pond and said that a mermaid lived there. For years I believed him.

As we approached a steep incline followed by a sharp dip in the road, the driver increased his speed, and for a second or two I felt that the car had left the ground. "Airplane ride," he chuckled. "You remember it?"

We would always urge my father on whenever we were approaching the incline, and in preparation press our backs against the seat to increase the sensation.

The car slowly passed the cane fields, but the airplane ride, experienced as a queasiness in my stomach, remained with me. We were just fifteen minutes away. I had not prepared myself. I had no idea what I would meet, what I would say. Nervousness sharpened my fear. I felt like asking the driver to turn around and take me back to the airport.

"I taking a little shortcut. We will reach in no time." He swung the car into a dirt road. Less than five minutes later, we emerged into a gravel road, and into the village of Lengua.

Thirty-three years, and it seemed as if nothing had changed: the square cedar houses built on long teak posts, the shaky wooden bridge, the landslips like raw wounds in the earth, the old Chinese shop, the stalls at the sides of the road displaying yam and dasheen, men and women walking unhurriedly. Just around the bend was the house. All at once, a complete and almost crippling exhaustion overcame me. I could not understand what the driver was saying. I suspected that he was asking for the exact location of the house, so with the greatest of effort I raised a hand and pointed to the bend. "A big concrete house." My hand dropped back to the seat.

And it was with this almost crippling feeling of exhaustion that I saw the house—a loose aluminium sheet fluttering against an eave, the side windows nailed down with wooden crosses, intersecting cracks and fissures on the wall, exposed bricks jutting out in areas where the mortar had fallen away.

The driver was still mumbling something. He took out my suitcase and placed it next to the gate. I reached into my pocket, withdrew my wallet and gave him forty Canadian dollars. He may have been surprised.

The corrugated iron gate had rusted down to mere nails, and the asphalt in the front yard was almost completely covered by clumps of knotgrass. I took up my suitcase and pushed open the gate.

~

Once, there had been a semicircular extension to the upstairs porch, forming a concrete canopy above the front entrance. My mother had planted her marigolds and chrysanthemums and petunias there, but the extension had broken off and was now a pile of rubble blocking the entrance.

"You sure it still have people living here?" the driver shouted from the car.

"It's okay." I walked over the broken bricks and concrete. I should have asked him to wait, but my thoughts belonged to another time. Laughing children, cricket matches, village council meetings, hastily called panchayats, a woman watering her flowers and singing her songs in a house, once formed the centre for all the activities in the village. Every single villager must have stepped inside these gates at one time or another.

The front door was open, so I entered. I heard the car speeding down the road. The door slammed shut. Maybe the hinges had rusted down.

As my vision adjusted to the faint light, I saw that the interior was not as bad as I had expected. Most of the furniture—the mahogany table and chairs, the maroon couch, the sewing machine, a glass cabinet, a space saver, and newer, unrecognizable pieces—had been stacked against the wall, but the floor appeared to have been swept and in the kitchen, where my mother had sung her movie songs, there were cups and plates at the side of the sink. I dropped my suitcase. A face appeared from behind a cupboard. I jumped, but the girl, short and very dark, appeared more startled than I was. She was clutching something against her chest.

"Who?"

"I used to live here," I said, not moving. I saw the disbelief, then the fear on her face. "I came to see my father."

"Which father?" She tightened her grip on what I now saw was a rolling pin. *Ballayna*, my mother called it.

"My father. Is he at home?"

She relaxed her grip on the rolling pin. I saw her staring at me, at my suitcase, and suddenly, almost too swift for me to be certain of the transformation, the disbelief on her face changed into a sneer. "Why you come back for?" But she did not wait for a reply. She pointed to the stairway. "In the front room."

While I was walking up the stairs, I realized that I had not brought a gift. I placed my suitcase in the hall and walked into the room.

Heavy curtains darkened the room, but I saw a figure on the bed, hands and feet stiff and straight. I drew the curtains back. His eyes were fixed on the ceiling. I went and sat on the bed. Just when I thought that he was sleeping, as some very old people do, with his eyes only partially closed, he looked at me. But there was no recognition in his eyes. It was as if he had not seen me, as if I were not on the bed, sitting next to him.

The years fell away and I remembered a boy about to leave for his first day at Naparima College, waiting with his father for the bus. And just before the boy boarded the bus, the father explaining that the most valuable gift a parent can give a child is a proper education. The father speaking solemnly about duty and then, uncharacteristically, revealing his pride that the boy had passed his common entrance for Naparima College.

I heard a soft, subdued whisper and I looked at my father's face, at the slack flesh, the slightly open mouth, the limp tongue, but the sound had not come from him. Just then, the girl came with a towel into the room. Not wanting her to see my face, I quickly got up and went to the window. I wiped my eyes and, when she had left, placed my head against the pane.

When I turned around, I saw that one side of my father's face was pressed against the pillow and his eyes were staring in the direction of the bookcase, filled with dusty hardcover editions of religious texts and the classics from which he had often read to me and sometimes quoted a favourite passage to a visitor. The *Ramayana*. The *Gita*. Keats. Wordsworth. Matthew Arnold. Dickens. They were all there. And on the top of the bookcase, the mural on which he had inscribed with Indian ink: *Reading maketh a full man*.

He was clutching the end of the coverlet across his chest. I wondered what he was thinking about, if he was still capable of rational thought.

When I went downstairs, the girl was sitting by the table in the kitchen, her fingers around an enamel cup. She saw me and got up. "You want something?" Her words were short, clipped and angry. I pulled out a chair and she explained, "Something to eat or drink?"

"How long has he been like this?"

Her fingers around the enamel cup were clasping and unclasping each other. "I clean up the place and make his food."

I felt that I should say, "The place looks clean." Instead, I repeated the question.

She hesitated a while. "I only start working here a year ago."

Perhaps she did not know. "Are there any visitors?"

She shook her head. "You want anything to eat or drink?"

"No, it's all right."

"You sure?" The voice was angry, insistent.

I relented. "Okay. Some tea."

She went to the stove and poured out water from a pot into a cup.

"Is he able to move around?"

Without turning, she said, "Sometimes. When he have to go to the toilet. But not alone. I only working here a year now."

She wiped a spoon and stirred the mixture in the cup. I felt that my questions were irritating her. She placed the tea on the table and stood at my side. There was a strong odour of some astringent soap. I sipped the tea. "It's good." Her fingers were pinching the long cotton dress. "The place looks clean."

"I fix up the bed in the last room for you. I put in new sheet and pillow."

"Thanks."

"I try to take good care of the old man."

I looked at her face. The voice still sounded angry,

but I felt that it was just the way she spoke. "It must be difficult for you."

She seemed confused by this unexpected sympathy. "I getting paid. Is my duty."

I took a long drink and finished the tea. "Did he tell you that?"

"I have to leave now." She went into the living room and took up a purse from the sewing machine against the wall. "I make up the bed in the last room."

"Does he say anything?" But she was gone.

I walked outside, wanting to see the direction she had taken, but in the darkness the road was barely visible. And with this darkness hiding the cracks in the wall, the exposed bricks, the rubble at the front, the knotgrass, the place looked just as I remembered. To the side of the house, just beside the fence, the branches of the mango tree, which we had pelted with small stones to bring down the fruits, seemed to be brushing and scraping the moon, and the sapodilla tree, caught in the shadows of the taller chenette tree, looked forsaken and dejected. I thought of a little girl tugging at her mother's dress, trying to get her attention.

~

The branches of the sapodilla tree had once formed a perfect bower. It was my sister's favourite spot, and whenever she was missing, we knew that she would be there with one of her dolls. On weekends, she would fill a basket with cakes, spread a towel at the base of the trunk, neatly arrange her cups and plates with sweet-drink and pieces of cake, and look on happily while my brothers and I ate. Little picnickers. It was a term my mother used.

My sister was ten years younger than I, just thirteen when I left for Canada. I knew nothing of her life, her marriage, her husband, her child. I knew little of the accident—it was at the time I had stopped opening my father's letters—and now I wondered whether she had been severely mutilated and in constant pain during the four days spent in the San Fernando hospital, or whether she was in a coma, free from pain and shock and anger.

In the distance, I heard the harsh hoot of a jumbie-bird and then the cry of a dog. I ran into the house and bolted the door.

That night, with my father in the front room, I walked through the dark corners and corridors, listening. I heard sounds I thought I had forgotten, and others I did not want to hear. I was no longer in control; I was carried from room to room, forced into the odours—decayed and bitter now—I had once cherished. I smelled the foreign fruits of Christmas, the moist birthday cakes, the oily sweets which followed the pujas, the special Sunday dinner prepared by my mother. But they were all dripping and rancid. I was pushed from one memory to another until, like a tired, shipwrecked sailor surrendering his will to the ocean (this is the image that comes to me), I just gave in. I allowed the guilt to wash over me, then the regret, the shame, and finally the fatigue.

Late in the night, I went into my father's room, held his bony, trembling hand and gazed into his eyes. But I no longer expected anything.

It was almost morning when I pulled the settee from the side of the bookcase and fell asleep at the foot of the bed, under a plaque on which my father had written the lines from the *Bhagavad Gita*: *And do your duty even if it is humble, rather than another's even if it is great. To die in one's duty is life; to live in another's is death.*

My dreams that night were broken, like the strands of some frayed garment floating in the air, just out of reach, rising higher and higher, not disappearing all at once but awkwardly losing visibility, as if swallowed in portions by a black hole. I dreamed that the entire family was travelling in the blue Consul on a trip to Mayaro beaches. I dreamed that I was in the car with my sister on the Beetham Highway, and just before the car skidded out of control, I was able to pull her out through an open door. I dreamed that I was at my mother's funeral and, although she was dead and in the coffin, she was smiling with me. I dreamed that when, thirty-three years ago, I was leaving for Canada, sitting at the front and the back of me were my parents and my brothers, and next to me, my sister. I dreamed that by us leaving together, the tragedy had been averted and we were all happy and safe in Canada.

I felt that I awoke a few times and saw my father staring at me, as he had sometimes done when I was sitting at the table in the hall, doing my home lesson from Naparima College. But that must have been another dream.

In the morning, my father's eyes were open. I thought at first that he was staring at some object above and behind me, perhaps the plaque on the wall, but then I saw that his eyes were not blinking and the coverlet around his chest was still. I remained on the settee for about forty minutes, then I got up and pressed his eyelids down. When the girl came into the room with a bowl and a towel, she looked at me standing by the bed, at my father's stiff body and then again at me. Without saying a word, she turned around and left.

I went back to the settee and closed my eyes. And waiting for the girl to return, not sure what I should do, weakened by indecision and fatigue, I fell asleep.

Someone awakened me, grasping and tugging at my shoulders. For a minute or two, I thought I was still dreaming and that I was being pushed into a narrow tunnel filled with murky water, but when I opened my eyes, I saw a man bending over me, his eyes red and bleary, his face unshaven, his clothes unwashed, smelling of sweat. I could not place his face. I looked towards the bed and saw that the sheet had been drawn up over my father's body, covering his head. I heard sounds downstairs, chairs scraping the floor, voices, a dull pounding, pounding.

"He was talking the truth. He was talking the truth all the time."

I was still drowsy; I could not understand why he was telling me this.

"Nobody ever take him on. They just thought it was an old man craziness talking. Ever since Ma dead, he only talking crazy talk. Nobody ever listen and then he stop talking. Just like that. But he always use to say that he not going to die until he see your face. The face of the first child. That is what keep him alive all these years."

"Ravin?"

He looked surprised. "What happen, you can't make out you own brother again?" He broke down into tears, began to cry uncontrollably, as if my lack of recognition offended him. With his words broken up by the sobbing and the shaking, he said, "You never ever come back for Malini and Ma funeral, and it was left for me to do your job. Drunkard Ravin had to do everything. Shave his head. Listen to the prayers. Light up the body. Throw the ashes the next morning in the sea. Fast for two months after. Everything that *only* you was suppose to do was left up to me. *I* had to do everything for Malini and for Ma."

I saw staring faces by the door. An old woman came into the room, placed her hand on my head, massaged Ravin's neck and burst into a low, wailing cry. It was a kind of signal: all the faces peeping by the door began to sniff and moan; each sound was distinctive, some soft and squelchy, others loud and insistent.

Ravin wiped his eyes with his shirt's collar. "At least you could do you duty this time." It was not an accusation, the way he said it, the expression on his face as if he was genuinely happy to see me.

For the next three days, I did my duty, did all that was expected of me, all the rituals the eldest child was obligated to perform. For three days, the house, the yard, was filled with people offering tears, advice, consolation. A tent was constructed, chairs arranged, coffee and biscuits purchased and placed on the tables. Everyone was busy, organized, efficient. Relatives and villagers filled the place as they had done so many years ago. I remember thinking that the house must have been shocked and delighted.

Then it was over. My father was cremated, his ashes tossed into the sea, the tent and chairs taken away, the place empty once more.

For the three weeks that I remained, I spent most of the time in a hammock which was fastened at one end to the trunk of the sapodilla tree and at the other to a wooden stake buried in the ground. It was the height of the crop season and the place was quiet except for the occasional vehicle, a dog baying in the distance, and kiskidees and blue jeans warbling their messages to each other. I felt wrapped in a soothing lethargy which was so different from the deadening fatigue to which I had grown accustomed.

Sometimes, I would see the girl peeping from a window, but during mealtimes she stood by the sink, washing wares, and we never spoke with each other. There was nothing to say, nothing that I wanted to hear, certainly not anything that could potentially threaten my languor. After I ate, I would hurry back to the hammock. Resting against the coarse material, I observed details that I had never noticed before or had forgotten. I watched the birds darting through the branches of the chenette tree, the dangling cornbirds' nests, the calloused bark of the mango tree, the mossy undulations on the trunk, the epiphytes—some in shocking bloom—peeping from between the leaves. In the evenings, I saw faint blotches tarnishing the blue of the sky, some faraway cane fields set afire.

Four days after the cremation, my brother came. I was half asleep in the hammock. He was walking unsteadily and he made a motion as if he were throwing a stone at the mango tree. "You remember." He squatted next to the hammock. "You remember the time you fall down from the tree and me and Devraj pick you up and drag you under here. I thought you was gone for sure." He smiled, and I saw that most of his teeth were gone. "Devraj was here for Malini and Ma cremation, but he couldn't make it this time. I know how all you foreigners busy all the time, making money so you could live in nice fancy houses." He exhaled a short, wheezing laugh and I smelled the stale rum. "I living in a little shack down the road, me alone. Wife and children gone now."

"Where?"

He scratched the side of a thigh and examined his fingernail. "I trying to control the drinking, but it getting harder and harder." He took out a cigarette from a pack and placed it between his lips. "You know, it had a time when I used to think that nothing bad could happen to our family. That we was protected. Of all the families in the village. I never see it coming." He lit the cigarette and took a deep drag. "First was Malini, then Ma and now Pa. The two of them never recover when Malini pass away, and when it was Pa alone, he just get worse. I used to visit him sometimes, but all he would do was quarrel and shout about everything. I could never please him. Then he stop quarrelling and shouting, and stop talking too. Is like he just lose interest in living." He flicked his thumb and the ash fell on the grass. "Thank god Devraj does send down a little something every month to pay the servant girl, because that is how he managing for the last year or so." He tossed the cigarette away.

"Where you working now?"

He seemed embarrassed by the question. "Here and there. Nothing steady. But is just me alone."

"What about the family?"

"Family? What family?" He seemed angry. I remained silent. "You didn't talk much to anybody during the cremation, eh? All these people who I didn't see for years. All them bitches who used to run to this house whenever they had a problem to fix."

I tried to understand his anger. "Everything was well arranged—tent, chairs, pundit, all the cremation material."

"The servant girl family. I help out here and there, but they do mostly everything." He withdrew another cigarette. "She used to take good care of him. Treat him like if she was his real daughter. She was the only one who could get him to say a few words. So why you never come back?"

The question was asked in a casual manner, but I felt that it was important to him. I considered my answers, the excuses I was now capable of believing, the lies accumulated over thirty-three years. I saw him looking intently at me, his eyes serious, sad, angry, hurt. I remembered the younger brother who would never complain when I struck him in sudden anger, but who would stand before me, forcing my anger to dissolve into admiration and guilt. And for the first time in thirty-three years I allowed entrance to the truth.

Against my parents' wishes I got married very young, chose a career in teaching rather than the legal profession and, in the worst blow of all, left everything behind and migrated to Canada, propelled by the false assumption that distance would somehow lessen their disappointment in me.

I had had grand hopes about Canada. There was this dream: a once-simple villager returning with a success only he had anticipated, stirring a solid pride in his repentant parents and in his fellow villagers, who had finally found something to celebrate. But nothing had gone right in Canada. One by one I saw all my bubbles bursting; perhaps they had been too grand and fanciful to begin with. I hated my job, hated the polite barricades which were thrust in my path. My wife, to whom I looked for encouragement, quickly constructed her private world and effectively shut me out. To her, I was nothing more than a visa to Canada; once she got in, my usefulness was gone. And—how shocking unsolicited knowledge can be—I had retreated in a manner not dissimilar to my wife, except that the landscape of my world was littered with doubt, guilt and fear. And selfishness. My self-pity was energetic, precise; it excluded everyone else, excluded my parents, my brothers, my sister, excluded everything but the fatigue. I was a beaten man. I could not return.

My brother's stare was unflinching. I knew that he

would not turn away until I answered his question. The words formed. I heard myself saying, "I was a disappointment."

Almost imperceptibly, his eyes widened. "You?" And then he laughed in an embarrassed sort of way.

But the lies were too comforting to be put aside entirely. "I retired from my job a few months ago. I was waiting for that time."

He cleared his throat and coughed in his cuffed palm. "You staying for the *bhandara*?"

I shook my head.

He got up. "Well, I will see you before you leave. And get a good barber to fix up you hair. The man who do the shaving *zog* you up." He bent over the hammock and passed his hand over my hair. "Take care." He walked away.

I never saw him again, but I took his advice the next day.

"A little barbershop under the house," the girl told me. "It have a little sign at the front. Is about half-mile from here. You will walk?"

I nodded.

"I does walk the same distance every morning and evening, but in the opposite direction." Her voice sounded friendlier than usual.

I was tired and sweating by the time I saw the sign. I stood by the gate and a dog began to bark.

"Coming now," someone shouted from the house. "Open the gate. The dog wouldn't bite."

Tentatively, I opened the gate. The dog sniffed my feet and wandered off. There were two wooden chairs and a table stacked with newspapers. I took the newspapers up the stairs, sat on a plastic chair in the gallery and read an article about a calypsonian who, at the height of his career, had shifted direction and was now singing gospel songs. The journalist did not approve; he felt the calypsonian was a traitor.

"Sorry to keep you waiting." I looked up from the newspaper. "Is you," she whispered, placing a hand against her mouth.

I could not recognize the face. She was middle-aged, attractive and, unlike the other women in the village, dressed in jeans and a jersey. She looked at me and giggled. "Look how they *zog* you up. Come inside." She motioned to a padded chair, then opened a drawer and took out scissors and a comb. "I see you in the cremation, but you was looking so serious-serious, I didn't talk to you."

I sat on the chair and gazed at her face in a mirror fastened to the wall. I tried to place her, but the face was not familiar.

"But things don't ever remain the same," she said in a chatty voice. "You remember when all the girls in Barrackpore Senior had a crush on you? You was the young, good-looking teacher fresh out of university, and all you had to do was look at one of us and the rest would get jealous."

"You went to that school?"

"You can't remember me? Renata. You dance with me and my friends for the school Christmas party. When you leave for Canada, I cry for weeks after." She burst into giggles. "And not me alone."

It was a time of my life I had completely forgotten. I felt like she was speaking about someone only vaguely familiar, perhaps a young man I had met in a taxi on my way from work. A happy, carefree, good-looking young man who must have imagined that his life would always be that way. Happy. Carefree.

She continued chatting, then she asked me, "I will see you again?"

I was surprised. To her I was not a tired old man, but the teacher with whom, more than thirty-three years ago, she had been infatuated. Her face in the mirror was serious.

"Yes."

When I returned to the house, the girl asked me, "You tired?"

"Oh, no. There's nothing wrong with a little exercise."

And for the first time, I saw her smile.

~

Twelve days later, as the plane circled the island, I peered out of the window, pretending I could see Lengua Village, and the house where so many dreams had been born and died. The house, free after all these years. I closed my eyes and felt lighthearted and optimistic. Just before I fell asleep, I imagined that I had buried my loss and, somehow, bridged my separation from the life I had known so many years ago.

Acknowledgements

I would like to thank my agent at Westwood, Hilary McMahon, and my editor, Diane Martin.

Also available in Vintage Tales

The Falling Woman by Shaena Lambert
Silent Cruise by Timothy Taylor